"Zombi[es] ... kick it up to a whole 'nother level . . . *Xombies: Apocalypticon* is more exciting, more action-packed, more gory, and more darkly humorous than its predecessor." —*BSCreview*

"Good characters and great action scenes . . . Fans of the original book should enjoy this one, and zombie fans looking for something different may enjoy it as well."
—*Monster Librarian*

"Walter Greatshell's *Xombies: Apocalypticon* actually succeeds in bringing something new and fascinating to this milieu . . . The Xombie tale is gory, wild, surreal, gross, and definitely action-packed. It has a macabre sense of humor and isn't afraid to step on toes or go places that might offend some readers. Yet it adds onto that with some great world-building and a fascinating biological puzzle that will certainly keep you guessing. If that sounds like your cup of tea, then I definitely recommend this one!" —*Errant Dreams*

PRAISE FOR

XOMBIES: [APOCALYPSE BLUES]

"A triumph, both epic in scope and entirely unpredictable, and anchored by one of the most refreshing and unique voices in modern horror fiction. Expect great things from Mr. Greatshell in the future."
—Nate Kenyon, author of *Sparrow Rock*

"Surprise after surprise . . . a heady brew of horror, science fiction, suspense, and adventure . . . *28 Days Later* meets *Lord of the Flies* . . . as sharp and bone-chilling as an arctic gale." —A. J. Matthews, author of *Unbroken*

continued . . .

Ace Books by Walter Greatshell

XOMBIES: APOCALYPSE BLUES
XOMBIES: APOCALYPTICON
MAD SKILLS

MAD SKILLS

WALTER GREATSHELL

ACE BOOKS, NEW YORK

THE BERKLEY PUBLISHING GROUP
Published by the Penguin Group
Penguin Group (USA) Inc.
375 Hudson Street, New York, New York 10014, USA
Penguin Group (Canada), 90 Eglinton Avenue East, Suite 700, Toronto, Ontario M4P 2Y3, Canada
(a division of Pearson Penguin Canada Inc.)
Penguin Books Ltd., 80 Strand, London WC2R 0RL, England
Penguin Group Ireland, 25 St. Stephen's Green, Dublin 2, Ireland (a division of Penguin Books Ltd.)
Penguin Group (Australia), 250 Camberwell Road, Camberwell, Victoria 3124, Australia
(a division of Pearson Australia Group Pty. Ltd.)
Penguin Books India Pvt. Ltd., 11 Community Centre, Panchsheel Park, New Delhi—110 017, India
Penguin Group (NZ), 67 Apollo Drive, Rosedale, North Shore 0632, New Zealand
(a division of Pearson New Zealand Ltd.)
Penguin Books (South Africa) (Pty.) Ltd., 24 Sturdee Avenue, Rosebank, Johannesburg 2196,
South Africa

Penguin Books Ltd., Registered Offices: 80 Strand, London WC2R 0RL, England

This is a work of fiction. Names, characters, places, and incidents either are the product of the author's imagination or are used fictitiously, and any resemblance to actual persons, living or dead, business establishments, events, or locales is entirely coincidental. The publisher does not have any control over and does not assume any responsibility for author or third-party websites or their content.

MAD SKILLS

An Ace Book / published by arrangement with the author

PRINTING HISTORY
Ace mass-market edition / January 2011

Copyright © 2011 by Walter Greatshell.
Cover art by Cliff Nielsen.
Cover design by Lesley Worrell.
Interior text design by Kristin del Rosario.

ISBN: 978-0-441-02012-6

ACE
Ace Books are published by The Berkley Publishing Group,
a division of Penguin Group (USA) Inc.,
375 Hudson Street, New York, New York 10014.
ACE and the "A" design are trademarks of Penguin Group (USA) Inc.

PRINTED IN THE UNITED STATES OF AMERICA

10 9 8 7 6 5 4 3 2 1

For Cindy and Max

ACKNOWLEDGMENTS

Thanks to my editor, Danielle Stockley, and to the great team at Ace and Penguin, whose real-life mad skills make my life easier.

I saw a young Indian in the Nation, who when present, and beholding the scenes of mad intemperance and folly acted by the white men in the town, clap his hand to his breast, and with a smile, looking aloft as if struck with astonishment, and wrapt in love and adoration to the Deity, as who should say, O thou Great and Good Spirit, we are indeed sensible of thy benignity and favour to us red men, in denying us the understanding of white men. We did not know before they came amongst us that mankind could become so base, and fall so below the dignity of their nature. Defend us from their manners, laws and power.

—WILLIAM BARTRAM

PROLOGUE

SWEET GIG

As Maddy Grant plummeted from the forty-second floor to certain death amid the blaring traffic of Ninth Avenue, all she could think was, *Stupid.*

Until then, it had been such a sweet gig.

She had said she was a college student, an incoming freshman at Columbia University, and it wasn't even a lie—Maddy fully intended to enroll at Columbia now that her situation was finally stabilized. Now that she had a job and a place to live and proper identification. A whole new identity: Brittany Higgenbotham, age eighteen, from Tempe, Arizona. The only thing she didn't have was references, but the woman who had hired her was so eager for a live-in nanny-slash-housekeeper-slash-whatever-else-she-could-think-of that she didn't care that it was Maddy's first job. All she cared about was that Maddy was cheap.

The condo was beautiful, a roomy three-bedroom on the West Side, just a five-minute walk from the park. Broadway and Times Square were not much farther. Maddy could hardly believe it: She was living in New York City!

Even in her achingly, fakingly sunny memories of growing up in the prairie suburbs of the West, she had always had a fascination with New York—so distant and out of reach, a fat, golden apple dangling from a high branch. More myth than reality. To her knowledge, she had only ever visited twice, years ago, once on a school trip and once with her parents, but somehow it was a deeply familiar place, the only place on the whole map that beckoned when she was lost and desperate. When she had nowhere else to go.

It was her second month on the job. Maddy's employer, an aging, fading starlet named Angela Brightly, was out for the evening, just as she was every evening, running out to clubs and parties and gallery openings, schmoozing with the rich and famous while Maddy babysat her two kids. Little Danielle and Sam knew that their mother was not just a swinging socialite but a struggling singer, actress, and model in fierce competition with all the newer models out there . . . most of whom hadn't had two children. The living room was full of pictures and artifacts of Angela's once-promising career, many cropped to remove the face of her ex-husband and manager. Her children had learned to accept the situation without fuss: *Mommy works hard so that we can have a good life.* They were the quietest, gloomiest children Maddy ever met . . . but they were certainly no hassle.

On that particular evening, Maddy made them dinner, read them animal stories from their collection of vintage children's books (television was a strict no-no), and tucked them both in. Then she changed into her sweats, made a big salad and some garlic bread, and plopped down in front of the TV. For dessert, she was looking forward to a nice slice of the cheesecake she had picked up at Zabar's that morning. Ms. Brightly wouldn't be home

for hours. It was going to be another quiet evening—
Maddy's favorite kind.

Then the fire alarm went off.

At first, she didn't recognize the noise; it wasn't the
shrill peeping of a room alarm but a loud bell coming
from outside. Annoyed that it was going to disturb the
kids, she jumped up and ran to the front door, peering
through the peephole. The emergency lights at the ends of
the hallway were flashing. *Shit!* She opened the door a
crack and could see other people on the floor sticking their
heads out as well.

"Is it a fire drill?" someone called above the deafening
noise.

A bald man across the way said, "I don't know."

"Either way, we better go down."

"It's probably nothing. Somebody burned the popcorn."

Suddenly, the elevator opened, and four firemen
emerged. They had shiny yellow helmets, fire axes, and
spanking new fire-retardant suits. The leader wore a tank
on his back. They advanced down the hall, banging on
doors, and shouting, "Everyone out! Now!"

People trying to ask them questions were jerked from
their doorways and shoved toward the stairs.

"Get out of the way! Move! All of you! Everyone out,
right now! Drop what you're doing and go! This is an
emergency!"

One of the firemen glanced straight at Maddy, then
hurriedly flicked his eyes away. It was a subtle, barely
noticeable thing, but suddenly she realized what was
going on. There was no fire, not even any fire drill—they
had come for *her*. She could scarcely believe it, but somehow they had found her.

Maddy shut the door and locked it, her heart slamming
in her chest. Her worst nightmare come true: *They found*

me. And yet, in a strange way, it was also a relief, the end of the suspense. Thoughts racing, she headed for the kitchen and spotted Sam and Danielle standing anxiously in the bedroom doorway. The poor things must be scared out of their wits. Maddy made an effort to look calm.

"It's okay, guys. Just a drill, it should be over soon. Go back to bed."

"Sam needs to go potty."

"Well, you're such a big girl, why don't you take him?"

The front door exploded inward. It was a steel security door with multiple dead bolts, but it blew off its hinges like cardboard. The whole building shook.

Jeez, Maddy thought, shielding the kids. She had been expecting a few more seconds at least.

The firemen poured in, shouting, "EVERYBODY ON THE FLOOR, NOW!"

Deafened, Maddy sprinted past the bedroom, grabbed the two children on the fly, and piled into the bathroom. She shut the door just as the lead fireman let off a stream of liquid flame that roared down the corridor and set off the sprinkler system.

There were no windows, no escape. Looking around the bathroom for something, *anything*, she yanked open the medicine cabinet and scanned the dozens of prescription bottles—Ms. Brightly was a total hypochondriac if not a drug addict—then grabbed a toenail clipper. As heavy boot steps squish-squished toward her across the wet carpet, Maddy used the clipper to strip the wires from a curling wand, then twined the bare wires around the brass door-knob and plugged it in.

Someone grabbed the knob. There was a bright blue spark and a loud snap, then a scream and a bone-jarring crash. The lights flickered, dimmed, and the men outside shouted, "Get back! Don't touch him!"

In the couple of seconds she had bought, Maddy hurriedly searched for a means of escape. The bathroom was like a desert, easily the emptiest room in the house; everything useful was bolted down. Still trying to act cheerful, she made the children lie down in the bathtub and covered them with an armload of towels and the toilet lid. They were both wide-awake, and intensely curious about whatever was going on.

"Them men shouldn't be here. It's too loud. My mommy's gonna be mad."

"Don't worry, I'll take care of it."

As axes began chopping at the door, Maddy reached up and pulled on the shower curtain rod. It was a fat enameled tube about five feet long, lightweight but sturdy. There was no way to get it down in one piece, not without tools—okay. Leverage. Sliding the shower curtain to the center and twisting it like a rope, she yanked the bar so hard it broke, landing her flat on her butt. *Ow.* She got up, wincing, and wrested the two halves out of the wall. The kids were fascinated.

"Oooh—you broke it. You're in *trouble*."

"Just stay there and be really quiet, okay? Just like two little deer in the forest."

"Like Bambi?"

"Just like Bambi, shh."

Digging around under the sink, Maddy grabbed a can of hairspray and a blow-dryer, then hunted around for a combustion chamber of the right size. Her darting eyes sought out shampoo bottles, the kids' potty, the plastic sheath for the toilet brush. Hmmm.

In front of the tub was a furry nonskid rug with rubberized backing—she flipped it over and placed the two halves of the shower curtain rod on either side, parallel with each other, then rolled them toward the center so that they resembled a fluffy pink scroll with metal tubes protruding from one end. Into these tubes she stuffed two pill

bottles wadded with toilet paper. Into the opposite end she
jammed the conical sheath for the toilet brush, minus the
brush itself. At last she tied everything together with
nylon stockings from the laundry hamper. It had to be
tight, practically airtight, but the rubberized backing made
a good seal. The only openings were the ends of the metal
tubes and the hole in the plastic sheath where the brush
handle had fit. Into that aperture, Maddy crammed the
barrel of a blow-dryer, so that the entire device resembled
a double-barreled shotgun with a pistol grip—a pink shag
blunderbuss.

The whole operation had taken exactly forty-seven
seconds.

She flicked on the blow-dryer as a boot kicked in the
splintered door. A wave of smoke and burning wet stench
poured in, and with it came a dripping, yellow-helmeted
man, ax held high. His face was pasty white, and his
mouth a rippling gullet lined with concentric rows of
inward-curving black teeth, needle-sharp as acacia thorns.

Sitting against the tub, Maddy sprayed hairspray into
the blow-dryer's suction fan. The aerosol's flammable
propellant gas—propane—filled the plastic chamber of
the toilet brush, while microparticles of sticky hairspray
compound flooded the dryer's nichrome heating coil.
There was a spark.

With a loud *pop*, both barrels fired at once, launching
the pill bottles straight into the man's face. Blue pills and
bits of orange plastic shrapnel exploded in all directions.
The man fell backward, bellowing in pain, but Maddy
didn't hesitate: She quickly loaded two more pill bottles,
ramming them home with the toilet brush, and fired again.
Then again and again. As the men fell back, she stood up
and followed . . . to the limit of the hair dryer's cord.

A blinded man was writhing at her feet; another one
was crawling away—probably the one who'd been elec-

trocuted. The other two were nowhere to be seen, but as Maddy stood there in the rain of the sprinklers, she realized she had a more serious problem.

The condo was full of dense smoke, getting thicker and more toxic every second. It was coming in through the front door—if it hadn't been before, the building now really was on fire. Dropping the fluffy pink weapon, ducking low, she approached the doorway and could see that the entire outside hall was in flames. The heat from the open door was murderous; she had to back off fast.

Making sure the apartment was empty of human—or inhuman—threats, she crawled on all fours to the kitchen and found the fire extinguisher. Empty! And the phone was dead! She couldn't believe it. Furiously grabbing a DustBuster off its charger, Maddy hurried back to the bathroom. She could hear the kids coughing in the tub.

"Okay, guys, we have to play a little game."

"I want my mommy!"

"I know, Dani, your mommy's coming. But we have to meet her outside, okay? You don't want to stay in here with all this yucky smoke, do you?"

"No. It hurts my *eyes*."

"No, I know it does, Sammy. Then you both have to do what I say. Get ready, this might be a little chilly . . ."

Maddy turned on the shower, soaking the complaining children from head to foot and draping wet towels over their heads. She then covered them with the clear plastic shower curtain and cinched it around their middles with another pair of dirty nylons, tucking the DustBuster in with them, nozzle downward. When it was turned on, the shower curtain inflated around the children's heads like a bubble—a bubble of filtered air.

"Okay, now everybody hold hands—we're gonna take a quick walk into the living room."

Leading the children, shielding them from the two injured men as well as the worst of the heat, Maddy hurried them into the living room and sat them by the open window. The street far below was hectic with sirens and the red and blue lights of emergency vehicles—real ones, she hoped. But even if they were, no rescue could come soon enough to save them. There would have to be another way.

"Listen, you guys, stay here by the window and wave so the nice men can see you. Breathe through your towels, like this. I have to go get something—I'll be right back."

Covering her upper body with the shower curtain, using the DustBuster to draw relatively clean air from the floor, Maddy searched the apartment for solutions, for some magic carpet to fly them out of there. What she wanted was rope, a nice, sturdy nylon rope—about five hundred feet of it—but the best she could find was bales of extension cord and old USB cable, pretty poor substitutes. Searching for something better, she began twining the available cables into a crude harness—a sling chair strong enough to hold the children.

But what to hold the harness? Some kind of parachute? A hang glider made with duct tape and garbage bags? A hot-air balloon? A chemical arresting rocket? Everything she needed was there in the apartment, but even a rope of knotted bedsheets would take too long—she had maybe two minutes left to assemble the raw materials and build anything. As it was, she could barely see; the smoke was becoming impenetrable, her makeshift breathing hood starting to melt, and she could hear the kids crying and coughing their little lungs out.

Maddy was nearly at the point of despair when she noticed the dining-room rug.

Hey. Flying carpet indeed—this was her day for miracle rugs.

In the center of the dining area, nearly covering the floor, was a handmade braided carpet—an Amish rope rug at least fifteen feet across. *Damn.* Quickly doing the math, a simple spiral algorithm, she figured it should be very nearly long enough . . . and hopefully strong enough. She couldn't believe she had almost missed it.

Moving as fast as possible, smoke and sweat stinging her eyes, Maddy shoved the dining table and chairs out of the way, then tried dragging the heavy rug into the living room. No chance—it was soaked from the sprinklers and weighed a ton. Okay.

Finding the outside end of the rope, she cut the binding threads with the toenail clipper until she had enough slack to tie it to a massive china hutch. Then, moving to the center of the rug, she freed the inner tip of the spiral, fastening it to her half-fashioned cable sling and unspooling the wires back to the living room. Her fingers were bleeding.

The kids started moaning for their mom at the sight of her, but Maddy had no time to reassure them—the sprinklers had cut out, the heat at her back was withering. Pressing the kids' shuddering chests together, she cinched the cable straps between their legs and up under their arms. It might pinch, but it would support them.

"Now hang on tight to each other!" she shouted, and threw them out the window.

The kids fell, screaming, until the slack ran out—till the wires drew taut and started stripping rope from the braided rug. With a not-too-painful jerk, their rate of descent slowed dramatically. It slowed *too* much, dropping them in fits and starts and finally stopping altogether, leaving them kicking and screaming down around the thirtieth floor.

Maddy was afraid the line might be tangled, but when she yanked on it, the rug grudgingly paid out more rope. The kids were just too light, the carpet's binding threads stronger than she thought—maybe because they were wet. Gravity was not enough; they would have to be lowered by hand. That was not good, because the dining room was an inferno: Wet or not, the rug was going to start burning through any second. And if they weren't down by the time it broke . . .

Maddy's brain was lit up like a Christmas tree, wires buzzing with all the mathematical variables, the myriad unknowns. She was in highest gear, and it still wasn't enough—some problems went beyond simple mousetraps.

Deeply worried that the rag rope couldn't support all three of them, she decided there was no choice. It was scary: Maddy didn't like heights and wasn't sure how to go about rappelling down the side of a building, especially not when she was shaking like a leaf. If only she could improvise a descender, some kind of friction device . . . but she was cornered; there was simply nothing left to use. Only her bare hands.

Okay . . . well . . . here goes . . .

But before she could climb over the windowsill, a hulking, helmeted figure lunged out of the smoke and pulled her to the floor. A raspy voice croaked, *"I gotcha now!"*

It was one of the fake firemen. He was burnt nearly to a crisp, his face and hands blackened, blistering, oozing blood. He was blind. Black lips peeled back from bloodworm teeth as he spoke.

"Where you think you goin'? You ain't goin' nowhere."

Maddy reached up and grabbed the taut rope, trying to pull herself up, but the man had her well pinned. He didn't seem to have any plan beyond restraining her, holding her in place and letting the fire do the rest.

Screw that.

Straining her skinny arms to their limit, Maddy pulled the rope down and crossed it under the man's chin . . . then let go. It sprang upward; the kids dropped another five feet, their weight stripping more line and causing the

coarse braid to saw against the man's throat. He flailed
against it, gagging. Maddy added to his difficulties by
kicking him away and sliding out from under.

"Come on, baby doll," he snarled. *"Stick around for
the weenie roast."*

She got to her feet, and as he leaped at her again,
Maddy ducked under his arms, drove her shoulder below
his center of gravity, and locked her hands together behind
his right leg. Using her body as a fulcrum, she rocked
backward, allowing herself to fall under his onslaught,
pulling his body where it wanted to go, guiding it up and
over her, unbalancing him, then centering both feet in his
groin and pushing as hard as she could with her legs so
that a man twice her size briefly became weightless, a
human missile following a trajectory that carried him over
the windowsill and outside the building.

But he had her. He had her sweatshirt in his clawed
fingers, dragging her out with him, headlong into the void,
so that in all of time and space, the only thing she had left
to grab was the rope, and suddenly the rug was unraveling
like somebody had harpooned a leviathan—two for the
price of one.

Falling, Maddy couldn't believe what was happening.
Stupid. How could she have been so dumb? Could have
just finished him off in the apartment, but oh no. Gone
straight for the carotid, the jugular, the basal ganglia. But
she was too nice—it was her biggest failing: not wanting
to kill anybody with her bare hands. Now they would all
hit the ground like a cluster bomb, kids first. That was if
the neck of her sweatshirt didn't choke her to death on the
way down—it *hurt.*

Kicking herself, Maddy didn't wait, didn't think, but
simply let go of the rope. That took the pressure off her
windpipe—at once, she and her attacker were in total free

fall. Oddly enough, even though their rate of descent increased, everything seemed to slow down. She had plenty of time to think.

The toenail clipper. Yes, there it was, still in her pocket. Maddy took it out and, with a swooping motion, reached behind her back, grabbed the man's fist, found his fat thumb, and with her other hand drove the clipper's steel beak deep under that big horny thumbnail.

His reaction was reflexive, instantaneous: He released her shirt as though it were a live wire, jerking his thumb away and hoarding it tenderly to himself, crumpling his whole body around it like a recoiling mollusk. Rolling away across windy space.

That took all of a split second, then Maddy fell onto the kids.

It was not exactly a devastating impact; they had been accelerating too, as the rug disintegrated ever more quickly. So it was back to babysitting again, humming "Rock-a-Bye Baby" as she and her charges hurtled together toward Ninth Avenue, and Maddy was barely able to find someplace for her legs before the rug spun apart entirely, its last outer coil twirling in the flames like an infernal lariat before abruptly springing taut, and the burning wooden hutch to which it was anchored—a piece of solid, Colonial-era craftsmanship, heavily freighted with family silver and wedding china—flipped over with a massive crash to charge like a loose cannon across the condo, billowing sparks as it gouged deep tracks in the parquet flooring. Other items of furniture piled up in its path, acting as a drag, so that by the time Maddy and the children touched down on the sidewalk, the impact was no more than a mild bump. *Then* the rope snapped.

The kids were all right. Maddy didn't wait around to see what would happen next. She ran.

ONE

MADDY AND BEN

Denton, Colorado, pop. 33,473.
Two years earlier.

HERE is what Maddy remembered of that night:
It had been raining for days. By Sunday night, the sky had finally cleared, and people had come out in droves to salvage something of the weekend. There was a big concert early in the evening, and the fairground was churned to mud. Everything had an ethereal glow—the cheesy soft focus of television flashbacks—and the carnival midway smelled of popcorn and wet sawdust.

Twiddling their plastic wristbands, Maddy Grant and her almost stepbrother, Ben Blevin, raised their voices above the hubbub. "That was *ridiculous*," Ben said. He was taller and darker than she was, with a seriousness that belied his sixteen years.

"I totally agree," Maddy said. "That was *amazing*." She was fifteen, buzzed from attending her first concert and secretly basking in the bronze godhood of her stepsibling-to-be.

"That's not what I meant. Can we go now?"

In the few months since her mom had started seeing Ben's father, Maddy had scarcely been able to think straight, jumping on every opportunity to hang out with her future relative. She knew it was sick, but she couldn't help it—she was well aware of her physical limitations. Pale, gangly-limbed, and freckle-faced, Maddy was not a troll; but neither was she a fairy princess . . . and she certainly had never been a magnet for the opposite sex. She'd never so much as been asked out on a date. So being thrown together into circumstances of enforced intimacy with a hunk like Ben was a godsend. Not that she pretended her new stepbrother had any such feelings for her.

Ben had personal issues she couldn't even imagine, issues he tended to keep to himself. For the first few weeks, she'd thought he hated her, and she couldn't blame him. It was one thing for your parents to get divorced, but to have your mother *die*—then to have to cope with your dad moving in with someone else—was beyond outrageous. Not wanting to intrude on his grief, she'd tried to be as invisible as possible, slinking around like a burglar in her own house, until one day he came up to her, and said, "Can we stop avoiding each other? Because this is getting ridiculous."

After that, things were easier. Not that they were BFFs or anything, but they could be in the same room together and sometimes even exchange words. The best, though, was being seen in public, especially at school. Maddy had never been Miss Popularity, but since Ben's arrival, she was suddenly in demand, all the bitch-queens cozying up for a backstage pass to her smokin'-hot new relation. And Maddy had played it for all it was worth . . . until Ben started going out with her best friend, Stephanie. That could have been a disaster, but fortunately it didn't last long. Maddy liked having Ben to herself. Being out with him made her feel better—made her *look* better. Ben was the ultimate fashion accessory.

"Oh, we can't leave yet." Maddy said. "I want something to eat. "

"How about a candy apple?"

"You know I can't eat those things. They gum up my braces."

"Well, then, let's get you some saltwater taffy."

"What? Didn't you hear what I—"

"Or some chewy, chewy caramel corn? Oops, sorry—the B word, I forgot."

"Very funny. I probably don't need all the carbs anyway." Maddy froze, staring. "Oh. My. God."

"What?"

"Don't look, don't look! I think that's her!"

"Who?"

"Marina Sweet."

"Oh God, no. Where?"

"Right there!"

Maddy's bedroom was a shrine to Marina Sweet. Pictures and posters and calendars showed doe-eyed Marina at all stages of her career: child sitcom star, flirty tween idol, touring sensation, international superstar, tarnished icon. Maddy's diary was an ode to this platinum-banged, platinum-selling recording artist, into which she poured all her girlish grief and yearning. She longed to *be* Marina, and on some level she felt that Marina was within her, a glamorous pop princess yearning to break free. Maddy had obsessed and fantasized and stared at Marina's tabloid residue for so long that she knew the other girl's life better than she did her own, as if by denying her own boring existence, she and Marina could somehow swap places.

Marina Sweet was the reason Maddy had begged her
mother to let her go to the carnival on a school night: to
finally see the legend in person. "Rare public appearance
for the increasingly reclusive star," was how some of the
news reports put it. Others were not so kind: "Small-time
venue for troubled starlet." Maddy didn't care; she wanted
to go.

Their folks were busy, so they made Ben take her to the
show. He wasn't happy about it, being about the only guy
in a sea of screaming teenyboppers, but Maddy had the
time of her life. Swept up in a blur of group euphoria,
dazzled by the lights and the sounds, she swayed and sang
to the music she knew so well, tears streaming down her
face. It was the most intense thing that had happened to
her since her parents' divorce.

Fortunately for Ben, the concert was short—shorter
than it should have been because Marina Sweet abruptly
disappeared. Disappointing her fans, she took off before
her big finale, the megahit single, "Soon, Ami." No thank-
you or good-bye, no curtain call, nothing. Everyone just
stood around stupidly, the musicians and dancers as confused as the audience, until a stagehand came out and
announced that Marina had left due to a "pressing engagement." The show was over.

"WHERE?" Ben asked doubtfully. "I don't see her."

"Right there! In the fun-house line. The one in the
hooded raincoat, with the sunglasses."

"*Her?* No way."

"It's her, I swear to God. She's incognito. I'd recognize her anywhere!"

"Are you serious? That girl doesn't look anything like
Marina Sweet."

"It's a disguise, don't you get it? That's what you have

to do to ditch the paparazzi—the trick is to do it before they even know you're gone. Leave right before the end of the show and slip out a side exit. Put on a wig and an overcoat and sneak away while everybody's still screaming for an encore. Stars *have* to do stuff like that, or the press will eat them up—look at what happened to Princess Diana and Michael Jackson. It's definitely her—come on!"

"Then how come nobody else seems to recognize her?"

"Cuz they're dumb! Come *on*!" Maddy grabbed his hand and pulled. "She's going into the fun house."

"This is *ridiculous*."

THE fun house was a portable plywood cave, painted black and red, with jigsawed flames and a fiberglass gargoyle suspended above the entrance doors. Tiny, two-seater cars rattled out of sight down the dark track, ferrying pairs of riders along its squeal-inducing itinerary before emerging a moment later and banging to a stop. The passengers were released, shaken but unharmed.

Maddy and Ben got in line behind the hooded girl, close enough to touch. For several minutes, they silently bickered over how best to get her to turn around, but before they could come to a decision, the object of their attention boarded a rickety black car and started off down the track. Following close behind, they got into the next car and belted themselves in. As the car jolted forward, Ben said, "I told you, it's not her."

"Is too. Shut up."

The cars passed over a fast-spinning roller and were catapulted through the swinging entrance doors, which read DANGER! KEEP OUT. Coasting along to the plunks of a banjo, they were carried up a steep incline and entered a cobwebby tunnel held up by timbers—an old mine shaft. Gleams of gold shone among the rocks, and an eerie voice chortled, *"We struck gold, pure gold. It's the mother lode, hee, hee, hee! You want some? Come on in . . . come take all you want . . ."*

The cars slowed. Flickering lanterns revealed several mangled bodies beside the track, then, bouncing up like a jack-in-the-box, their killer: a crazed miner holding a bloody pickax. A deep voice bellowed, "IT'S MY GOLD, ALL MINE!"

Maddy grabbed Ben's arm. Just in time, the car shot forward, clearing the ax but hurtling toward a dead end. A sign across the tracks read, BEWARE! MINE COLLAPSE. Just beyond was a pile of rubble, with arms and legs sticking out. At the last second, the car lurched sharply right.

Then they were in a greenish-lit tunnel, passing a dead canary in a cage. Sickly-faced corpses lay in postures of agony, clutching their throats. Voices gasped, *"Air . . . need air . . ."* As the car approached a patch of darkness, lights strobed to reveal a host of hideous ghouls blocking the way. Stiffly closing in, the zombies all held bloody picks and shovels, having already massacred the passengers of an earlier car, whose bodies lay half-eaten on the floor. Maddy shrieked, huddling tight with Ben.

Again, the car shot free around a blind curve.

Their faces were so close together that it would have required only the slightest effort to kiss. Suddenly, before Maddy knew it, Ben's lips were touching hers. She felt the warmth of his body in the dark, his arms around her, and she responded, heart hammering with fear and yearning. Fear that what they were doing was wrong, but even more that she might screw up her first real kiss—she wanted to do it right.

He sat back. "Oh my God," he said.

"It's okay," Maddy said. "I mean, we're not really related or anything."

"I know, but still . . ."

"Don't worry, I won't tell anyone."

"I must be insane."

"Why? Because I'm not pretty enough for you? Like *Stephanie*?"

"No, because you're gonna be my *stepsister*."

"So what? That doesn't make you a pervert."

"Oh no?"

"No—we just kissed, that's all."

"Oh, that's all, huh?"

"Yeah."

He mulled it over. "I don't know, man. That was a pretty intense kiss."

"Really?"

"Uh-huh."

"I thought so, too."

Around them, all was red and rumbling. Lava glimmered in the crevices, and blackened skeletons littered the floor. Screams echoed as if from a deep pit. Something about the room made Maddy's head hurt; suddenly, she didn't feel so well. She hoped the ride was almost over.

Entering the final straightaway, they saw the other car again. It was not far ahead.

"There she is," Maddy said.

"Watch this," Ben said, unbuckling his seat belt.

"Ben! Don't!"

"No, it'll be funny, watch."

As he jumped off the slow-moving car, the lights suddenly winked out. Everything went silent, and both cars shuddered to a total stop.

"Ben?"

There was no sound, nothing.

"Ben, this isn't funny. Get back . . . get back here buh . . . before you get . . ."

That was weird—Maddy could barely say the words. Her head felt all woozy, and her stomach began to whirl. She could feel the blood throbbing in her temples like a kettledrum. *Seasick,* she thought. Nearly retching, she knew something was seriously wrong, but she was tired, so tired. Feeling her head start to droop, she roused herself to stand, hanging on to the car for dear life. The floor rocked like the deck of a ship. *I have to get out of here.* Steadying herself, she let go and tried to walk.

"Help . . . help us . . ."

Outside. If she could just reach the outdoors. *Follow the tracks—the tracks lead outside.* Barely coherent, Maddy clung to this basic fact like a lifeline. Feeling her way along, swaying through the dark, she saw something looming up in her path. Someone or something . . .

"Ben?"

Not Ben. The other car, with its lone passenger still seated, as though primly waiting for the ride to resume. The car sat on the brink of a gaping devil's mouth, a leering Day-Glo-colored face with twining black horns and demonic tattoos.

Trying to speak, to say, *Marina . . . please . . . need help*, Maddy reached for the hooded figure.

When it turned, she screamed.

TWO

NEWS CYCLE

FUN-HOUSE TRAGEDY

Special to _The Examiner_

Every year, millions of teenagers attend traveling carnivals, lured away from their PlayStations and TiVos by the lights, the sights, the sounds, and the smells of an earlier generation's notion of interactivity. Like their parents and grandparents before them, they go seeking old-time fun and thrills, and perhaps the slight aura of danger: the time-honored sleaze of the traveling show.

Sometimes they get more than they bargained for.

Sunday night at the Denton Fairgrounds, teenagers Benjamin Blevin and Madeline Grant climbed into car four of the fun-house ride at Ridley's Laff-O-Rama. As they clattered along the dark track, ducking plaster zombies and rubber skeletons, they could hardly have imagined that the corny fake horror was about to turn very real.

Just as the teens jerked around the ride's final curve, less than twenty feet from the swinging exit doors, the car stopped. They probably thought it was part of the ride. But as they waited in pitch-blackness for whatever final thrill was in store, they might have noticed a strange sensation of nausea or dizziness . . . or perhaps nothing at all. Perhaps they merely went to sleep, unaware that leaking fumes from a faulty generator had turned their Tunnel of Love into a Tunnel of Death—literally a gas chamber. Dozens of other cars had passed through safely, their occupants complaining of nothing worse than a sudden headache. It was the terrible coincidence of a snag in the ride's chain drive that doomed Ben and Maddy to their fates.

As the teens quietly succumbed to lethal fumes, the ride operator, Cecil Bluth, 27, noticed that his control lever had gone dead. The cars wouldn't budge.

"I thought it was kids messing around," Bluth says. "Happens all the time. They'll jump off the cars while the ride's still in motion and fool around, then jump back on. Or they'll just throw trash at the exhibits. I'm always picking off spit wads, gum, you name it. If anything blocks the track, it sets off an alarm—there's an automatic shutdown. Usually happens at least once a night. I send Bernie to do a walk-through and verify ain't no safety hazard, which there almost never is. This time it was different."

Bernie is Bernard Wornovski, 36, the carnival's veteran mechanic, who entered the plywood archway as he had a thousand times before but never would again.

Cecil Bluth says, "Just before he went in, Bernie mentioned it was weird that nobody was yelling for help. He called out to let them know not to panic, but there was no answer. Most folks freak out pretty quick when you leave them in the dark, so we thought that was a little strange. Then when I didn't hear back from Bernie right away, the hair really pricked up on my neck. That's when I called 911."

(See *Tragedy*, p. A8)

THREE

DREAM THERAPY

PEPL r gud I lik thm dr. stevnz iz nis she iz mi fren soz ners claybrn and dr. wali nrs clabrn taks me swimn evre morning aftr brekfs mi favrit aktvt iz swimn i lik it

"MADDY, are you awake?"
   "Mmmm . . ."
   "Maddy, wake up. Time for school."
   "Mmmm-*nuh*!"

I yuz tu b norml i yuz 2b lik yu i had mad skilz thats wat pepl sa enywa i don no i don rely rmembr bfor tha aksidnt i wish i cud but I cant thas ok i cn stil dans

"WAKE up, sleepyhead."
   The voice was inescapable, persistent as an usher with a flashlight. Maddy's mind retreated like a toad under a

rock, but the more she withdrew into comforting darkness, the more that voice followed her down the hole. At the same time, some part of her knew she was being unreasonable, that it was high time she woke up, but she couldn't help it—she was *soooo tired.*

It had felt like the longest night of her life, an endless, restless sleep, densely cluttered with crazy dreams. Not ordinary nightmares of falling or fleeing, but an exhausting monotony of being stuck with needles, wired to machines, shackled to treadmills. Being walked and talked to death by infinitely patient doctors with big shiny clipboards and bigger, shinier grins. And the games—so many tedious games and puzzles, like some kind of waiting room in Hell. Then the questions! She couldn't even understand half the stuff they asked, but they would keep after her, pestering and cajoling until she came out with something they liked.

Showing her a picture, they might ask, "Do you know who this is?"

"Nuh . . ."

"That's you, silly! That's Maddy Grant. Now you try saying it."

"Muh-Maddee . . ."

"Good, good—don't give up."

"Gaaant. Gant."

"Try rolling your tongue: Grrant, Grrraaant."

"Gwaaant. Maddee Gwaaant."

"That's good! Excellent! And who's this?"

"Nuh . . ."

"That's your mommy! Bethany Grant. Can you say mommy?"

Then they might reward her, let her watch TV, play on the computer.

Oh, they tried to make it fun, to pretend it was all a big sleepaway camp, but it wasn't. Therapy, they called it. To

Maddy, it was more like school . . . only a million times more boring than any school she remembered. Not that she remembered much—only that she used to like school and didn't care at all for this dream therapy.

I dont lik tu rit its boren I hat ritn this jrnel but its tharpee jus lik tokkin is tharpee bla bla bla evrethnz tharpee tharpee suks eksep swimn yr not supos2 pee in tha pool but i sed 2 ners clabrn no thas tharpee

yestrda mi parnts cam tu vizit an we wen on a ltl feeltrp to see sum anamlz I luv anamlz

HER last dream: a van ride through the country, the picnic by the river—chicken salad sandwiches, potato chips, pickles. Tepid peach tea. Danish butter cookies from a tin. Her parents, smiling and praising her . . . and Dr. Stevens.

AFTER lunch, they wheeled her back in the van and drove the rest of the way, arriving at a sleek, mirrored building. A chrome cube with rounded edges, sitting on a grassy hill surrounded by pines. Maddy could see herself in the glass doors as they pushed her up the walk. She knew it was her because of her braces; otherwise, she wouldn't have recognized the drooling, slack-faced creature in the wheelchair. Not her face. So pale and puffy, with a childish pink bow in her hair. The sight was frightening—she jerked her eyes away, wishing she could wake up. Maddy hated mirrors.

The mirrored building was a funny place. The people there were just as nice as Dr. Stevens, but everybody talked too fast, gobble-gobbling together like turkeys. Occasionally, her mother might lean down and speak to her,

"Maddy, how would you like to go back home? Back to your old room? All your things are still there, just the way you left them, and there are a lot of presents waiting for you. Doesn't that sound like fun?"

"Nyeah . . ."

"That's what these nice people want to do, honey: to help you be yourself again so you can come home. Be the Maddy we remember. To skate and ski and go to the mall with Stephanie. Do you remember your friend Stephanie? She misses you. We all miss you, honey."

Mom was crying again. Maddy didn't quite know why, and didn't like it.

Dad stepped in. "Beth, stop, you'll just upset her. It's okay, honey—Mommy's fine, see? Funny Mommy!"

"MR. and Mrs. Grant, so pleased to meet you. Members of the press, Congressman Lawlor, welcome. I'm Dr. Plummer, the head man here at the Braintree Institute. And this must be Maddy! I've heard a lot about *you*. Dr. Stevens tells me you're quite the character. You are, aren't you? I can always tell. Welcome, welcome to Braintree.

"Well, I know you folks have been briefed about our program here, but let me walk you through it so you can maybe get a better idea of what we're hoping to accomplish with your daughter.

"It's been over a year since her trauma, and I know that Maddy's therapy has met with limited success. This is not unusual for her type of injury. She's had all the most innovative rehabilitation techniques, including alternative therapies like acupuncture, but she seems to have hit a cognitive plateau. You're concerned that she may never function at higher than a kindergarten level. You have expressed interest in exploring avenues that are a bit more . . . aggressive? Perfectly understandable. That's why

Dr. Stevens recommended you to our department. We specialize in something called Deep Brain Stimulation, or DBS.

"Now, in standard DBS, a pair of very fine wires is implanted in the brain, where they act as a kind of low-voltage pacemaker to reactivate damaged brain tissue, restoring a certain degree of lost function. It's a proven and reasonably effective procedure. But it's only a halfway measure—nobody expects a full recovery.

"That's where we come in. I specialize in an experimental form of DBS known as Remote Cortical Augmentation, or RCA. The basic principle of RCA is the same as DBS: a matter of stimulating the brain using wires. But where our work differs is in the degree of stimulation . . . and the precision. See, in DBS, the level of accuracy is relatively poor—you're throwing darts in the dark and hoping to luck into the target. When it works, the results might be dramatic . . . or they might not. And oftentimes any improvement is temporary as the brain becomes dulled to the stimuli.

"Just as with standard DBS, our procedure involves implanting a set of wires. Only instead of two, we implant two bundles of thirty wires each, all much finer than the ones typically used in DBS—less than a micron in diameter. The bundles are designed to unravel in a controlled way as they penetrate the cortex, sending branches into specific regions and giving us a wide range of potential targets—a nearly limitless combination. We call this the Christmas Tree.

"Once the array is in place, we test each point of contact to measure its neurological effect. The effects are then mixed and matched to produce the most successful combinations, just like single notes combining into chords of music. Over time, using a powerful computer, we are able to develop increasingly complex formulas for bypassing cognitive deficits, awakening the brain to whole new avenues of being. It's like conducting an orchestra. Finally, these chords are programmed into a portable, rechargeable data processor, about the size of an MP3 player, which is fitted to the cranium under the scalp and delivers a constant stream of directed pulses.

"This is for basic functioning. But the most promising aspect of the technology is that it is not static: The patient's personal data unit is wirelessly linked to a larger computer network, allowing the system to keep evolving, refining and customizing itself to the specific needs of its wearer. Like the human brain itself, it *learns*.

"At the heart of all this is a very unusual computer. Step this way, please.

"What you see here is our computer lab. Help yourselves to a donut! All looks pretty ordinary until you take a closer look inside our mainframe. Notice anything unusual? That's because our system's core is nothing less than an actual organic brain. Sounds like something out of a science-fiction movie, but it's quite real, and will soon be coming to a store near you. A highly simplified brain, not a human brain, but a brain nonetheless, comprised of millions of living neurons.

"See this box? This is it. Inside this shock-absorbent casing is a gel capsule containing a rudimentary form of intelligence, cultured from leech cells and sandwiched within a matrix of conductive fibers. It's smaller than a golf ball. Nerve signals are translated into optical pulses, which are then interfaced with specialized software. Why leeches? Leeches are used because their neurons are very, very large, and their structure is quite well understood— plus not many people have an ethical objection to using leeches. I know the thought of a leech brain might creep some people out; well, I can promise you that these leeches won't suck your blood, but they will give you a piece of their primitive mind. You may wonder what that's worth. Let me show you—come this way.

"This is our Simulation Room. Up on that screen is a 3-D computer model of a hypothetical city—a composite of different urban centers around the US, with pedestrian and traffic patterns, commercial activity, weather cycles, industrial development, you name it. Even fluctuations in capital and stock projections. The Leech-Tron has been running that program continuously for seven months, factoring in a hundred random events every second, and as you can see, it has grown incredibly complex.

"Now over here, in this studio, is an actual physical replica of the same city, made to the same exact specifications out of polystyrene foam and other raw materials, perfect down to the tiniest detail. That's our Demonstrator. If you'll follow me out onto our observation platform, you can see the entire practical model in operation.

"Welcome, ladies and gentlemen, to the Rat Race."

IN Maddy's dream, she was on a platform above a brightly lit toy city. It looked like the world's most elaborate model train set: hundreds of intricate buildings that covered the entire floor area. The model was in a kind of auditorium or soundstage, with lights and cameras dangling from cranes, and a network of catwalks up in the rafters.

Between the miniature buildings (and some of them weren't really so miniature) were streets and canals and elevated trains, all seething with hectic activity. It was noisy. It smelled like a pet store. But the most remarkable thing to Maddy was that it was not just a sterile clockwork, a toy store's gaudy Christmas display. It was alive. It was populated . . . or perhaps more accurately, it was *infested*.

Infested with rats!

Maddy laughed with delight—it was the funniest thing she had ever seen.

Rats everywhere, rats wearing little hats—black caps with blinking blue LEDs. Many of them also wore specialized body harnesses with side pouches and Velcro straps, like miniature pack mules.

And so *many*. The avenues were full of them, stopping and starting, yielding and passing, getting on and off trains and boats, most carrying loads of one kind or another, all moving in orderly lines as though trained for the circus—a perfect simulacrum of urban commerce. Or perhaps not perfect in that it was *too* perfect: There were no bottlenecks, no traffic jams, no pileups or police sirens. Just a smooth flow of furry bodies and pink tails, as orderly as the movement of blood cells through capillaries. Or ants in a nest.

Above her left shoulder, Maddy heard her father say, "This is amazing."

"Isn't it? Everything you see is controlled by computer. It's constantly refining the live model to match the simulation, down to a fraction of an inch. If you can believe it, we started with only one rat. Once the computer mastered that, we tried ten, then added about ten a week until we reached a thousand. The rats are manipulated, using very crude neural implants—nothing like the sophistication of the human prototype—but you can see it's enough to govern a wide range of behaviors. The truly remarkable feat here is not the implant itself but the logistical challenge: Every rat has its own complex series of functions, and each rat's mission intersects either directly or indirectly with every other rat, so they have to work at a high degree of organizational efficiency. Combine that with the need to keep them healthy, to feed and sleep them in rotating shifts, to cope with every conceivable variable, intended or otherwise, and you can understand the tremendous sophistication required to keep it running smoothly. Fortunately, we leave most of that to the computer. Thanks to its organic component, the system has great flexibility in adapting to random events, just as a living organism must. It forms new synaptic pathways as needed, quadrillions of them, far beyond what we can predict or understand. Fortunately, we don't have to."

"But why? Why build this whole thing?"

"*We* didn't build it, Mr. Grant. *They* did. They're still doing it, see? When anything breaks down, they fix it. The rats are the hands of the computer."

"But what does this have to do with our daughter?"

"This city is a complex system, just like your daughter's brain. The computer doesn't know the difference—it's all just urban renewal."

"I don't know. It seems so bizarre . . ."

"Okay, well, look at me. Do I seem bizarre or unusual in any way to you?"

"No . . ."

"That's good. Because just seven months ago, I suffered a severe stroke. Oh yes. Completely out of the blue. I was paralyzed, a vegetable, unable to walk or talk. My wife nearly signed a Do Not Resuscitate order. Almost pulled the plug."

"Oh my God."

"That's right. But look at me now. You see, Mr. and Mrs. Grant, I'm not only a doctor here at Braintree—I'm also a client."

FOUR

BLINDS

WEIRD. Maddy was amazed at how clearly she could remember her dreams. Normally, they evaporated upon waking like so much dry ice, all details lost in the fog. This was more like adjusting the focal length of a microscope: The harder she thought about her dreams, the sharper and more elaborate they became, so that it was necessary to scan the endless recollections as if fast-forwarding a DVD. *I must still be sick,* she thought. Scrolling, scrolling—no end in sight. *I'm delirious.*

The torrent of memories was fascinating . . . and disturbing. She'd never had such dreams, not even in her worst fevers. They were like a whole lifetime passing before her eyes. Not her lifetime, thank God, but the lifetime of some alternate-universe Maddy Grant—a drooling basket case who could barely walk or talk. Yet in these dreams she *was* that girl, as though her brain had somehow recorded things that had happened to someone else. It was creeping her out.

"Maddy, wake up."

"I'm *awake*. God."

The venetian blinds next to her bed were driving her crazy. Dust had collected on the beige horizontal slats, and all she could think was, *Why don't they make them vertical? Or just hang curtains.* It had to be a pain to clean these things, dusting each slat individually, and the scattered dust would only float back down and make them dirty all over again. Waste of energy. Plus the metal slats were unnecessarily heavy, noisy, and fragile, and the string-pulley mechanism overly complex. The whole thing was an accident waiting to happen—one crimped slat, one tangle, and it was history. It reminded her of a failed contraption from the dawn of aviation, one of those early technological bloopers. And why *venetian*, anyway? Were they really invented in Venice, and if so, what gave the Venetians license to design a window blind? The sun wasn't especially intense there, was it? You think Venice, you think canals, gondolas, bridges, churches. You think blown glass. You don't think crappy window blinds from an old detective movie. Egyptians or somebody like that should have the franchise on blinds—some ancient culture from a desert climate, who could do it right. Think of those rooftop windcatchers in medieval Cairene architecture. Now that was an elegant technology.

"Maddy."

Maddy turned toward the voice. It was a smiling, sharp-featured woman with a steely gray 'fro. *Dr. Stevens,* Maddy recalled. It was strange to see her in real life, because this wasn't quite the same Dr. Stevens from her dreams. That one was godlike and benevolent. Angelic. Capable of miracles. This was just a middle-aged woman with thin, cracked lips and an oddly ambivalent smile. She seemed to have shrunk substantially.

"Where am I?" Maddy asked. It hurt to talk. "What happened?"

"Don't worry, you're safe. You've had a bit of an accident, but you're doing fine. Your folks are on their way in now—they should be here any minute."

"What accident?" Maddy suddenly realized that her fingers were bandaged, and when she raised them to her head, she found more bandages covering her scalp. Her heart jumped in fright. "What is this?"

"You don't remember anything?"

Maddy tried to think back—back past the vivid dreams of that long, long, restless night, seeking the last time she had been fully awake. It was like trying to swim through molasses . . . but the harder she tried, the more clearly she could visualize shapes and colors through the muck. Faces, places, random familiar images flipping like pictures in a photo album. Marina Sweet. Colored lights over the trees and the wheezing sound of a calliope. With each mental effort, she felt a peculiar rush of acceleration, almost like changing gears on her bike.

Suddenly, she could smell popcorn and damp sawdust. The carnival. Craving a candy apple. Ben. Going in the fun house. That kiss in the dark. And at the end . . .

"Where's Ben? *What happened to Ben?*"

Even before Dr. Stevens answered, Maddy already knew. She had heard the doctor talking to her parents about it . . . but in the dream. That was just a dream!

"Now please remember that your daughter has suffered a significant brain injury. Considering she's just awoken from three weeks in a coma, she's doing exceptionally well—it's a miracle she's alive at all—but she's still in what we call a minimally conscious state. That means we're not quite sure what she may or may not be aware of. It's important that you don't overreact to her impairment—try to appear relaxed and upbeat. Reassure her that you haven't changed, that there's nothing to be afraid of."

"*We understand. Don't we, honey?*"

"*Normal. Yes, okay. I'll try. Thank you, Dr. Stevens.*"

"*Come this way.*"

"*I'm still just so thankful that you could squeeze her in here, you have no idea. It's a long trip for us, but just knowing that she's getting this level of care makes it so much easier to cope. That other hospital—*"

"*Of course. I understand, Mr. Grant. Just remember that your daughter is also providing a valuable benefit for us—we're a private research clinic, not a charity hospital. Medicine is our business. If Maddy wasn't helping us develop the next generation of neurological treatments, she wouldn't have been enrolled in the program. Many are denied, most of whom are very deserving people. For instance, we turn away many injured vets simply because their type or degree of brain trauma does not fit the narrow parameters of our study. So don't thank us too much for your daughter's care. We need her as much as she needs us.*"

"*Certainly, certainly.*"

"*Here we are. Maddy? Look who's come to visit: It's your mom and pop.*"

"*Oh my God, oh my God. Maddy! Baby!*"

"*Muhmm . . . fah . . .*"

"*Oh dear Lord . . . Maddy . . .*"

"*Bem . . . wuh Bem . . .*"

"*It's okay, baby, we're here. It's us.*"

"*. . . wah know wuh Bem . . .*"

"*What's wrong? What's she saying?*"

"*She's been asking about Ben Blevin since this morning. It's actually a sign of significant improvement that she remembers.*"

"*Oh my God. Have you told her?*"

"*We were waiting for you. We wanted her to have as much emotional support as possible.*"

"Oh God. My poor baby. Do you think we should tell her now?"

"I'm afraid that's up to you."

"Bem . . . wah Bem . . . gahhh . . ."

"Oh dear God . . . Maddy? Baby, I'm so sorry. Ben has gone up to Heaven to be with the angels. He's passed away. Do you understand, sweetie? But Mommy and Daddy are here, and we love you. We're here with your friend Dr. Stevens. You're safe now."

"Bem . . . Bem . . ."

"Baby? Maddy? It's Mommy. Doctor, I don't think she can hear me."

"From what we know, she's physically capable of hearing you, Mrs. Grant. It just may be that she doesn't comprehend what you're saying . . . or perhaps simply doesn't want to. That's not surprising. Give her some time to let it sink in. With therapy, we're hoping she'll continue to improve, but part of that will be accepting a profoundly different reality than the one she may remember prior to her injury. That goes for you two as well. You're all in it for the long haul. Today is the first day of the rest of your lives."

It was no dream, none of it. Twisting her hospital wristband until it hurt, Maddy cried, "He's *dead*?"

"Ben passed away, I'm afraid. It was too late to save him. It's a miracle you survived."

"No way . . . you're lying. I can tell you're lying."

"I'm so sorry."

"He can't be dead, okay? He *kissed* me! I can still feel it!"

Releasing a dose of sedative into Maddy's IV, Dr. Stevens said, "There there, it's going to be all right."

"No! He kissed me—he *liked* me!"

The room blurred, everything spinning. She tried to fight it, clinging to the bed rails and sobbing *"No, no . . ."* Then the tornado carried her away.

FIVE

SCRATCHES

WHEN she woke up, Dr. Stevens was still waiting.

"Ben," Maddy croaked.

"Madeline, that was a long time ago. It's over; it's time to let Ben go. You have a new life to look forward to. Don't you think he would want that?"

She glowered at the doctor as if seeing her for the first time. In a flat, weary tone, she said, "You never had any children, did you?"

"Now now, shhh."

"No, wait, I'm wrong." Maddy strained to sit up. "You *did* have a child. But something bad happened, right? It died, or disappointed you . . . or both."

"Hush now, that's enough."

"So you gave up. You turned cold and made it all about the work. I'm the work, aren't I? People like me. We're just substitutes for what you've given up—holy shit, you *hate* us. You're lying to me, and you're lying to yourself. You think I'm Pinocchio, but I'm a human being. You're the one made of wood."

Dr. Stevens blinked as though dazed. She laughed weakly, and said, "Miss Grant, you're just experiencing a drug reaction. Try not to speak."

Maddy collapsed back onto the pillow, all doped up. She was sweating, and her eyes burned with tears. "What do you mean, a long time?" she demanded. "How long have I been here?"

"Fourteen months."

"Fourteen *months*?"

"Yes—shhh, don't scream. You were comatose when we first brought you here, and since then you've been through extensive rehabilitation. For most of that time you were unconscious, or delirious. Someone should have cut your nails sooner; that's how you scratched your hands, I'm sorry. But I'm happy to tell you you've turned the corner. Thanks to your recent surgery, we're confident of a full recovery . . . perhaps within days. You may not realize it yet, but the change is striking."

"MADDY! OH, OH, MY BABY!"

Before Maddy could react, her mother swept in like a tornado and fell upon her, sobbing hysterically.

"Oh God oh my sweet baby . . ."

"Hey, Mom. Ow."

Her dad was there, too—her real dad, Roger, not Ben's handsome father, Sam—but he kept his distance, sagging tearfully against the doorway. Roger Grant knew Maddy didn't like big emotional displays—she had suffered enough melodrama during the divorce to last a lifetime.

"Mom, I'm not an infant. Come on, it's okay."

Her mother sobbed against her awhile longer, then sat up and fumbled a pack of tissues out of her purse. Her face was a disaster.

"Oh my God. I'm sorry, sweetie. It's just—it's just that I never thought I'd have you back again. Look at you! I can't believe it!"

She dissolved once more into wracking sobs. Maddy's father came forward and put his arm around his ex-wife's shoulder, saying gently, "That's enough now, Beth. Maddy's just woken up; she probably doesn't need us going to pieces right now."

"I CAN'T HELP IT!"

"Okay, okay . . . relax."

"MY DAUGHTER IS ALIVE! CAN YOU UNDERSTAND THAT?"

"Yes, yes—shh."

"MY LITTLE GIRL IS BACK! SO JUST—JUST LET US ALONE FOR FIVE SECONDS! *JESUS!*"

"Fine. Absolutely. Sorry—go ahead."

Maddy asked, "You guys haven't gotten back together by any chance, have you?"

Sniffling, her mother gave a rueful chuckle and blew her nose. "No, honey."

"We just both wanted to be here for you."

"Divorce or no divorce, you're our only daughter."

Maddy looked at her folks, so broken up. It must have been horrible for them. They looked old and worn-out, as if they were the ones who belonged in the hospital. They were so . . . pitiful. It was disturbing to see them this way, nothing like the uncritical childish adoration she'd felt for them in her dream. In the dream, they were her heroes, they were back together again, reunited as a family, and it was all so effing wonderful. Stupid.

Maddy felt bad about not sharing the moment—obviously this was a huge deal to them—but from her point of view, she hadn't gone anywhere. Apparently she'd snoozed through all the really rough stuff. Her most meaningful event was Ben's death . . . and obviously nobody cared about that anymore. Ben Blevin, the first boy she'd ever kissed, was old news.

Maddy looked past her parents to Dr. Stevens, who was standing unobtrusively in the corner.

"So . . . when can I go home?"

"Soon. We'd like to keep you a few more days, just for observation."

"Haven't you observed me enough by now?"

Her folks laughed gratefully at her wry tone—this was the Maddy they remembered—but the doctor only smiled and said, "Not quite."

SIX

THE PROCRUSTEAN
READING ROOM

THE Braintree Clinic was different in her dreams. In
dreams, it was much bigger inside than out. In dreams,
it was old. She remembered it as a magic box, a brightly
mirrored portal into a strange castle riddled with crazy
catacombs and pools of white light. It echoed.

The reality was less impressive: a generic silver module five stories high, with a pleasant view of trees. Braintree was obviously very well funded, everything gleaming
and state of the art, but Maddy thought it was a little lame
how they wanted it to look like something out of *Star Trek*
when behind the chrome veneer it was really the same old
crap. The inefficiencies drove her crazy, not to mention the
health hazards—she could practically smell formaldehyde
leaching from unstable compounds in the furniture. And
forget cracking a window! Wandering the faux-futuristic
halls, she half expected to turn a corner and find herself in a cavern full of enormous, rusty machinery. But
Maddy knew there could be no such place there—that it

had to be some kind of residual memory from the fun house.

The fun house. Maddy had read news reports of the carnival accident, but thankfully she didn't remember very much of that night. And it was hard to tell which of her memories were true, so she was always looking for independent confirmation. Verifiable facts. There were still a lot of gray areas, neutral territories where dreams and reality battled for turf in her head. However much she would have liked to make peace with both sides, they could not share the same ground; they did not mesh. They could be remarkably similar at times, but they occupied separate universes. Nevertheless, she homed in on any points of congruence she could find, seizing them like handholds—intersections along the tightrope where her fumbling mind could find purchase.

One such place was the Reading Room.

In her dreams, she had spent a lot of time there, and was surprised to find it much as she remembered: a cozy library and study center, all wheelchair-accessible. She had overheard Dr. Plummer call it the Procrustean Science Reading Room—she wasn't sure why. Unless maybe because it had the pleasant, crusty smell of old books.

It was Hell.

Even wide-awake, she was still a little scared of those books. They figured prominently in her most recent nightmare, a long, weird episode in which she craved books like a drug, cracking their covers and inhaling their contents. No matter how many books she devoured, nothing slaked her terrible thirst. The frustration caused her to rip many of the books apart, cutting her fingers to ribbons as she sought richer marrow to suck. She found a computer, and that helped for a while, but in the end its flow of sustaining manna became a trickle of thin gruel, another starvation diet. Out of desperation, Maddy mangled the computer, too, chasing the spring to its source, enlarging the well. But the dream ended before she finished.

Perusing the shelves, she knew the books were just books. They did not beckon like insanely addictive fruit. She couldn't crack them like coconuts and drink their words in one gulp. Proof of that was in the fact that she barely recognized most of the titles, much less remembered their contents. Maddy had never been a big reader; books were not high on her list of favorite entertainments, and these looked especially dull: mostly kids' books and elementary study manuals. Plowing through the whole library sounded like the worst kind of drudgery. She couldn't imagine doing it. And yet . . .

There were her bloody fingerprints. Volume after volume imprinted with her own dried blood, irrefutable DNA evidence of her very recent lunacy. Pages torn and taped together—like her fingers. A great many books missing, replaced by new ones.

Maddy picked up a pristine copy of *The Compleat Shakespeare* and flipped through it. She had always found Shakespeare unreadable, but this was clearly a moron-level abridged version, the watered-down Kid Lit edition. Skimming *Titus Andronicus*, she flinched, ripping out a handful of pages. *Ow. Damn.* There was a bead of blood on the exposed base of her thumb—a paper cut!

Sucking her hand, Maddy thought, *What kind of sadistic shit is this?*

Likewise, the "computer" was bogus. It resembled a real computer on the outside but was some sort of cheap imitation, agonizingly slow and clumsy, with limited Internet access and a keyboard that was basically a medieval torture device. She would think she was getting somewhere only to have the picture abruptly scramble. No wonder she had been so frustrated. Whether or not she had ever really taken the device apart, at the moment it was whole and showed no sign of having been fiddled with . . . except that its CPU was locked in a metal cabinet. That was new.

Out of curiosity, Maddy took two paper clips from the desk and picked the lock. In minutes, the computer was laid bare. As she tinkered with its circuits, she suddenly realized there was someone watching her. A guy.

"What are you doing?" he asked.

Flushing red, trying to cover the evidence of her shame, she said, "Nothing."

"Is that a computer?"

"That's what I'm trying to figure out."

"Did you take it all apart like that?"

"It's supposed to come apart."

"Yeah, with tools. You use your teeth, or what?"

"Ha-ha, very funny."

"Sorry, I don't mean to bug you. I don't know if we've met before. Are you a patient here?"

"No, I'm a brilliant junior neurosurgeon. Duh, I'm a patient. Which I assume you are, too, unless you shaved your head for kicks."

"No, I'm a patient." He held out his hand. "Pleased to meet you. My name's Dev."

"Maddy Grant." She reached to shake, then hurriedly retracted her bandaged hand. "Sorry."

"What happened to your fingers?"

"Nothing," she said. "Couple of paper cuts."

"*Paper* cuts?"

"Sometimes I cut myself."

"How?"

"It's because the pages are too sharp." Annoyed by his concerned look, she said, "It's not on *purpose*."

"What do you mean, they're too sharp?"

"The paper is wicked sharp and brittle. I think it's been heat-treated or something. It's some kind of stupid dexterity exercise."

"Where is this paper?"

"Up my butt. Where do you think? Inside the books!"

"Which ones?"

"All of them!"

"Wait—you really got all cut up like that just from *reading*?"

"I told you, the books are weird. You'll see. You don't notice at first, but all of a sudden the pages start ripping out, and next thing you know, there's blood all over the place. And those cuts *sting*, man. It's obviously some kind of stupid test because the computer is just as bad—you ever get cramps in both hands at the same time? That's why I'm simplifying the interface. The doctors deny it, but the purpose of their experiments is obviously to make every task here as hard as possible, so we have an easier time recovering back home."

"That sounds a little messed up. Death by a thousand paper cuts?"

"It's the only thing that makes logical sense. And it works—I swear, I am so psyched to be leaving tomorrow."

"How long have you been here?"

"Over a year. But I've only been fully conscious for a couple of days now. Before that, it's all a big acid trip, complete with flashbacks. What about you?"

"I don't know."

"What do you mean, you don't know?"

"I mean I don't know. I can't remember anything for more than a few hours at a time. That's why I'm here, so they can hopefully cure me."

"That's horrible!"

"It's not so bad."

"How do you remember anything?"

"I remember basic stuff like my name. Anything else important I write on my arm—see?"

"Wow. Huh."

"Yeah. So you're some kind of mad genius or something?"

"Oh yeah, that's me." She scoffed. "I'm a real Young Einstein."

He looked at the intricate circuit board she was soldering with a glowing twist of live wire from a cannibalized light fixture. "No kidding."

She shook her head. "Anyway, it's not like there's anything else to do around here. I'd kill for a TV. Just make sure you tape up your hands before you try reading any of this kiddy lit. You should actually write that down."

"Thanks. Maybe I'll just browse for now." He obviously thought she was a maniac.

Maddy reassembled the computer while Dev scanned the shelves. She stole glances at him while she tinkered. With his hospital pallor, shaved head, and blue and black scribbles on his left arm, he looked very punk; but there was something endearingly childlike about him. Innocent. Physically, he might resemble a creepy skinhead . . . but so did she. Other than that, she would have never guessed he had such a serious problem. Actually, he was cute in a skinny way—he had the rangy build and slight twang of a Southern farm boy. Both of them were wearing the same baggy green scrubs, nothing underneath, and Maddy was struck by the intimacy of that, as though they were in their pajamas—or their underwear. For all she knew, he could be a dangerous psycho, but they wouldn't let someone like that roam around the hospital, would they? It suddenly occurred to her that she was alone in a room with a mental patient. Of course, so was he.

"Kiddy lit, huh?" he said, interrupting her thoughts. "I don't s'pose you got any recommendations?"

Wary though she was of the library, his snide tone made her defensive. "There's some good stuff, yeah. I like *James and the Giant Peach*. Or *Matilda*—did you ever read anything by Roald Dahl? *Charlie and the Chocolate Factory*?"

"I saw the movie."

"I also like *Bartholomew and the Oobleck*, *Pagoo*, *The Clambake Mutiny*, *The Pushcart War*, *Harriet the Spy*, *The Egypt Game*, *The Magus*, *I Claudius*, *Ulysses*, *The Golden Bough*, *Sexual Personae*, *Gray's Anatomy*—" She unconsciously began talking faster, as if rolling downhill. "—*Applied Kinematics*, *Interpretation of Nature and the Psyche*, *Strength of Materials*, *Fundamentals of Acceleration*, *Chemicals and Compounds*, *Molecular Engineering*, *Probability in Engineering*, *Principles of Mechanical Design*, *Automotive Engineering*, *Velocity Problems*, *The Coriolis Component*, *Algorithms and Computing Machines*, *Anatomy of LISP*, *Pattern Recognition*, *Cybernetics and Motor-Neuron Compatibility*—" She was blazing, the syllables all running together. "—*Neue Bahnen der physikalischen Erkenntnis*, *Computability and Logic*, *Philosophiae Naturalis Principia Mathematica*, *Engineering Thermodynamics*, *The Joy of Cooking*, *Behavior of Slaughter Plant and Auction Employees to the Animals*—"

"Whoa, stop, I get it. Damn."

Maddy's mental gears spun down. "What, sorry?"

"No, it's cool—you're a brainiac. That's awesome."

Feeling tears spring to her eyes, she said, "You're a jerk."

"What?"

"I know everybody thinks I'm retarded. *I'm not retarded.* I may not be as smart as everyone else around here, but I'm not stupid."

"Wait, I don't—"

"At least I'm not an asshole!" Maddy ran from the

room and along the corridor. The fluorescent ceiling lights were all strobing, making her feel like she was running in slow motion. Not wanting anyone to see her cry, she ducked down the fire stairs to her floor and walked casually past the nurses' station. Once safely inside her room, she fell sobbing on the bed.

Why, Ben? she thought. *Why did you have to leave me here all alone? I wish you'd taken me with you. I wish we were together right now, and this was all just a bad dream.*

SEVEN

REPORT

POSTOPERATIVE ANALYSIS:

Subject, Madeline Zoe Grant, exhibits rapid cognitive improvement in all areas, including neuromuscular/response. Cortical sensitivity to stress factors nominal within test parameters—dopamine inhibitors at saturation. CT, fMRI, and EEG scans show subthalamic efficiency at 410% above normal. Patient exhibits confusion, fear, and frustration from increased neuroactivity, but attributes this to physical debility and external situational factors. Is largely unaware of accelerated performance; complains that the test regimen is "for retards" or "boring." When asked why she started tearing pages out of the practice material, replied that she didn't want to read anymore because "it hurts my hands"—by which she meant that she could not turn the pages fast enough to keep up with level of reading comprehension. Similarly, when given a standard computer, Subject soon developed mild tendonitis from manipulating the mouse and keyboard—her joints and tendons cannot keep pace with her neural processes. Likewise, at full engagement, her visual scanning capacity surpassed the scan rate of the computer screen, rendering it useless. Despite such handicaps, Subject was able to complete doctoral-level examinations in applied calculus, celestial mechanics, nuclear physics, molecular biology, advanced chemistry, statistical analysis, semiotics, political theory, and a number of specialized fields of study. Based on test results, she has memorized significant portions of the reference library, both printed and on disk. When provided with only the first proof from Euclid's *Elements*, she was able to logically extrapolate the entire field of geometry, moving into levels of fourth-dimensional theory so complex that no one on staff is qualified to interpret it. We have forwarded her notebook to specialists for evaluation. Likewise, her Intelligence Quotient exceeds our ability to quantify it. But she herself does not yet recognize the change, in fact is unable to comprehend it . . . perhaps the one thing she can't comprehend. When her brain is challenged, it automatically shifts the burden to the computer unit, which elicits greater and greater degrees of processing power from her own dormant neurons until she can solve the problem, thus giving her the illusion that every problem is equally simple. Reading a textbook of theoretical physics is no different to her than flipping through *The Cat in the Hat*. For that matter, her critical intuition is so acute that some of the staff have reported feeling uncomfortable around her because she is so adept at "reading" people, i.e., deducing from their clothes or manner (or any number of other factors) exactly what they may be thinking. I experienced this myself in regard to the Program. Nevertheless, Subject doesn't yet grasp the magnitude of her own abilities, still thinks she's a mediocre student, weak at math and Spanish, and because of this may be able to transition more easily back into the life of an ordinary teenager. Whether or not she can succeed at this—or for how long—will determine the next phase of occupational therapy. For the present, Subject is fit to be released to the care of her family. Get her the hell out of here.

EIGHT

DRIVE-THRU

THE car ride home was difficult. It didn't start out badly—Maddy was just so glad to be out of the hospital that everything around her had a heightened reality, a saturated Technicolor brightness that made her feel like she was in some kind of Disney musical. Bright golden sunlight, blue sky, brilliant autumn leaves . . . even the stiff breeze was a joy.

She felt strong enough to stand, but they didn't let her: An orderly wheeled her to the curb and helped her parents load her in the car.

God, the car, Maddy thought, looking at the old Suburban. This piston-engined monstrosity with its American flag and Support the Troops sticker—were they all insane? When she was belted in, her parents just sat there for a second. She realized that her mother was getting all worked up again.

"Let's just go."

"Oh, honey, it's just such a *miracle* . . ."

"I know, but can we go? Really—just go. Please!"

They drove. After a while, her dad said, "Boy, I bet it feels good to be out of there."

"I guess. Yeah."

"So what's the first thing you want to do, now that you're back among the living?"

"Go to Disneyland!"

"Really?"

"No."

"Oh."

"Daddy, I just want to go home. I feel so out of touch, like a stranger . . . but I think I'll be fine if I can go home and decompress for a while. Reconnect. Go someplace familiar, surrounded by my own things. I want to lie on a bed and know it's *my* bed. I want to wear my own clothes, clothes that smell like me, and walk in my own shoes. I want to hug Mr. Fuzzbutt until he squirms to get away. I want to feel the way I used to feel, like everything just feels *right*—the way it's supposed to."

"Of course you do, honey. That's perfectly normal after being away for so long. Dr. Stevens said so."

"But that's what's so weird. I don't feel like I've been away for any time at all. It's like it all happened to another person . . . but that her memories have somehow gotten mixed up with my own. I can't really explain it."

"Well, honey, Dr. Stevens said—"

"I know what she said! I *know*. That doesn't make it any easier."

Her mother said, "Honey, everything will be just the way it was, I promise. We've left your room exactly the way you left it. Because that's the same thing we all want. It's what we've been praying for all these months, and the reason you're here talking to us now is because the Lord answered our prayers—and I'm sure He's not finished yet. Just give it time, be patient. You'll see."

"I am. I'm trying."

Maddy couldn't bring herself to tell her folks that she also wanted *them* to be the same. To give up this stupid divorce baloney and get back to being the wonderful, omnipotent deities she had revisited in her dream, who used to laugh and dance and steal kisses in the garage. Who flirted in the kitchen and held hands across the dinner table. Most of all, who sheltered and protected *her*, making it possible for Maddy to trust, to hope, to live the worry-free life of a child. She needed that again.

But that was all years ago, before the fights started. Before her dad started staying away longer and longer, and finally moved out altogether. Before they sat her down one day after school and broke the terrible news to her, so that well before the accident, Maddy was already damaged, a shut-down shell of herself.

She couldn't tell them she wanted to love them again. Trust them again the way she had in the dream. Like when they were big, and she was little. She wanted to let go of the monkey bars and let them catch her. But she couldn't just yet . . . and wasn't sure she ever would.

It was several hours getting back home, so Maddy had plenty of time to catch up on current events. Her parents talked nonstop, with the radio on, taking turns as though afraid to let loose the reins of their upbeat patter.

Had it always been like this? This terror of silence, of space? She made a great effort to act interested in Aunt Trudy's gallbladder surgery and Grandpa Simon's new wife (she was *Mexican*!), but after a while she just had to tune it out, it was such a catalogue of trivia. Even the radio seemed unusually insipid—Maddy usually loved country music, but something was wrong with this stuff. Its mind-numbing banality depressed her. Much better to watch the country itself flow by. Nature was a relief.

Engrossed in the fractal patterns of the trees, she realized that her mother was asking her something.

"Hm? What, sorry?"

"I just asked you what you might want to do about food. It's about time we took a little snack break, don't you think?"

"Sure, yeah—whatever you guys want."

"Do you have any preferences?"

"No, not really. Anything's fine."

"Burgers?"

"Okay."

They pulled up to a drive-thru and ordered. Faced with the familiar and yet oddly unappetizing choices, Maddy felt a brief twinge of anxiety, but then her subconscious kicked in and her vocal cords took over: "I'll have the bacon cheeseburger, onion rings, and a large diet soda." She realized as she automatically recited the words that this was not what she wanted at all but merely the same stuff she had always ordered in the past: "Maddy's favor-ites." But that was another Maddy—a stranger to her.

With this thought came an intense rush of panic, and it was all she could do to control it. She shuddered in the backseat, sweating furiously, and pressed her hands over her face until it passed. Fortunately, her folks were too busy paying, then checking the bags of food to really notice.

"Honey, are you okay? You're white as a sheet."

"I'm okay. Little carsick. I have to go to the bathroom."

"Wait, let me help you—"

"No, that's okay. Back in a sec."

Maddy bolted from the car and made her way to the restroom. Her legs felt like rubber bands, and once inside, she collapsed against a toilet, dry-heaving her guts out. After a few minutes she climbed to her feet and tottered to the sink. Looking in the mirror, she thought, *Maybe I'm dying*.

Taking off her ski cap, she inspected the bandages on her head, peeling the edge back to see the stitches. Lovely.

Anne Frankenstein. Under the skin at the back of her scalp was a smoothly curved thing like a limpet, about three inches long, which she knew to be the implant. That was only the top part; the rest was sunk into her skull, with ultrafine metal roots branching deep inside her brain. Weird. At least the stubble meant that her hair was coming back—the doctors said that would soon cover everything.

With a shock, she suddenly realized that her braces had been removed! Wow. Then a lady with two kids came in, and Maddy pulled herself together, splashing water on her face. The kids gawped—*Mommy, look!*—and the mother shushed them up.

"It's not cancer," Maddy said, drying her face and putting her hat back on. "I'm just a freak of modern science."

Her father was waiting outside the door.

"You okay?" he asked.

"I'm *fine*, Dad—jeez."

"Well, you still look a little shaky. Your mother was worried. It's nothing to be embarrassed about."

"I'm not embarrassed. Everything's just a little weird, that's all."

"Hey, it's weird for us, too, you know."

"I know. I'm sorry."

"Nothing for you to be sorry about, kid. Just don't be afraid to tell us whatever we can do to make it easier for you. That's why we're here, okay?"

"Okay. Well, I don't think I can eat this food."

"That's okay. No appetite?"

"No. Not really."

What she hesitated to say was that everything about the place screamed bloody murder. Maddy was no vegetarian, she had eaten meat all her life without giving it a thought, but suddenly . . . suddenly she could *see* the whole process, reverse-engineered from Finish to Start. Every single thing she looked at seemed to bloom before her eyes, deconstructing, peeling back layer from layer to its fundamentals, all the pieces branching from a central truth—which, in the case of the fast-food franchise, was grim death. Institutional hell.

She could read it in the cheerfully generic architecture and packaging, in the equally generic (but less cheerful) employees and patrons. The jolly artifice was a disguise, the inviting red gloss on a poison mushroom. It was all a false front, and beneath that plastic façade of pleasant order was an appalling dungeon of suffering, filth, and darkness. It was not a restaurant but a machine, the shiny ass end of a cold, impersonal thresher that reduced living, feeling flesh to frozen cakes of slurry.

Of course, Maddy had always known that animals were killed for their meat, but the scale of the killing had been unimaginable and very remote. Now the horror was laid out right in front of her, the whole mechanism mapped out in her head like a mental PowerPoint presentation:

A burger disassembles as if by magic, its tepid gray patty flying into a heat sterilizer, then suddenly rock-hard into a freezer, where it slips into a stack of identical frozen disks, to be shipped backward by refrigerated truck to a factory, where it instantly thaws and joins a great vat of raw pulp—a combination of meat, chemical additives, and pathogen-rich fecal matter—that is sucked through a grinder and reconstitutes as red slabs of flesh on a conveyer belt. These hunks of muscle tissue are then ingeniously pieced together to assemble a dead cow . . . which, dangling from a hook, abruptly starts gathering blood and offal into itself, filling up its body cavity like the bag of a vacuum cleaner and zipping shut, to be neatly upholstered with new cowhide. Suddenly, it starts to twitch—it's alive! Dropping to the floor, the cow jerks to its feet and flinches as its fractured skull abruptly claps solid. It ambles backward into daylight, joining a line of other cows.

That was the process in a nutshell: millions upon millions of domesticated cows, pigs, and chickens raised in sheds, pumped full of hormones and antibiotics, crammed into trucks, bludgeoned to death, ripped apart and churned up with their own spilled offal, then simply heated sufficiently to sterilize the germs. Sold.

It wasn't just livestock that died of stupidity: People were part of the chain, too. So eager, they were lining up for the pleasure, compliant bovines herding themselves. Oblivious to the killing, absolutely disconnected from the sources of their food. Absolved of any complicity. That was the trouble, that willful, insatiable innocence. No less credulous than the cattle, they came drawn by the addictive chemical allure of fat, salt, caffeine, and high-fructose corn syrup, driving up in droves to pay bottom dollar for the bargain of obesity, constricted arteries, and diabetic shock. Ironic that it was called a chain restaurant—all that was lacking to complete the cycle was that they didn't then feed the human remains back to the animals. *That's a waste,* Maddy thought. *No doubt someone is working on that.*

They returned to the car. Her mother was worried about her lack of appetite, but her father signaled her to play it cool, let it go. To Maddy's relief, she went along— that was a first. Trying to be equally accommodating, Maddy nibbled some onion rings.

As they neared the outskirts of their hometown, she became fraught with more conflicted feelings, more things she had never thought of before. She couldn't understand it: She had always taken her life for granted as the best of all possible worlds . . . or perhaps the *only* of all possible worlds:

What of consequence could possibly lie beyond these perfect houses, this pleasant sea of lawns? TV and radio gave no plausible clue, nor did anything else in this care-

fully cultivated mindscape. It wasn't just the grass being
weeded and raked around here. It scared Maddy to realize
that all her life she had been living such a shallow existence, a big fat lie, its limitations made bearable only by
certain childish assumptions, the first of which was never
to question its rightness. Even her parents' divorce—a
commonplace event among her peers—had not under-
mined Maddy's faith in the essential concepts: *God*, *Country*, *Family*. Why should it be any different now? And yet
somehow, home no longer felt like home.

She kept pushing these alien feelings down. Focus on
the positive! And there was a hopeful tingle of anticipation, certainly, but it was curdled by the same kind of nauseating total awareness that had spoiled her lunch.

The houses all looked the same. Generic. Impersonal.
Mindlessly repetitious. Street after street, subdivision after
subdivision, orderly as an immense circuit board, her once-
beloved neighborhood sprawled across the countryside,
reducing the life cycles of its inhabitants to impersonal
blips in a computer. The machine again—the same machine. Was that what it was all about? *Farming us, fatten-
ing us like cattle . . .*

No! This time Maddy was determined not to give in to
it. Talk it out—that was what she had always done in the
past. She needed to get over herself and trust her parents
like she used to. Before the divorce. Love them like she
did in her dream. Why should that be so hard?

"Could I ask you guys something?"

"Of course, honey."

"Why do we live all the way out here?"

"What do you mean?"

"Well, I mean, we've always spent so much time in the
car. You're both always complaining about the traffic and
the gas prices. I kind of think that even had something to
do with the divorce, right? The fact that you guys never

had any time together? What with commuting to work and driving me everyplace. Couldn't we have just lived a little closer to the city?"

Caught off guard by this peculiar non sequitur, her parents fumbled for a reply. Her dad was first to come up with something:

"Maybe, but your mother and I decided even before we got married that the first thing we wanted to do was make sure we lived in a place where it was healthy to raise a child. A real neighborhood, away from all the crime and pollution, with decent schools and a sense of community—like we had when we were kids. We wanted you to be safe."

He said these last words with a crack in his voice, sad eyes welling up in the rearview mirror.

Sidestepping the emotion, Maddy pressed on.

"Okay, but what about the larger issues? I mean, don't crime and pollution just get worse if people like us bail out? What happens to those people who can't leave? Is that fair? I mean, how safe are we in the long run if millions of kids grow up without a stake in perpetuating the culture? No wonder there's crime. And you guys are always complaining about taxes, but isn't it taxes that subsidize this suburban lifestyle—all the roads and utilities and everything? Wouldn't it be more patriotic to all work together to make better cities and schools for everybody? Leave nature alone? Look how dead it is out here—there's no creativity, no individuality. No sense of history. And speaking of pollution, just think how much carbon dioxide we've generated driving a hundred miles a day for all these years. Plus the oil spills. And isn't it ultimately people like us who are responsible for this war? If not for oil, we wouldn't even be in the Middle East. We should have a bumper sticker that reads, Support the Sheiks."

Her parents listened with baffled unease, then her father said, "Well, honey, that's true I suppose . . . but our whole economy depends on oil. It's because of oil that we have the standard of living we have in this country. Would you rather live like this or like someone in the Third World, with no car, no television, no refrigerator or air conditioner? No cell phone or modern convenience of any kind?"

"But Dad, that's not the choice. There are plenty of alternatives to oil. And for sure better technologies than this primitive, internal-combustion deathmobile. The basic mechanism hasn't changed for over a hundred years—obviously it's all about money! I can't even believe we still drive these things. We might as well still be hand-cranking an old Model T."

"Well, Maddy, what would you have us drive? A bicycle?" Her folks laughed at the absurd notion.

Maddy considered the question, and immediately began assembling materials in her head.

"No. But something clean. Preferably that flies. That way, you not only eliminate traffic but the need for roads."

"Flies! That's good. Hey, I'd like that, anytime we ran into traffic, we could just—zoom! Up in the air."

They were humoring her; Maddy barely heard them. An ideal city rose from the plains of her mind—a city swarming with clean, green, bubble-topped vehicles.

"Something solid-state," she continued. "Without moving parts to wear out. Frictionless . . . silent. Okay: Redundant contrarotating turbines with piezoelectric actuators, magnetic-repulsion bearings, universal GPS-based guidance algorithm so nobody needs a pilot's license. Hydrogen-biofueled using on-demand electrolytic solar nanoconverters—it'd be easy."

"Easy!" Her folks hadn't understood anything she'd just said.

"Sure. The technology's pretty much available in one

form or another. It just has to be put together and mass-produced."

"Oh, is that all?"

"Well, if we don't do *something*, we're screwed."

They were quiet the rest of the drive into Denton. For some reason, their street was blocked off, but the cop waved them through the barricade. At last they pulled up into the driveway of their house, a prefabricated split-level ranch on a hump of lawn, sweating under a veneer of powder blue vinyl siding. So familiar and yet so . . . not.

It had never really felt like home after her dad moved out. During the divorce, he'd bought a small condo in a nearby town. Feeling needy, Maddy hoped he would stay—maybe her folks could be persuaded to set aside their differences for one night. Under the circumstances. Attempting to broach the subject, Maddy realized that her mom was crying again, weeping quietly into a handkerchief—not at all like the sobs of gratitude and relief she had been crying earlier. Clearly, she was upset about something.

"Mom? What's wrong?"

"Nothing. Don't worry, honey. It's just . . . everything that's happened today. It's been a little much for me—I'm a bit overwhelmed. Don't pay any attention, I'm being silly. Come on, let's go inside."

They unloaded her hospital things from the car and went up the walk, her parents on either side as if ready to catch her. Dad unlocked the door and held it open. The living-room drapes were pulled; it was dark inside. As Maddy stepped over the threshold, the lights suddenly came on, and fifty voices shouted in unison, *"SURPRISE!"*

NINE

HOMECOMING QUEEN

IT seemed as if everyone in the neighborhood was there, as well as her entire extended family: all the distant cousins and nieces and nephews and great-great-aunts, most of whom she barely knew, all rushing up to greet her. There were balloons and streamers and a mountain of presents. A table loaded with pink cake and lime sherbet. From one end of the room to the other hung a banner reading, WELCOME HOME, MADDY!

Her legs weakened, and she was helped to sit down.

What was there to say about the party? The best thing about it was that it didn't drag on too long—everybody had obviously been told in advance that she still needed time to recover. That she might be a little . . . off.

Actually, after the initial weak spell, Maddy felt pretty good. She knew she looked like death but began to enjoy playing it up a little bit—why the hell not? Hadn't she earned it? For the first time all day, she actually had an appetite. People jumped to fetch whatever she asked for; she hardly had to lift a finger. *Cake? Sure. Chips? Okay,*

*and could I also get some of that dip? Pizza? Oh, thanks.
How about a nice lime float? Sure, why not?*

They were all so eager to help, she felt like Snow White
among the Seven Dwarfs. It was fun being the center of
attention, basking in public sympathy: Drama Queen for
a Day.

They didn't crowd her, but most folks were clearly
amazed by her "miraculous" recovery—Maddy was reminded that for over a year they had been accustomed to
seeing her as a near vegetable. She knew she had been home
a number of times during the course of her rehabilitation,
staying at a nearby hospice and even attending special-needs
classes at her high school. Apparently these outings had
made her something of a local celebrity: That poor Grant
Girl. Ugh. While she hated the idea of everybody gawking
at her in such a helpless, unattractive condition, it did amuse
her at first how freaked out they were by her unexpected
return to the living. Then it started to become annoying:

People cooing and petting her as if she were a cat, or
talking too loud, enunciating each syllable as if communicating with a deaf foreigner. Being overly hearty, bellowing how *terrific* she looked . . . or the opposite, clucking
about how *awful* she looked—right in front of her! And
then practically jumping out of their skins when she said,
"*Hello*, I'm right here." The one person she would have
liked to talk to was Ben's dad, Sam Blevin, but he wasn't
at the party.

"Weh-heh-hell. If it isn't the unsinkable Maddy Grant.
Hello there, young lady. Welcome home."

It was burly Leo Batrachian, principal of her school
and deacon of her church. Maddy had rarely ever spoken
to him before.

"Thank you, sir."

"I'm delighted to see you doing so well. It's really
quite remarkable. The difference."

He was studying her as though appraising a piece of furniture.

"I know. That's what they tell me. I don't really remember much that happened while I was . . . out."

"No, I wouldn't think so. It's such a shame what happened to you and that poor young man . . . but we can take comfort knowing he's in a better place. As for yourself, it would seem your work on this Earth is not finished. Incredible what they can do now. A new medical procedure, I understand. Something experimental, using wires?"

"I guess."

"Well, however it's done, I'd go so far as to call it a miracle. And I've seen a few! On the news they said it could revolutionize the treatment of a great many mental disorders, from Alzheimer's to—"

"It was on the news?"

"Oh yes. Of *course*. And now that you're home, they'll certainly want to interview you. I know Eyewitness News and Action Six both wanted to have camera crews here today, but the hospital prevailed upon them to allow you a quiet homecoming with family and friends. No doubt they'll be out in force two weeks from now, recording your return to school. Having seen you myself, I can understand their interest—it's truly a marvel."

"School? What do you mean, two *weeks*?"

"Yes, didn't you know that? Your parents were encouraged by your doctor—Dr. Plummer, I believe—to enroll you in classes at once, as a matter of helping speed your adjustment. Immersion Therapy. Back on the horse, as they say! I apologize; I thought you knew. You've been given a clean bill of health, and having spoken to you now, I can't think of any reason you shouldn't return to us posthaste. All your friends are eager to see you. You'll be a year behind the rest of your classmates, but I think that's a small enough price to pay, don't you? Holiday's over, my dear!"

He chucked her playfully under the chin without actually touching her.

Maddy could tell from the principal's demeanor that there were things he was holding back. He was a very large man, stout but not flabby, and she had always thought of him as a powerful, intimidating presence, someone to be given a wide berth. You did not want to be called into his office. The horror stories were legion.

Yet hunkering before her now, his head bared as though paying obeisance, Principal Batrachian wasn't nearly so imposing. In fact, he was utterly without substance, a plus-sized empty suit. His respiration, dilated pupils, rapid eye movements, and awkward posture all suggested he was deeply anxious about something. Studying her.

Maddy didn't press it—most of her well-wishers were equally reticent, equally strange. It had to be unnerving to see someone you knew go from being a human to a zombie to a human being again—she was getting used to the reaction. But the principal had always been such a larger-than-life, almost God-like figure, that Maddy was disturbed to see through him.

"Mr. Batrachian, did you know that stars are like carbon factories? That's where the carbon in our bodies comes from. It's what makes life possible."

"Oh . . . yes?"

"And when a star collapses into a white dwarf, those carbon molecules inside it crystallize to form a diamond. Imagine that: a single diamond with more mass than our whole planet."

"That's . . . very interesting."

"I think so, too. Eventually, of course, the white dwarf cools off and becomes a brown dwarf. Goes dark. For all we know, there are millions or billions of these giant diamonds floating around the universe."

"Really. Hmm."

"Yup."

"Well, the Lord moves in mysterious ways," he said. "It certainly wouldn't surprise me."

"Why do you think God would make these diamonds?"

"I couldn't begin to say."

"Do you think God works according to the laws of physics?"

"God works according to His own laws."

"Are those the same as the laws of physics?"

"I wouldn't say so, no."

"Did God make us according to the laws of physics?"

"No. He made us by an act of Creation."

"Just like the rest of the universe?"

"Yes."

"Including the diamonds?"

"Including everything."

"Did He make Himself?"

"That's a mystery."

"Unlike those diamonds?"

"Well, I'm not sure about the diamonds."

"But you're sure about God."

"Of course."

"How is that?"

"Faith."

She shook her head. Not wanting to offend him, she said, "I don't know."

"Maddy, God loves you and promises eternal life. What use are those diamonds?"

"They're real."

Batrachian's face hardened. "So is your immortal soul. Would you trade that for a diamond you can never possess?"

"Why should I have to trade?"

"Think of Adam and Eve, or the Tower of Babel. You know God expects us to choose between Faith and Knowledge. One path leads to salvation, the other to . . ."

"Sorry, sir, I don't believe in Hell anymore. And I don't think you do, either."

"Why do you say that?"

"Because right now you're less afraid of Hell than you are of me."

Turning pale, the principal excused himself and fell into hearty conversation with someone else.

The next time her mother came by to see how she was doing, Maddy asked, "Mom, why isn't Mr. Blevin here?"

Taken aback, Beth Grant said, "Wouldn't you rather talk about this later? When we can be alone?"

"I'd prefer to talk about it now, actually."

"Well, honey, after what happened, Sam and I aren't seeing each other anymore. He moved away."

Maddy was shocked. "When was this?"

"It's been months now. I think it was too painful for him. Seeing you always reminded him too much of Ben."

"But that's why I wanted to talk to him."

"I know, honey. But I think that would be very difficult for him. I'm sorry. That's why I didn't tell you sooner because I thought you should be the one to bring it up."

"So you're back on the market, then."

"No. Actually your dad's moving in with us for the time being."

"Seriously?"

"We've been discussing it, and he and I both feel it's better for all of us to be together right now."

Maddy smiled for the first time in a long, long time. "That's great," she said. "That's really great."

TEN

SOLITAIRE

IN the week after the party, everything settled down to a low hum. The first few days were blissfully free of obligation, and Maddy found that by sequestering herself within the four walls, she could dull her attention to the competing info-streams, more easily tune them out, or perhaps they just dried up of their own accord. Either way, she was at least able to savor the musty, all-U-can-eat banquet of the familiar. This house, her home, with all its deeply ingrained smells and textures, evoked a familiar history as sticky sweet as maple syrup.

Maddy spent most of her time zoned out on the couch. She was not bored; in her mind, she surfed the curious patterns of megadigit prime numerals and plumbed discrepancies in the Standard Theory, eking and tweaking her own equations for a comprehensive Unified Field Solution that she mentally filed alongside solitaire on her list of pleasant ways to kill time.

If other people were around, a lot of what she did was just playacting, performing the role of Maddy Grant, all-

American girl, as she knew they expected her to be. But the more she did it, the more she realized how impossible it would be to inhabit this mythical Maddy, to actually will the silly creature into being. To become herself again.

What had Maddy Grant been all about? Inspecting her room was like browsing a museum . . . or a mausoleum. It was all there. Physical vanity, mostly—she had been a typical teenager agonizing over every blemish. Self-conscious, self-loathing, even occasionally self-mutilating (although this mainly manifested itself in biting her nails too short), the girl was a bundle of postpubescent neuroses, some of which could be at least partially attributed to her parents' divorce. The positive stuff was not much better: hanging out at the mall, obsessing about boys, and worshipping some inane pop star. Marina Sweet—Jesus. *What a dip I was,* Maddy thought, looking at all the Marina memorabilia.

"We weren't sure what to do with all this," her mother said over her shoulder. "After what happened to Marina."

"Why? What happened to her?"

Her mother shrank back. "Oh, honey, I'm sorry—I thought you'd remember. We told you. It happened so long ago . . ."

"What? What, for God's sake?"

"Marina Sweet is dead. She died in a plane crash."

Maddy was startled, and shocked that she was startled—as if the news of some platinum-bobbed teen queen's death should mean anything to her now.

"Oh," she said.

"I'm sorry, baby." Her mother took something down from a shelf in the closet: a box of magazine and newspaper articles. "I saved these for you in case you wanted them. It happened right after you and Ben went to her concert. At first I blamed her in some way for everything, but then I realized it wasn't her fault."

Her mom handed her a clipping, and Maddy read it at a glance.

POP SINGER SUFFERS BREAKDOWN

Associated Press: Former teen sensation Marina Sweet is reportedly in seclusion today, following her sudden disappearance during a stage performance in Colorado. The remaining dates of her 12-state concert tour have been canceled.

"Marina is suffering from exhaustion, pure and simple," said her father and longtime manager, David Sweet. "She apologizes to her fans and looks forward to going back on the road as soon as possible. For the time being, she needs to rest and focus on writing the songs for her upcoming studio album. We ask that the press respect our family's need for privacy during this period of recuperation. Thank you."

When asked where his daughter was recuperating, Mr. Sweet replied that it was a private psychiatric facility near the family's home. He denied rumors that her collapse was due to substance abuse, saying only, "Marina treats her body like a well-oiled machine. She's a consummate professional, totally focused on her long-term goals, and I deeply resent any suggestion to the contrary."

There was another article stapled to the first one. It read:

MARINA SWEET DEAD AT 15

UPI: Teenage superstar Marina Sweet has been confirmed dead after a fiery helicopter crash. Also killed in the accident were her father, David Sweet, 47, and the helicopter's pilot, Paul Talbott, 33.

The popular teen entertainer, best known for playing the character Amber Grease in the popular *Middle School* films, and for her syndicated TV show *Sweet!*, was returning to her home after being treated for exhaustion, when the helicopter in which she was traveling appears to have lost power, going down in a mountainous area of northwest Idaho. By the time searchers located the remote crash site, fire had consumed most of the wreckage.

All across the country, spontaneous candlelight vigils are being held, and several suicides of young girls have been attributed to grief over the death of their idol.

Maddy shrugged, reluctant to let her mother see how she felt. "I'm okay," she said. "Let's get rid of this junk."

ELEVEN

MOUSETRAP

TRAPPINGS of a life so circumscribed it was suffocating: watch TV, surf the Internet, play video games, eat, sleep, wake up—lather, rinse, repeat. None of it any good now. All she saw when she looked at the TV or the Web was the crude technology: flat images made of fluorescent chemicals, poorly simulating the color and depth of life. It was incredible to think she had spent hours of every day staring at this crap! For *years*. Especially since there was no reason for it to be so bad—Maddy could think of a hundred ways to simplify and improve the experience, starting with eliminating the video screen altogether. Human beings already had a built-in screen, one that was 3-D and stereoscopic: their eyes. To fully replicate the sense of sight, it was simply necessary to refract images into the pupils, turning each eyeball into a portable, personal camera obscura.

Unfortunately, that wouldn't change the fact that the shows themselves were totally unwatchable, not to men-

tion the incessant, hectoring commercials. She sat with
her folks in the evening to view their favorite programs,
and it was a nightmare: grindingly repetitive legal dramas,
hospital dramas, police dramas; vacuous "news" about
celebrities and diets; fake comedy and true crime; depressing "inspirational" programs and flat-out lies. Maddy
was first astonished, then disgusted by the lack of substance, which was clearly by design—anything that might
disturb the national slumber party was forbidden.

"God, what the hell happened to TV while I was
gone?" she asked.

"What do you mean, sweetie?" asked her dad.

"It's gotten so *evil*. Every show is like every other show,
and it's all just to crush any sense of shared humanity or
larger purpose."

"But that's silly, sweetheart. It's just harmless entertainment."

"Harmless? This stuff is in every home, every day,
pushing this horrible agenda. No wonder people need
antidepressants."

"What agenda?"

"Are you serious? That we should all be *terrified*. About
crime, about money, about our health, about our looks.
And for everything that scares us, somebody's selling the
cure. Except it's all just bullshit, intended to distract us
from what we should really be worried about, which is the
assholes who are twisting human civilization into a giant
pig farm. Terror as a tool of mass manipulation—isn't that
the definition of terrorism?"

Her mother said, "I'm sorry, honey, but could you
just try to watch your language? Please? For me?"

"Sure, of course—sorry, Mom. I guess I'm still adjusting."

Trying to dispel the awkwardness, her dad said, "Listen, if you don't want to watch TV, we don't have to watch TV." He clicked the set off. "We'll do whatever you want to do, Mads."

"Can we just talk a little while?"

"Certainly. That would be nice. What would you like to talk about?"

"Well, first I just want to apologize to you guys. I know I've been kind of bitchy since I got home, and I don't mean to be. I want to let you know I'm not all depressed or anything. It probably seems like I hate everything all the time, which is not true—there are a lot of beautiful things going on that I never noticed before. I'm just not used to talking about them."

"That's wonderful, honey," said her mother. "Like what?"

"Well, for instance, I really like that we're all together like this. I wanted to thank you guys for that. I know it's been tough for you, and I appreciate it."

"Oh, baby, I'm so glad."

"We should be the ones thanking you," said her father. He took his wife's hand, and they beamed at each other. "You helped us realize that what really matters is family. Through thick and thin."

They all stood up and hugged over the coffee table, weeping. After a moment, they settled back into their seats.

Wiping her eyes, Maddy said, "Also, I love crystals."

"Oh?"

"They're so amazing, don't you think?"

"I guess they are at that," ventured Mr. Grant.

Mrs. Grant said, "It's so nice in the morning when the sun shines through them, and they make little rainbows all over the room."

Maddy nodded in polite agreement. "Oh, definitely. It's also fun to play around with hypothetical variants on the four basic cell-unit types and the geometric tessellations of the seven crystalline systems, just to see what happens. Why stop with the fourteen Bravais Lattices? I've worked out Face-Centered, Base-Centered, and Body-Centered Dodecahedral and Octoclinic Systems—you name it. The theoretical configurations are infinite."

"My goodness."

"It's better than Legos."

Her folks sat nodding for a moment, then looked at each other. "Well!" her dad said heartily. "And on that note, I'm gonna go brush my teeth."

THE Internet was another level of mindlessness altogether, though at least she could bypass all the "user-friendly" junk and write her own programming code. Still, technology was the holdup: Everything was slow—agonizingly slow. The sad fact was it was not all that different from the crude level of consciousness she had experienced in her brain-dead state. To go back to either of those conditions now, Maddy would feel like a goldfish stranded in a puddle. Flopping around and gasping for breath. Which was exactly what she was: a big fish in a little pond.

So she pretended.

She was good at pretending: Santa Claus, the Tooth Fairy, angels—she had once fervently believed in them all. One summer her camp counselors dug up an old Ouija board and held a séance, at which Maddy truly thought she had witnessed the raising of spirits. Clearly, she could believe anything. But to resurrect the spirit of Maddy Grant, she needed others around her just as credulous— fortunately, good old Mom and Dad were also sitting at the table, hands joined, intently waiting for the candles to flicker.

They baked cookies, did dishes together, ironed and

folded laundry, played cards and board games in the evenings. All three participated with determined enthusiasm, pushing themselves to conform to their own highest expectations of how a happy family should act. Her folks fulfilled their roles as a loving couple, Dad having moved back in to complete the family unit, and Mom pretending to forgive his infidelities. Maddy was pretty sure they weren't sleeping in the same bed, but it was the thought that counted. The hope. And, taxing as the effort was, all three of them did sense something real stirring, a spark of normalcy in the damp tinder . . . or perhaps they just wanted it so badly.

They even had a chance to perform their dog and pony show in public, on the open-air stage of their front porch, before a select audience of reporters and TV cameras. And the act must have been convincing, because the resulting news stories all presented them as exactly the sort of close-knit clan they were pretending to be. Everybody in the world called with congratulations and support. So it must be true.

All that grinning was exhausting, however, and when it was over, Maddy compensated by spending her last few days of freedom lounging on the couch. From time to time, there would be the irritating *thud thud thud* of some kid's car stereo passing outside, or a loud motorcycle setting off all the car alarms.

It got her thinking about a magnetohydrodynamic pulse emitter—something focused, that could jam a specific target without frying the whole neighborhood. Easy enough—there was toluene-based paint thinner in the garage; it would work as the propellant in a crude flux-compressor, utilizing parts from her dad's old motorcycle to harness the reaction—why had she never thought of this before? The muffled chrome tailpipe, properly insulated, would serve as the EMP cannon. A stator winding, some simple capacitors—bye-bye, bass thumper!

Maddy was contemplating principles of harmonic resonance when there was a shriek from the kitchen. It was her mother. She jumped up to see what was wrong.

"Mom?"

"Oh, I'm sorry, honey. Did I disturb you? I'm so sorry. It was a mouse in the cupboard—it startled me. Are you okay?"

"Yeah. I wasn't really napping."

"No? You need your rest; are you having trouble sleeping?"

"Not really, I just think I'm all caught up."

"Oh. Well, it's these *mice*. I don't know how they get in, but every year, as soon as the ground starts to freeze, they come inside. Just these little gray field mice. They're harmless, but they scare the bejesus out of me when they catch me by surprise. And I hate the smell—can you smell it? That mouse-pee smell."

Maddy nodded sympathetically. She knew about the mice, one of her mother's seasonal pet peeves, along with squirrels in the attic and mildew in the basement. Mice nested in the walls during the winter and returned to the fields in the spring. Personally, Maddy never minded them; she thought they were cute. Over the years, her dad had tried many methods of getting rid of them, including an easily discouraged cat, but ultimately her mother didn't have the heart to kill them, and anyway, the mice were too clever.

Theatrically sniffing the air, her mom tried tracing the mouse funk to its source.

"For some reason, there are more of them than usual this year," she said. "They must have had an early litter."

Maddy asked, "Why don't you hire an exterminator?"

"Oh no—it's not as if they're rats or something. It's too expensive, and I don't want any poison bait lying around for the cat to find, or dead mice rotting in the walls—ugh. We went through that. I just wish there was some other way to get rid of them."

The thought of mice in the walls caused something to trip. With a hitch in her voice, Maddy said, "Mom? What's wrong with me?"

"Wrong with you? Nothing, honey. Why do you say that?"

Before she knew what was happening, Maddy was sobbing. The words all came pouring out in a rush:

"No, there's something *wrong* with me! It's like I can see through everything! Why does it all seem so flimsy all of a sudden? You know what it is? It's like I went away, and everything I knew was replaced with some cheap, crappy substitute. Even the people! I don't know how else to describe it. You know those computer pop-ups, that spyware? Whenever I focus on something, that's sort of what happens in my head: All these thoughts come up, just exploding out of nowhere—this mass of overlapping images littering my screen until I can barely think straight.

"Whatever it is I'm looking at becomes pure hypertext, telling me more than I ever wanted to know about it. But it doesn't *matter* what I want, it's too *late*—I already know it. I *know* it. And once I know it, I can't forget it or ignore it . . . because it's *true*. And that's depressing because nothing is as simple as I used to think it was. It's like the smarter I get, the stupider I feel. Looking at people I used to love is like looking at bugs under a microscope—I just see all these strange, mechanical *things*. Even you and dad. It doesn't lend itself to empathy or compassion, you know?

"I used to think people could be good or bad, ugly or beautiful, happy or sad. Smart or stupid. It was all so simple:

Some people I wanted to be like, others I didn't, but most
fell in between, neither wonderful nor awful, but just . . .
normal. I always thought of myself as one of those, and I
guess I must have been pretty comfortable there. I never
realized it at the time, but there's some kind of solace in not
being either too perfect or too imperfect. It's the consolation
prize: the consolation of being ordinary.

"But now I see that it's all a game, just animals following patterns of instinct and brute conditioning, like rats in
a maze. I don't know exactly how or when it happened,
but somehow my whole stupid pageant of girly fantasies
just died, and I must have slept through it. Where's my
fairy tale, Mom? What happened to my white wedding
and my handsome prince? Who killed them? Was it your
divorce or my own puberty? Or was it the doctors at the
clinic? Did they take it along with my braces and a chunk
of my head? I don't know, I don't know. And I'm starting
to think I'll probably never know . . . will I? *Will* I?"

Her mom listened, unable to comprehend or contribute
anything more than her own tears. The doctor had told her
there would be times like these.

"I don't know, honey," she said, "but I promise it'll be
all right. Just hang in there, okay? It'll be all right."

Late that night, as if sleepwalking, Maddy went to the
kitchen and cut the tops off some empty two-liter soda
bottles, smeared peanut butter inside the bottles, and
sprinkled in a few mouse turds. Then she taped the tops
back on upside down, turning them into closed funnels.
She propped the bottles upright amid the canned goods
and went back to bed.

In the morning, they were full of mice. Every single
one in the house. On the way to school, Maddy's dad
pulled over, so she could release them into the fields.

TWELVE

ON THE QUAD

RETURNING to school was an interesting experience. Maddy had always felt more or less insignificant at school, a minor player of modest talents who tended to disappear into the woodwork. Neither the smartest nor the dumbest, the cutest or the ugliest, the nicest or the meanest, the strongest or the weakest, she was solidly, safely embedded in the boring majority: the prairie-broad middle ground of the "average."

That was okay; Maddy was accustomed to it, accepting and even defending her role in the pecking order. Because after all, who could complain about being normal? Everybody wanted to be normal. If you couldn't be a star, the next best thing was to be average, an ordinary person whose mediocrity neither merited nor begged special attention but consigned one to the bland horde of the mainstream, those plodders and pluggers whose dull reliability in tedious yet essential work enabled all the fruits of human civilization.

But they weren't going to let her be normal.

News crews were waiting at the front of the school, and when she told her dad to drive around the block, they found more reporters staking out the rear.

Maddy was accustomed to thinking of herself as a gray pigeon in the thrall of brilliant and beautiful parrots, social animals like her best friend, Stephanie. Stephanie wouldn't have been afraid of all this attention; she would have loved it. Maddy just wanted to be left alone.

"Dad, drop me off around the corner."

"Are you sure?"

"Yeah. I just need a minute alone to get psyched up for this."

"But you're gonna be okay?"

"I'll be fine. Really."

She kissed him good-bye and got out of the car. As soon as he was out of sight, she walked to a nearby convenience store and browsed the automotive shelves. Making chemical connections in her head, she bought various items and took them behind the store, where she fashioned a peculiar device out of plastic bottles and volatile compounds. It looked like a toy spaceship. The warhead was a can of degreaser with a steel penetrator made from a lug bolt. It took a few minutes to assemble everything, then she had to hurry with it down the street—she didn't want to be late for school.

A few blocks over, she found what she was looking for: a clear view of the local TV news affiliate. Estimating trajectory, she angled the device just right and lit it off. It went *shoosh!* and streaked upward, arcing high over the town common. A second later, there was a crash and a puff of flame—the station's big satellite dish was on fire. People came out, yelling and screaming, and in minutes the news trucks started showing up.

Maddy passed them going the other way. The front of the school was clear of media people. She slipped onto campus unnoticed, grateful that she hadn't missed the bell. Nobody even gave her a second glance . . . just as usual.

There was a tap on her shoulder.

". . . Maddy?"

"Steph! Hi!"

"Oh. My. *Gawd*. This is *ridiculous*!"

They fell into a tearful hug, Stephanie's shrieks drawing a throng of curious onlookers.

Maddy broke it off first, feeling awkward. Wiping her eyes, she said, "It's ridiculous all right."

"Oh my God, you are like totally normal! Guys, you know who this is? This is my friend Maddy Grant! From Special Ed!"

People crowded around, ogling her. Her name bounced around the crowd: *Maddy Grant, Maddy Grant—it's her. No way. Yes it is—check her out. Damn! Chick is busted!* Some of the girls made perfunctory gestures of welcome and sympathy, but most of the onlookers treated her like a two-headed snake.

Maddy said, "Thanks . . . I guess. This is a wig."

"Oh my God," Stephanie said. "I can't believe how incredible you look. You've lost so much weight!"

"Yeah. Hospital chic—it's the next big thing."

"I'm *serious*! This is just—you *totally* have to hang out with us today so everybody can get used to seeing you like this. For the past year, you've been so . . . different. Do you even remember any of that?"

"Not really. It's like a weird dream or something."

"Wow, that must be *so* weird! God, I can't even believe you can *talk*. Last time I saw you, you were like . . . severely mentally disabled. I mean really out of it, you know? We all felt so bad for you, seeing you like that. It was sad, dude. People are gonna shit when they see you, seriously. I mean, we all heard about you on the news and all that, but it's not the same as seeing you in person. I tried to call you about fifty times, but your phone is always busy."

"We've had to leave it off the hook. Why didn't you just come over?"

"Mr. Batrachian said we shouldn't. He made an announcement saying you needed time with your family, and that we shouldn't bug you until you came back to school. Scared the crap out of me, man. Everybody was thinking you'd maybe be able to sing the Alphabet Song or something at the next assembly. Nobody expected you to just show up today, totally normal! I'm blown away."

"Me too."

One of Stephanie's friends, a blond girl Maddy didn't know, said, "I heard they're putting you back in Special Ed."

"Yeah—just until I get up to speed."

"But then they're going to make you finish junior year, right?"

"Yeah."

"That sucks."

"Yeah, well . . . you know."

"But I guess you sort of missed it."

"Sort of."

Smoothing over the rough spot, Stephanie piped up, "God! I can't believe I can talk to you again—it's been so long! Did you hear that Marina Sweet died?"

"I know."

"Everything just seemed to happen at once. And then Ben's funeral. I mean, it was so terrible what happened to you and Ben . . . but at least he was at peace, you know? We all went to the funeral. His dad had him cremated and all, but still, the whole ceremony made it easier to let go."

While Maddy had been terribly jealous during the brief

time that Stephanie and Ben had dated, she now felt her friend's pain like a bridge between them. She wanted to say, *I loved him, too.*

But she couldn't bring herself to say it because Stephanie was saying something else entirely. Not with her mouth, but with her evasive eyes, her guilty tone, her whole manner. Maddy could read between the lines, the myriad hidden "tells" which came across much more clearly than the actual spoken words. Stephanie was saying:

With you it's been harder. All these months and months afterward I keep thinking I've moved on, then somebody will mention you're back from the hospital, that you're making progress, or I'll see your folks wheeling you around town or catch sight of you between classes . . . and I keep being reminded that it's not over. I can't count how many times somebody got my hopes up only to realize nothing had changed . . . nothing would change. I couldn't stand to see you like that, so I've sort of been avoiding you. I got another girl to take your place and started living my life again. I gave up on progress and stopped hanging on hope. So many times I've wished you could just quietly die like Ben, all nice and neat. So I could forget.

A gap of uncomfortable silence opened between them, their smiles so tight Maddy could almost hear the tendons creaking. The strain was broken by the school bell.

"Shoot, there's the bell," said Stephanie with relief. "I gotta go. We'll talk at lunch! Meet me over by the Media Center—that's where the upperclassmen hang out."

Maddy heard:

This is to tell you I've moved on, and I can't look back. I'm telling you this right up-front so I don't hurt your feelings, okay? It's not my fault. I know you've been through a lot of horrible stuff, and I'm really sorry, but I don't think I can ever go back to the way we were. I don't want to. Maybe I just need more time, but I'm a senior now, and

I have other things to think about—please don't push it.
You don't belong with us. You're so different, Maddy, I
don't even know if you're still really you anymore.

There it was: the very thing Maddy had been asking
herself all week. Staring back at Stephanie, she desperately wanted to shout, *Yes! It's me! It's me! The same girl*
who used to play Barbies with you after school. Who went
Goth with you in seventh grade. Who cleaned you up when
you got sick at Ryan's party. Who brushed your hair and
kept all your secrets. Your best friend.

But Maddy could only nod, and say, "Okay." She barely
believed these things herself, and none of it made any difference anymore. They were strangers to each other.

Then Stephanie and her posse were gone, a flurry of
bouncing ponytails, gray woolen skirts, black stockings,
and shiny heels flashing up the marble entrance. Upstairs
with the rest of the senior class.

THIRTEEN

SPECIAL NEEDS

MADDY, on the other hand, was going downstairs. Down to the Special Needs Room in the basement.

It was okay—she actually was looking forward to it because her vague memories of that place were all good. She associated it with the homey smells of oatmeal cookies and warm laundry. Snack times, playtimes, nap times. Feelings of love and acceptance, which she desperately needed just then.

She had been told she had friends there, and a woman who was practically a second mother to her: Miss Sally McNulty, whose pillowy arms and huge enfolding bosom offered refuge from any storm. Maddy didn't really remember much about Miss Sally other than those few vague impressions, but they were enough to take the sting out of being denied her seat among the seniors . . . or even, for the time being, the juniors.

Who cares? she thought bitterly. *I'm Special.*

It helped to know she was only going to the special-needs class for a short period of evaluation—a few weeks at most, just to ease her return. As soon as she proved herself capable, they would transfer her into the regular system, and things would get back to normal. Perhaps she could even skip straight to senior year! That would be fantastic.

But something was wrong.

On some level, Maddy had expected it to go wrong, had come to realize by now that nothing was going to be the way she hoped it would be. That she was fated to be disappointed by everyone and everything . . . and ashamed at her own disappointment.

Shame was the main thing, and as she stared into the Special Needs Room, her cheeks burned with it.

There were twenty or so students milling around the big, colorful space, several in wheelchairs and the rest basically ambulatory but with varying degrees of mental or physical impairment. At least half clearly had Down Syndrome, while others wore protective headgear or specialized shoes to accommodate their disabilities. A few drooled, screeched, or twitched and flapped their arms like chicken wings.

Had she really been one of these people? This had to be the wrong place . . . and yet Maddy knew very well it wasn't. She wanted to back out, to run, but before she could react, they saw her.

With a delighted cry—*Maddy!*—the students rushed forward and caught her up in a moist-fingered scrimmage of affection. Pulling her inside the room, they barraged her with questions and random, incomprehensible details about themselves, so that Miss Sally, emerging from the back in an apron, had to shout to make herself heard above the din.

"Everyone sit down! Sit down please! I'm sure we're all pleased to have Miss Grant back among us, but you gotta give her space to breathe!"

The class reluctantly sat down on the floor mats, all taking their prearranged spots. Maddy sat as well, feeling weirdly regressed to infancy. The walls were covered with finger paintings and construction-paper collages, elementary handwriting exercises and spelling tests with words like COUGH and PLOUGH—some scrawled with her name. On the shelves stood a variety of animal figures sculpted from Froot Loops or macaroni, a couple of them also identified as hers. Worst of all, there was an exhibit of class photos, and Maddy was startled to see herself as she must have looked only a few weeks ago: bound to a wheelchair, mouth gaping open, her head canted back at an awkward angle. She was gazing worshipfully at Principal Batrachian.

Miss Sally studied Maddy from across the room, peering curiously over the tops of her reading glasses. She was nearly as wide as she was tall, ruddy-cheeked and heavily freckled, with tiny features bunched close together in the middle of her face.

"Well, if it isn't Maddy Grant. Look at you, girl! You are truly a sight to behold—if I didn't see it myself, I'd never have believed it."

The warmth of the words did not mesh with the woman herself—there was a glaring disconnect. Miss Sally was a ball of hostility and self-loathing, a spinning pulsar of repressed emotion. Her whole body seethed in a perpetual state of crisis, her veins stretched to their limits and her enlarged heart straining against the pressure, all building to some eventual critical mass. At this rate, she didn't have long to live.

Maddy knew immediately what it was: fear. Miss Sally wasn't in here teaching disabled kids out of love or saintly compassion, but out of an all-consuming desire to be needed. She was *using* them for her own frustrated ends—

just as she used food—to assuage her own feelings of
worthlessness. She needed to feel needed, and these kids
were the ideal captive audience. Something bad had happened to her when she was young and impressionable,
and so she hid out in Special Needs, the neediest of the
bunch. Which was going to be a problem since Maddy
clearly no longer needed her.

This insight led Maddy to a broader revelation: Looking at the composition of the photos, she realized that
Miss Sally was serving higher needs than merely her own.
This was not just about her; the torment was bigger than
that, the damage more difficult to rationalize. Sally Mc-
Nulty's murky fishbowl concealed a bigger fish. By using
these kids, she was earning brownie points with someone
else . . . someone she had loved and feared since childhood and who exploited her obsessive worship for reasons
of his own. That someone was Principal Batrachian.

Was charity just a by-product of guilt? An extension of
greed? Not selfless but essentially selfish, exploiting the
helpless to assuage personal fears of helplessness? The
weak exploiting the weak? If that was true, saints must
be the biggest sinners of all. Evil must be inextricable
from good since good couldn't exist without it. Evil was
necessary.

Mulling over this disturbing idea, Maddy let herself
drift through the morning routine, doing simple language
and math puzzles and participating in silly dance-along
exercises. It wasn't so bad. At first she resisted, but the
other kids were having such a good time that when they
clamored for her to join them, she couldn't say no.

Finally, lunchtime rolled around. It was a relief to get out
of the windowless basement and into the sunlight. Maddy
trailed the other kids out onto the quad, then split off in her
own direction. Miss Sally's voice stopped her short.

"Excuse me—Miss Grant!"

"Yes?"

"Where are you going?"

"Over to have lunch?"

"Lunch is this way."

"No, I mean with my friends."

"Your friends. How nice! Well, we like to stick to-gether if you don't mind—it makes it easier to maintain the group dynamic."

"What?"

"You understand. Where would we be if everyone just wandered off in their own direction? Who's to make sure they get back to class, or prevent them from leaving school grounds altogether? Imagine! That's why we have our own little corner of the cafeteria set aside just for us."

"But I—"

"I know you're feeling very independent, but please think of the others. They're your friends, too. They won't understand, and their feelings will be hurt when they can't follow your example. Come on, be a good sport."

"But I was supposed to meet someone. I don't even belong in this class!"

"Oh, I'm sorry. I believe that's for others to decide, isn't it?"

"As if it isn't obvious."

"There's more to it than test scores, Miss Grant. Personal conduct is also one of the criteria. Leadership. The ability to put others before oneself."

"Are you serious? I'm not trying to earn my merit badge here. I just want a few minutes free to myself."

"I'm not going to stand here arguing with you. Maybe you'd prefer to tell it to the principal. Don't be a rotten egg—come on!"

The other kids were becoming impatient with the delay.

When they noticed it was Maddy holding them up, they all began clamoring for her to get a move on—they were hungry and didn't want to lose their favored place in line. Also, the regular students pouring onto the quad were starting to pay attention, to notice her.

With a sigh, she gave in and followed.

FOURTEEN

DIP VAN WINKLE

FOR a week, things went on that way. Maddy commuted from the stuffy seclusion of home to the stuffy seclusion of Special Needs, with very little peer interaction along the way to hamper the smooth transition. She encountered Stephanie once or twice in passing. As the novelty of seeing the "zombie girl" wore off, people lost all interest in her, averting their eyes and ducking away to avoid facing another awkward exchange. It was so stupid, because Maddy would have loved nothing more than to have a conversation about something other than herself. She was as sick of that topic as anyone—sicker!—and just wanted to forget about the operation and "amazing" recovery. But she knew she still looked like death, and who wanted to be friends with death?

Furthermore, the whole world had aged a year in her absence. A year was a long time; it would take them a while to catch up . . . and her as well. During that time, Veggie-Maddy had apparently served as a powerful reminder of life's preciousness and fragility. Everyone took something from her tragedy. But now that they could talk to her, and realized they didn't want to, those emotional epiphanies felt cheapened.

I'm a time-traveler, she thought. *Dip Van Winkle.*

At least the local media had forgotten about her, focusing all its attention on the "terrorist attack" on the TV station. Maddy had to laugh about that.

Then, suddenly, it was Friday. She'd survived her first week . . . or perhaps *survived* was the wrong word. More like *inhabited.* No one had been overtly mean, but since Maddy couldn't or wouldn't stop making everyone uncomfortable, they quickly dug a moat around her, diverting all their social energies to either side and leaving her marooned on a quiet little island of her own. In one way, Maddy found that a great relief—nothing was required of her other than she show up, shut up, and be counted. In another way, it was a major drag—nothing was required of her.

Waiting for her dad after school, Maddy could see Stephanie's group dispersing for the parking lot, all the cheery senior girls calling to one another, making their plans for the weekend. She didn't resent them for it . . . or tried not to. It wasn't their fault. All week long, she had become more and more aware of the gulf between them— not just the seniors, but everyone in school—and had decided not to fight it. Maddy had no more desire to join in that weirdly inane chatter than they had to inflict it on her. So why bother?

She watched Stephanie get into her sporty little red car and pull out of the parking lot. But instead of heading away down the street, Stephanie turned up the school driveway to where Maddy was standing. "Hey, kid," she called. "You want a ride?"

"Hey, Steph. I'm waiting for my dad."

"No kidding, doofus. He called to say he can't make it. Get in."

Shaking her head, Maddy plopped into the seat. "He called you to give me a ride? Unbelievable. Thanks."

"No problema. Actually, I'm kind of glad. I feel like I haven't had a chance to talk to you at all this week. How's it going?"

"Fine, I guess."

"Have they said when they're going to get you back into regular classes?"

"Not really."

"Oh, come on, man! You can't let them keep you in Special Needs. The longer you're in there, the more you're going to fall behind the rest of your class."

"I know."

"Tell your folks to get on them or something. This is ridiculous, seriously."

"I know."

They drove in silence for a few miles. Turning onto Maddy's street, Stephanie asked, "So listen, are you really doing okay? Because it's freaking me out not knowing."

"I think I'm okay. I mean, I'm not *deeply despondent* or anything—actually I feel pretty good. Everything's just very different from the way I remember it. But that's probably just me."

"Bullshit. It's not just you. We're all trying to figure this out; it's weird for everybody. It's weird for me, too."

"I know."

"Stop saying 'I know'!" She pulled up hard before Maddy's house. "It's really annoying since you obviously don't know, and neither do I. You have to start dealing with this shit."

"I know—sorry. I mean I will. Well, thanks for the ride." Maddy got out of the car and shut the door. "Maybe I'll see you next week."

"Hold up a second. You want to go to the mall tomorrow?"

Maddy was caught short. "Tomorrow?"

"Yeah, tomorrow. Like, the day after today."

"Sure. Okay."

"Cool. I'll pick you up at ten."

"Ten. Great." Maddy watched the car disappear, then went in the house.

FIFTEEN

THE MALL

THE next morning, they went to the mall. Maddy avoided telling her folks until the last second because she knew they would make a big thing out of it, and she just didn't have the energy. It wasn't until Stephanie's car beeped its horn that she said, "I'm going out. Bye!"

Turning off the vacuum cleaner, her mom called, "Maddy, wait! Where are you going?"

"To the mall with Steph. Gotta go!"

"With Stephanie? But, honey, that's great! Why didn't you say anything?"

"Just did! Love you—bye!"

Maddy had been going to the same mall forever, but she never reflected on exactly *why*. Over the years, she and Stephanie probably spent more of their weekends loitering mall stores than all their other recreational activities combined—i.e., they were typical American kids. As in most towns of its type, there was little else to do in Denton except go to church. It had been many years since the mall killed Main Street, and nobody missed it, with its meager town library and depressing local-owned businesses, certainly not two hormonal teenage girls. The mall, on the other hand, was their alpha and omega; it was their doorway to a wider world they knew only from television.

As Stephanie's car came in sight of the sprawling complex, Maddy laughed to realize its implications. "Jesus Spends," she murmured.

"What?"

She caught herself. "Nothing. Just thinking of all the stuff we did here."

"Hell, yeah. We were hard-core. We *owned* this joint."

What had made Maddy laugh was the shocking resemblance of Denton's two major temples of worship, the megamall and the megachurch. How had she never recognized their similarities? They were so obvious: the same plastic cathedrals, the same seas of SUVs, the same eager customers seeking easy answers. It was no accident that these institutions were remarkably alike, not only architecturally but philosophically. Both traded on human insecurity. Both enforced conformity. Both pitched their wares on TV. Whereas traditionally their ideologies might have been opposed, they had learned it was more profitable to reinforce each other's base. Play down the Sermon on the Mount in favor of the gospel of P. T. Barnum. Reassure their patrons that God loved a winner, and the only sin was in feeling guilty about it.

"Sick, dude," said Stephanie, as if reading her mind.

"What is?"

"This! You and me! It's gonna be awesome. You ready?"

"Ready when you are."

"Let's hit it."

The girls' mall-going had peaked in seventh grade, then sharply declined as Stephanie outgrew the thrill of following boys and actually started dating them. Since

Maddy had no gift for this, being plainer, quieter, and terminally shy around the opposite sex, that put a crimp in their friendship. But it wasn't until Stephanie hit on Ben that things really got difficult.

Ben.

Maddy still vividly remembered the feeling of seeing them together, like being punched really hard in the stomach. She would have rather been punched. But, as with most high-school romances, their relationship fell apart after only a few weeks. Maddy didn't really know the whole story because neither of them talked about it afterward. Sometimes she wondered if it was because they realized the pain they were causing her. Whatever happened, it was certainly irrelevant now; Maddy had no bad feelings about Stephanie, nor of revisiting this shrine to their adolescence.

"What do you want to do first?" her friend asked, as they entered the busy concourse.

"Whatever you want to do."

"Don't do this to me, man. 'What do you wanna do?' 'I dunno, what do *you* wanna do?' Come on."

Maddy was a bit dazed. She remembered the mall being huge and exciting, sleek as a space station. This place was oppressively grim and shoddy, a cheap mockup of the shopping Mecca she knew so well. It was ugly if not positively unsafe. There was no fresh air, and queasy saxophone music oozed like poison from the ceiling. "I'm still getting my bearings. You lead the way for now."

"Just like old times, huh? Okay, then." Going up to the mall floor plan, Steph closed her eyes and randomly poked the map with her finger. Opening her eyes, she said, "Ew, that's no good." She tried again and hit a lingerie store. "This-a-way!"

For three hours, they cruised the small boutiques and the big department stores, Stephanie gushing over designer labels as Maddy feigned interest. It was almost unbearable, but she refused to disappoint her friend the way she had her parents. If she was ever going to make it in this world, she had to learn to get along with people, no matter how boring or idiotic they seemed. But why did they all have to be so boring and idiotic? It was maddening. *This is why people do drugs,* she thought. *Or get lobotomies.*

Stephanie noticed Maddy's glazed look and suggested they stop for lunch. Maddy gratefully agreed.

Eagerly digging into her pile of General Gau's chicken, wontons, and pork fried rice, Steph asked, "So how's it going? Are we having fun yet?"

"Sure." Maddy picked at her salad, nervous about pesticides and *E. coli* contamination. She couldn't even look at Stephanie's food.

"What's going on? Tell me."

"I don't know. I wish I did. I'm sorry. I feel like I'm ruining your day."

"Fuck you, man. I'm here because I want to be here. Because I missed you. So don't give me that bullshit; tell me what's going on in your head. Like, what was that all about back there about the shoes?"

"I just didn't understand how anybody could wear them."

"What are you talking about? Those were expensive-ass shoes! I'd kill for those!"

"They're not even shoes! At least with men's shoes, you can see they were designed for a human foot, but with most of those women's shoes, it's impossible to tell what kind of weird hoof goes in there! They're like some bizarre alien artifact. Whatever they're meant for, it's not human."

"I think you're being a little extreme."

"Yeah, I'm being extreme because I think it's strange

to want to wobble around all day on two pegs like a double amputee. It's stupid!"

"People just want to look good. Heels make women's legs look longer."

"Where did this idea come from? You know what I think the problem is? All these things were designed by Dr. Frankenstein."

"What!"

"Think about it. A mad scientist is not going to appreciate a woman's body as anything other than crude potential, an unrealized ideal. They're looking for some abstract concept of aesthetic perfection that has nothing to do with physical reality. That requires that they unnaturally distort them, turn us into freaks."

"It's not mad scientists who are checking out my legs. And I happen to like those shoes! Does that make me a freak?"

"Obviously, that's just cultural conditioning. Commercial manipulation mixed with sexual exploitation, preying on women's fears of inadequacy induced by lifelong exposure to artificial physical ideals. In other words, brainwashing. Stockholm syndrome. Drill that into girls long enough, and they become the enforcers of their own oppression."

"Oppression!"

"Same thing as with the diet industry, the cosmetics industry, the fashion industry, and the boob-job industry. As to why straight men like it, with enough time, any nonsense can be imposed as a cultural norm. I'm sure plenty of Japanese guys used to get off on seeing women's feet bound up until the bones fused into horrible little gnarled stumps. Likewise female genital mutilation—that's still standard in parts of the world. I can't believe I never realized before just how much of our society is based on blind conditioning. Everything could work so much better than it does! It's kind of terrifying."

"Maddy, come on. Do you realize how lame this sounds? I mean, dude. You're like some crazy radical feminist all of a sudden. Since when did you start hating men?"

"Hating men? How can I hate men when men have obviously been just as brainwashed? Why else would they need all these sports bars, if not to distract them from a rigged system that punishes their individuality, pits them against each other to see who can be the most soulless drone, humiliates them when they fail, then criminalizes their aggressive instincts? Oh, and chops the protective covering off their junk. Why else would they care about strangers chasing a ball, or watch a car go around a track five hundred times? It's the same reason a captive lion paces in its cage. They're not *made* for this."

"It's called civilization."

"Then why isn't it more civil? This is less rational than a baboon colony. It just has more stress."

"Maybe we should go see a movie," Stephanie muttered. "There's less talking involved."

The multiplex was at the far end of the mall. On the way, they passed the pet store, Petropolis, all the puppies tussling or snoozing in bales of shredded newspaper. "Aw, cute!" Stephanie said.

Not so long ago, Maddy would have melted at the sight of these baby animals. This was the same store where she had bought her cat, Mr. Fuzzbutt, and it had always been one of her favorite places in the mall—an opportunity to fondle all the furry creatures her parents wouldn't let her have. These toys loved you back!

But this time she felt a chill. Her eyes were drawn to stacks of small, cramped cages in the rear, each one containing a lone puppy or kitten. They looked miserable,

paws sore from standing on metal bars all day. Other
sections held birds, rodents, or more unusual creatures
like ferrets and snakes. Some of the birds had nearly
plucked themselves bald, reminding Maddy of patients at
the Institute . . . patients like her.

This is sick, she thought.

Like a kick in the head, she realized how the pet store
worked. How the pets themselves worked. She tried to
slam her mind shut against the awful knowledge, but it
was too late—before she knew it, she knew it.

The dogs had all been genetically engineered, bred and
inbred to exaggerate their most extreme physical attributes. It was purely cosmetic; any useful traits they might
have once had as work animals were corrupted, making
them bundles of disabilities and behavioral tics. For that
they were labeled "purebred." They were about as cute as
abused war orphans, half-crazed from the lack of any
meaningful purpose to their existence.

The poor things!

Where Maddy had once found them adorable, she now
realized they were grotesque mutants, barely functional as
living organisms, utterly dependent on human beings to
keep them alive. They were treated like merchandise.
Their only relief was an occasional rotation in the front
window, but the sickliest ones never got a break. If they
missed their sell-by date, they went out the back door and
were sent to discount brokers, who auctioned them online
to the highest bidder. Any that still did not sell were
picked up at lot prices by medical supply houses for lab
experiments. Experiments like her.

"Let's go," she said, not trusting herself to explain.

"How come?"

"Because if we don't, I'm gonna throw up."

"Whoa! We're outta here."

Maddy had not been to a movie in over a year, but the

general choices were exactly the same as she remembered: a big-budget fantasy flick, a CGI family movie, an
action thriller, a romantic comedy for women, a raunchy
comedy for men, and a cheesy horror film. Half the movies were in 3-D. None of them appealed to her.

"I feel like I've seen all these movies a hundred times,"
she said.

"Come on, Debbie Downer. I think we both need a
good laugh. My treat." Stephanie bought two tickets to the
raunchy comedy. Since it was a special occasion, she also
insisted they splurge on snacks: a giant buttered popcorn,
a king-size bar of chocolate, and two buckets of soda.

"This is insane," Maddy said. She was still nauseous
from the pet store. "You know, there's more salt and oil in
this thing than in the whole Gulf of Mexico."

"At least it's not real butter. I thought as a vegetarian
you'd appreciate the lack of animal products."

"Oh, I do. I just also like my food to be, you know, *food*."

The theater was mostly empty, a dim and restful hideout
from the bustling mall. Maddy was glad she had come—
she desperately needed to clear her head. They chose their
favorite seats in the far back, where they could munch and
chat and make amusing comments about the movie.

The lights went down, and a series of commercials
came on. Though Maddy knew this was nothing unusual,
she found it much more grating than ever before. Why the
hell were there commercials in a movie theater? She didn't
pay for that. At least on TV you could mute the sound or
change the channel. Movie commercials were acts of
brute coercion. And the commercials themselves were so
annoying, all aimed at male adolescents: caffeinated soft
drinks, fast cars, antiperspirants. There was a long military
recruiting film showing attractive people engaged in
bloodless combat, a highly stylized montage of deadly
machines and heroic deeds. It was blatant propaganda.

Maddy understood that military recruitment was necessary. What she didn't understand was why it was necessary to lie about it. Tell the truth: We Pay You To Shoot People And Maybe Get Shot. Human beings were violent by nature, especially teenage boys; most craved an excuse to kill and die for something. Clearly, the idea was to shield softhearted folks from the notion that the fundamental purpose of any soldier was to kill. Not disaster relief, not playing ball with Arab children, but killing. Even the most patriotic dad might try to talk his kid out of something like that. These commercials were for the *parents*.

Then came the movie trailers—a string of cookie-cutter gutter comedies exactly like the one they were about to see. Maddy didn't know if she could take it.

Fortunately, she didn't have to. Before the movie even began, there was a problem: no sound.

"Oh, come on," Stephanie groaned.

"Typical," Maddy said. As usual, nobody was making any effort to do anything.

Stephanie yelled, "Sound!"

The movie kept playing in silence. Maddy got up. "I'll go tell them."

"Hang on a minute. I'm sure they're dealing with it."

"The projectors are all automated. There's probably no one up there."

Taking her drink, she walked up the aisle to the exit, sensing hopeful eyes watching her. They would sit there forever now that someone was handling things. Of course, the only usher was far at the end of the corridor, in the lobby. Unbelievable.

Nearer at hand was an unmarked door with an electronic keypad, monitored by a surveillance camera. Hmm. Keeping her face down, Maddy slipped into the women's room, grabbed a big wad of toilet paper, and soaked it with water. Leaving the restroom, she came around under the camera and did a fair imitation of a basketball layup, plastering the camera dome with wet toilet tissue. No one took any notice.

Then she attacked the keypad. It was easy to see which four keys were smudged with finger grease, and she rapidly tried various permutations of those digits until the lock popped open. On the other side of the door was a short passage leading to a stairway, where she could hear the din of machinery. She cautiously climbed the stairs and peeped through a doorway at the top. It was the projection room. The sight was impressive: a long attic space lined on either side with roaring movie projectors, like cannons in a Spanish galleon—cannons of light. Each projector faced a tiny window overlooking a different theater. They were timed to operate with minimal supervision, a fact the projectionist obviously took full advantage of.

The projector for her theater was last on the right. Its controls were so simple, Maddy realized she could fix it herself—it was just a matter of flipping a switch. She did so, listening to the movie's eighties soundtrack kick in as she took a sip of her soda. On the wall next to her was the room's temperature-control panel and a heavy-duty circuit breaker. The projector bulbs were very hot; without constant cooling, the room would quickly become an oven.

Finishing her drink, Maddy opened the thermostat and unwired the temperature regulator. There was about an inch of slack, barely enough to poke the sensor bulb through her cup of ice and leave it hanging there. Immediately, she heard the big cooling plant shut down, cutting off the breeze from the vents. As an afterthought, she jammed open the main circuit breaker with the twisted cup lid. In the dead air, she could already feel a lot of heat starting to build. A trickle of meltwater ran down the HVAC circuit panel into the power coupling feeding all the projectors. The instant the cooling unit started up again, that water would act as a power conduit, creating a feedback loop that would short out both electrical systems.

She returned downstairs, peeking to make sure the coast was clear. There was a commotion in the lobby, with Stephanie yelling at the center of it. Maddy knew she hadn't been upstairs for more than a few minutes, but Stephanie must have gotten worried. That was okay—it was a good diversion. Maddy slipped out the exit and waited on a bench in front of the theater. Just in time, a bunch of mall security guys showed up. They spotted her right away.

"Is your name Madeline Grant?"

"Yeah."

The men relaxed. One of them raised his walkie-talkie. "Givens here. We found her. She's right outside the theater." Speaking to Maddy, he said, "You know, your friend is very worried about you."

"Why?"

"She says you disappeared on her."

Another man said, "She told us you may be delirious."

"I'm not delirious. I just needed a minute to think."

Now Stephanie appeared, yelling, "Oh my God. Oh my *God*. Where the hell *were* you?"

"Right here."

"I have been freaking out looking for you! I called 911! I called your mom and dad! I didn't know if you passed out and hit your head or been kidnapped or—"

There was a resounding boom from somewhere deep in the building, and suddenly the power cut off. The mall went dim, lit only by skylights. The music died.

The head of security, Givens, said, "What the hell just happened?"

For a long fraction of a second, everything was dead quiet, the shoppers all frozen in their tracks. Then the other shoe fell: Battery-powered emergency lights winked to life, followed by the sprinkler system and fire alarm. As cold water rained down, people screamed in surprise, triggering a general panic.

The security men shouted, "Out! Everybody out! Follow the lighted exit signs!"

Maddy and Stephanie joined a mass of people heading down the fire stairs. Stephanie's hair was plastered to her head, and she was hysterical, crying, "Oh my God, what is going *on*? I don't even *believe* this!" She was so distracted she barely noticed as Maddy took a little side trip, ducking into the darkened pet center and opening all the kennels. The dogs automatically ran in the direction of light and people, got scooped up by friendly hands. Cats were another matter, defeated by the sprinklers, but Maddy picked up as many wet kittens as she could carry and handed them off to kids in the crowd. The other beasts she left to their own devices.

Stephanie never even realized she was gone, or wondered why she was breathing hard. They returned to the car and went home. As she dropped Maddy off, Stephanie looked at her old friend with an expression of horror and furious incomprehension. "What just happened back there?" she demanded. "What the fuck was that?"

Maddy only shook her head. Truth was, she herself had no idea.

Stephanie's face collapsed. Voice quaking, she said, "I can't do this. I just can't do this."

"It's okay. I'll see you tomorrow." Maddy got out of the car.

"I can't do this. I just can't."

"Bye, Steph."

"Bye."

The car drove away.

SIXTEEN

JONAS AND LAKISHA

MONDAY came quickly. Tuesday even quicker. Life in Special Needs was settling into a well-worn groove.

As the week wore on, Maddy started remembering the kids. Not as a faceless group of walking disabilities but as individuals. It was a strange thing because they were so completely different from the people in her dreams that she hadn't recognized them, assuming the dream entities to be inventions of her subconscious.

But they were quite real . . . and she had loved them. Two of them in particular:

Jonas and Lakisha had been her closest friends for what felt like a lifetime, a dreamlike eon that was really less than a year. They did everything together, creating whole worlds of mystery and adventure from within the confines of the school basement. The basement itself seemed a much different place then, not creepy or claustrophobic at all, but instead a land of possibility, full of interesting hideouts and forbidden curiosities—and warm oatmeal cookies. Maddy's impressions from that time were nothing but pleasant, the swaddled pleasures of infancy.

Lakisha's favorite game had been dress-up: She loved digging through the Lost and Found bin, dressing herself and Maddy in the most outlandish costumes, then modeling the outfits for the rest of the class. It had seemed the height of sophistication at the time. Lakisha was beautiful. Lakisha was funny.

Looking at her with new eyes, Maddy saw that "fashionable" Lakisha was a very damaged girl. She had multiple, profound learning disabilities . . . but also tremendous energy and need for attention. She could not sit still for more than a few seconds at a time and was forever disrupting the room with her playful, manic outbursts. Though basically gentle with others, she wore a protective helmet and mouth guard, so she wouldn't hurt herself when she started slamming her own head against the wall.

What disturbed Maddy the most was the realization that she was at least partly responsible for Lakisha's frenzy.

"She misses you," said Miss Sally, cleaning paintbrushes. "She knows you're avoiding her and doesn't understand why you don't like her anymore."

"I like her fine! I just can't handle having her hanging on me every second. It's too much."

"That's funny."

"What?"

"Her hanging on you all the time. I remember when it was just the opposite."

"That's not fair. I'm not the same."

"But she is."

"How is that my fault?"

"It's not. But you can't blame her for being hurt . . . or for acting out."

"Great. So what am I supposed to do, then?"

"Miss Grant, you surprise me. And here I thought you were so smart."

While Lakisha wouldn't leave her alone, Jonas kept his distance.

In Maddy's dream world, Jonas had been like a big brother to her: wise, protective, and infinitely kind. In memory after memory, his were the strong arms holding her up, his the kind hands guiding her useless ones. He was the one who lifted her in and out of her wheelchair; he was the one who pushed it. He sang for her and danced with her. And something else: He was the only one who dared step forward when Principal Batrachian took one of the kids into the changing closet—Miss Sally had to physically hold him down.

But how much of that was real? What did it mean? Maddy didn't know . . . and really didn't want to know. None of it made sense anyway, good or bad. Jonas the Hero? Jonas the Brave? It all had to be a fantasy since Jonas was plainly a very shy retarded boy, grossly obese, reeking of urine, with caked spittle in the corners of his mouth. That was the only reality that mattered.

I was one of them. I was one of them.

However hard she tried, Maddy couldn't escape that recurring thought. *I was Special, too.* Her eyes kept finding their way to the picture on the wall—that idiot grin. She wished she could tear it down, hide it, burn it. She didn't want to be reminded that she had ever belonged here, that it was only by dint of extreme medical intervention that she wasn't stuck that way for the rest of her life.

The worst part of it, the really unbearable thing, was that some major part of her yearned to return to that state. Its simplicity beckoned her, bleeding through her consciousness until she could barely differentiate memories that took place before the carnival accident from those that happened after, as if her whole life prior to the operation had been spent in moronic bliss. The demarcation line was not the accident, not the brain damage itself, but the *repair*, suggesting that the difference between Normal Maddy and Brain-Dead Maddy was much less significant than the change effected by the operation . . . whatever Maddy that had spawned.

IT was on Wednesday that everything finally came apart.

Taking her place at the end of the lunch line, Maddy found herself surrounded by curious bystanders. It was a bunch of guys from the water-polo team, chlorinated jocks with green-tinged hair and bloodshot eyes. It wasn't too long ago that she had idolized these guys, giggling with other girls about which one was the cutest. Now the thought embarrassed her. The boys conferred together in loud stage whispers, so that she heard mention of her name and "that guy who died." Finally, one approached her.

"Hey, you're that chick."

"Excuse me?"

"You are. You're that chick. The one who had the operation."

"Oh. Yeah . . . I guess."

"Awesome! Do you really have a computer chip implanted in your brain?"

Another one interrupted, "Can we see the scar?"

"Shut up, dude!" the first one said. "Can't you see she's a retard?"

A third said, "Don't say *retard*, man—it's not cool. The word is *mentally disabled*."

"She ain't retarded! Are you?"

"Maybe I am," Maddy replied.

"No way!"

The rudest one, a short, stocky boy, demanded, "How come you're with the retard class? She's retarded, I told you!"

"You don't have to be retarded to be in there," said the taller kid. "Last year, I knew a kid whose big toenail got infected, and they put him in Special Ed until he could walk again."

"Bull*shit*, man."

"Yuh-huh—Wayne Drabinski."

"Wayne Drabinski—who the hell's Wayne Drabinski?"

"Just some retard."

Maddy erupted. "Hey! Could you guys please back off?"

"Hey, whoa. I'm *sorry*. What's your name?"

"Beverly Hills."

"Seriously, what's your name? Don't pay any attention to these assholes."

Trying to cut him some slack—he couldn't help being stupid—she sighed. "Maddy, okay?"

"Yeah, that's it. Does it hurt to have wires stuck in your brain?"

Another blurted, "What was the accident like? When that guy died?"

Feeling her face getting hot, Maddy tried to ignore them. A lot of people were watching them. She could see Stephanie at the edge of the crowd. Why was the line moving so slowly?

The first one said, "*Blevin*—Ben Blevin."

"Yeah, Ben Blevin. Wasn't he your stepbrother or something? I heard you were in the Tunnel of Love when he died. That must have been *awesome*."

"Shut up, man," said someone farther back.

"Hey, I'm just saying! Did you and him plan that? I mean, did you set it all up on purpose so you could get it on? Because that would be dope, seriously. I would pay to see that."

The other boys pretended to be shocked, saying, "Shut the fuck *up*, Eric!" But they didn't mean it; this was a moment of over-the-top hilarity they would repeat again and again. Eric was their idol, and he ruled.

Maddy turned and stepped near the one named Eric. The inner workings of his pea brain were scrolling across his forehead like a stock ticker.

"Why are you trying so hard?" she said in a low voice.

"Huh?"

"What are you ashamed of? Is it because your friends would treat you differently if they knew the truth?"

"What?"

"Maybe they've already noticed how nervous you are in the locker room, so careful not to give yourself away."

"Yeah, right."

"Is that why you got into swimming? The Speedos and waxed chests?"

The crowd tittered, and the boy lashed out. "Step back, bitch."

"Something happened, didn't it, a long time ago? Something that made you feel different from the other boys?"

"*Fuck* you."

"Wait—don't lose your place in line. Nobody's judging you. You were a child; it was innocent curiosity."

"*You're* the freak—"

"That's been your defense mechanism all these years, hasn't it? Accusing others in order to shift attention from yourself? Hanging around people too dumb to see through the act. But it's so *obvious* . . ."

"Fuck you up, bitch."

"It's easier to change the subject than to change your sex."

Eric was ready to explode, his ears bright red. One of the other guys spoke up: "Come on, dude, she's just messin' with you."

"Then she better shut her fucking mouth before I do it for her."

Shifting her attention to the other boy, Maddy studied his features, his body rhythms, and said, "You've been feeling tired, haven't you?"

"What? Shut up, I'm not talking to you."

"Seriously, how's your game?"

"My *game*?"

"You've been skipping practice, right?"

"What're you, stalking me?"

"I don't have to—your hair's not bleached to the root, and your hands aren't pruned. Also, you've lost weight recently. It shows first in the face, around the eyes. You're cold all the time. And your color's funky—haven't you noticed? You're a ghost, kid."

"Yeah, so I've had the flu, so what?"

"No. This has been going on too long for that. Your blood cells are destroying themselves."

"Are you serious, you crazy bitch?"

"Idiopathic autoimmune hemolytic anemia—I'd bet on it. You should go to the doctor before you have a massive coronary."

"What! Yeah, like I'm gonna go to the doctor because—"

"You should. Just to rule out leukemia. Or AIDS."

"Give me a *break*."

"And Eric? It's not a crime to be into water sports. But you have to find someone your own age. Don't obsess about the past, and try not to abuse the Internet—you never know who might be watching."

With the crowd laughing and jeering him, Eric went berserk, fighting the intervening boys to get at her. Maddy felt a hand on her arm, gently pulling her out of line.

"Come on," said Stephanie. "You should get out of here."

"What do you care?" Maddy said, jerking free and running from the cafeteria.

Sobbing, she left the building and fled across the Great Lawn, drawing stares from students and the attention of faculty yard monitors, who gave chase. Seeking a restroom, Maddy ducked indoors and passed bright classrooms with row after row of identical desks . . . and it suddenly seemed to her that the people behind those desks were also identical, all reading identical books, thinking identical thoughts. Robots. Disposable, interchangeable robots. Existing only to perpetuate the status quo.

Maddy had been a good little robot, too. Only now she was defective, she didn't fit in. They used euphemisms like *special* and *gifted*, but what they really meant was defective. Unstable. And it was no big mystery what happened to defective machines: They got thrown away.

Maddy crashed through the office doors and burst in on Principal Batrachian. He was in a conference with several teachers, and they all jumped up in surprise as Maddy vaulted over his desk and plunged a cafeteria fork into their principal's fat throat.

As they wrestled her off, Maddy was babbling unintelligibly about heavy isotopes, atomic decay, and planned obsolescence. It took three burly EMTs to get her to the ambulance.

SEVENTEEN

RETURN TO SENDER

THE hospital again. Elvis on the speakers (or was it just in her head?), singing "Return to Sender."

Wheeled around on a gurney, dipping in and out of consciousness, Maddy could tell at once that nobody at Braintree was surprised to see her. The doctors all had the sympathetic, slightly condescending manner of people who were not accustomed to being proven wrong. Dr. Stevens loomed overhead, talking in slow motion.

"Well, Mr. and Mrs. Grant, just as we anticipated might happen, your daughter Madeline has experienced a bit of difficulty adapting to the RCA interface. It's nothing to be alarmed about—I'm confident that with the right conditioning, we can get her back on track. It's just a matter of fine-tuning the program to distribute her psychic workload more evenly. Avert this kind of crisis in the future by repeatedly inducing the appropriate response in a controlled environment. A conditioned reflex. For that reason, it's very important that we keep her here at the facility—I wouldn't recommend outpatient therapy again until we have greater confidence in her ability to cope."

"Dear God. How long do you think she'll have to stay here this time?"

"Well, it could be worse. If it had gone to court, she could have been permanently institutionalized. Short of that, I do think an open-ended commitment of at least six months would be conservative."

"Six months!" cried Mrs. Grant.

The doctor said, "I realize it's difficult, but this is the time when intervention can make the most difference in your daughter's recovery. Her damaged cortex is knitting right now, generating new synaptic pathways that will decide her personality for the rest of her life. Once her brain fully incorporates the implant, it will be much harder to modify. Whatever glitches still exist, she'll have to live with them permanently. And these things can be progressive, leading to a complete mental breakdown, as we've just seen. Better to get it right the first time."

"If you'd gotten it right the first time, I wouldn't be back in here."

"Well! Good morning, Maddy. Feeling better, I hope?"

"Jeez, Doc, give me a chance to wake up. Hi Mom, hi Dad. How long have you guys been here?"

"Hi, baby. All night—we rode with you. Are you okay?"

"I think so. I'm not quite sure what I'm doing here. What was that about six months?"

"Dr. Stevens was just telling us that they'd like you to stay here for another six months of therapy. Inpatient this time. Do you understand?"

"Yeah . . . I think so . . ."

"What do you think of that? Your dad and I hate the idea, but the doctor thinks it could make a lot of difference. You can call us anytime you want, and we'll drive right over. We won't make you do it if you don't want to."

Maddy thought about it.

"If it'll mean I don't have to go back to school."

BY the next day, Maddy felt better already. Her head was perfectly, beautifully clear. She had slept soundly, and for the first time all week she could really hear herself think. When Dr. Stevens and Dr. Plummer came in, she said, "Hey, I feel pretty good. What if I'm all better? Do I still have to stay here for six months?"

Dr. Stevens said, "Actually, Maddy, that's what we're here to talk to you about."

Dr. Plummer placed a thick file folder in Maddy's lap. It had her name on it.

"What's this?"

He said, "Open it up and take a look."

Maddy opened the folder. Inside was a sheaf of documents, a plastic billfold, a zipper bag containing a set of keys and a fancy cell phone, and a sleek device that resembled a tiny computer modem.

"What is all this?"

"It's yours. Take a look."

Maddy opened the wallet and was a bit disconcerted to see a brand-new photo ID with an unflattering picture of herself. She couldn't remember ever having that picture taken. Then again, she didn't remember a lot of things. More intriguing was the money in the wallet, a wad of twenties—at least a couple of hundred bucks—and a credit card. Like the ID, the credit card had her name on it. There it was, in big, embossed letters: MADELINE Z. GRANT. Which was quite interesting because Maddy was fairly certain she would remember if she'd ever owned a credit card. It was something she'd been bugging her mother about for years.

"What's this for?" she asked.

"Well," said Dr. Plummer, "you may be glad to know that your next phase of treatment doesn't involve puzzles or tests or doctors poking at you. It doesn't involve living here at the hospital at all. That kind of clinical examination can no longer tell us what we really need to know, which is how that new brain of yours responds to real-world stimuli. In other words: field-testing."

"Wait—didn't we just try that?"

"We did, but in sending you home, we assumed it would *reduce* your stress—that the benefits of familiarity would outweigh the risk. Unfortunately, we were wrong."

"Great."

"This time, we'd like to apply similar stresses, but in a controlled way, strictly monitored, with fail-safes in place to prevent another overload. So, starting tomorrow, you'll be transferred to an off-site treatment facility, our Practical Recovery Unit, where you can explore your potential more effectively. In a real-world situation."

"Meaning what, exactly?"

"Meaning you'll essentially be living independently, in a private dormitory. We'll be tracking your progress via this wireless modem, but you'll have considerable discretion over the use of your time . . . and money. That being the major point of the exercise."

Dr. Stevens continued, "Before you get too excited, keep in mind that maintaining proficiency in your studies is part of your therapy, as is managing your day-to-day living expenses. The debit account is just a loan until you find a job, after which you must establish a payment schedule as part of your budget. The whole program is loaded into your PDA."

"What if I don't pay? I'm still a minor—what if I just go nuts with the card and party my brains out?"

"That will indicate to us that your impulse-control center is not being properly stimulated. We would have to find out why, and that could require intensive sessions in the fMRI lab—perhaps even more surgery."

Ugh—Maddy's worst experiences in the hospital involved that dreaded fMRI machine. Being strapped down in a narrow tube for hours on end, her head held in a vise, as the thing magnetically scoured her brain.

"I get it. No thanks, I'd rather count my pennies."

"Good. So you're interested?"

"Do I have a choice?"

"Of course you do—the program's purely voluntary."

"What happens if I don't do it?"

"A Thorazine drip and indefinite clinical confinement."

"Where do I sign up?"

EIGHTEEN

HARMONY

THE next morning, Maddy ate a big breakfast of sausages, eggs, and blueberry pancakes, and was accompanied by Dr. Stevens to a waiting van.

"Where exactly am I going?"

"The town of Harmony. It's not far—we're on the outskirts here, about ten miles away I'd say. It used to be an industrial area, but in recent years it was bought up by developers and has been transformed into a very picturesque planned community."

"Okay, good. Well . . . bye, then, Dr. Stevens."

"Bye, Maddy. Have a good trip, and remember to just relax; stay centered. Everything you'll need to know is on your PDA. We'll be watching you, so don't worry."

"Thanks. I'm fine."

Dr. Stevens slammed the door and waved as the van took off.

The silver cube of the clinic vanished in the trees as they drove down a long, descending road into the valley. It was a very scenic drive, densely forested on either side.

In fact, the road was pretty rugged, unpaved and deeply rutted in spots, more like a logging trail than an actual highway. There were no signs and numerous twists and turns, but the driver seemed to know where he was going. He was a startled-looking man with receding hair and a double chin, though he was neither old nor fat. His name tag read: DR. RUDY MCGURK.

"Is this a shortcut?" Maddy asked.

"Yeah—it's restricted access. DARPA money. All this back in here is private, government property."

"Isn't that an oxymoron?"

"What?"

"Nothing."

"I know—you think I'm stupid or something. I just didn't hear you."

"Private, government? Government generally means public."

"Not here it don't, sis."

The air became hazy, filtering the sunlight and washing out the shadows. There seemed to be a greasy, sooty film over everything—and a *smell*: rotten eggs.

"What's that smell?" Maddy asked.

"Coal fire," Rudy said. "Used to be a strip mine around here, until it had to be abandoned."

"The fire's still burning?"

"Oh, it'll probably go for the next thousand years. It's burning away underground, following the coal seam."

"Is that safe?"

"Well, every now and again a sinkhole might open up in the fairway, but other than that, you'd never know it was there. Actually, it creates an interesting thermal effect—there's no snow accumulation, and the valley stays fairly temperate all winter long, so it's kind of a golfer's paradise."

"What about, like, toxic gases?"

"I wouldn't worry about it."

"Oh yeah? Then what about these guys?"

They had come to a fenced checkpoint with concrete barricades and a guard station. Guards in gas masks waved them through.

"Those are just to filter out the dust," Rudy assured her.

Beyond the fence, it was all smooth sailing, the van carried along on a ribbon of freshly laid asphalt. The trees thinned, becoming first denuded and scrawny, then mere blackened skeletons.

Burnt-over woods gave way to a smoggy vista of gray rubble, a blasted moonscape that abruptly changed to parkland, the rolling green sprawl of a golf course. It still stank. Fumes hung heavy in the air, and here and there were dead zones: staked-off patches of smoldering, scorched earth, with warning signs like orange pirate flags.

Out of nowhere, houses appeared, a pristine residential area. Block after block of identical prefabricated units, with people mowing lawns and washing cars. There was a lot of new construction going on—the place was booming.

"Yeesh," Maddy said, "who would want to live here?"

"*I* live here," Rudy said.

"Oh. Sorry."

"We bought one of the last lots, and were lucky to get it. There's no property tax, plus you've got year-round golfing, tennis, shopping—"

"It's great. Absolutely. I was just being stupid."

The town center consisted of a large shopping plaza radiating from an old mine complex, with a restored railcar and a huge central structure like a tin-roofed cathedral. The sign on it read, MUSEUM OF INDUSTRY AND CULTURE.

Shiny bright though it appeared, the village was devoid of character, if not actually grim. Maddy thought Rudy McGurk and Chandra Stevens must have a pretty odd notion of the picturesque. Aside from the mine complex, it was all plastic. There had been obvious efforts to make it quaint—plantings and antique streetlights and Norman Rockwell façades for the chain stores—but nothing could disguise the essential hollowness at its core. At least the air was clearer, or maybe she was just getting used to it.

Dr. Stevens had been right about one thing: Downtown was quiet—quiet as a Sunday morning. The shopping plaza looked closed; there was no traffic to speak of and few pedestrians in sight.

The van pulled up in front of a budget motel advertising weekly rates. It wasn't until the driver set the emergency brake and started getting out that Maddy realized they had arrived.

"Wait—what's this?"

"We're here," Rudy said. "All ashore that's going ashore."

"*Here?* This motel?"

"Yes, ma'am."

Slightly unnerved, Maddy allowed herself to be led through the door into the lobby. What was there to say about it? It was a motel lobby, with generic motel-lobby furniture and motel-lobby pictures on the walls. Nothing to suggest it was a halfway house for potentially violent headcases. She couldn't decide if that was good or bad.

There was a frosted-glass window labeled CHECK IN. Rudy pressed a buzzer, and the glass slid back, revealing a burly Middle-Eastern woman. Smiling, the woman said, "Ah, yes," and took Maddy's documents. "Welcome to Harmony Suites. I hope you enjoy your stay with us." Typing something into the computer, she printed it out and gave it to the driver to sign.

"Well, this is as far as I go," he said, scribbling. "Good luck."

Maddy was uncomfortable with the idea of his just leaving her here. Accepting her files back, she asked, "Is someone supposed to meet me here or what?"

"Who?"

"I don't know. A counselor or something. Dr. Stevens said I would be strictly supervised."

"She meant electronically. Via your implant."

"Oh yeah." *Stupid.*

"What did you think the external modem was for?"

"Riiight. Robo-chaperone."

"Exactly. That's the whole point. Stay within a kilometer of this, and you got a high-speed wireless connection at all times. GPS, Bluetooth, you name it. It also acts as a wireless charger, converting radio frequencies to electricity, so you don't have to worry about your batteries running low. Nothing can happen to you now without your doctors knowing about it, and we're just up the hill."

"I get it. Should have given me one of these before."

"Well, the technology is so new, there are still major gray areas in terms of state and federal law. Off the reservation, Braintree simply doesn't have as much authority to protect its proprietary technology in the event of loss or seizure. It's an unacceptable risk. If anything goes wrong, the clinic needs to know that they'll have first crack at their property. Not some clumsy first responder. Not some well-meaning doctor or hospital lawyer. Not some judge. You were too vulnerable to unwarranted intrusion before; here, we have reasonable confidence of primacy."

Primacy. Property. Maddy didn't like the sound of that. By *first crack* did he mean at the modem . . . or her skull?

"Well, that's about it," he said. "We all set?"

"Yeah . . . I think so."

"You're gonna be fine. Try to enjoy it, and remember that everything you need to know is right up here." He tapped himself on the head.

"Okay."

"You take it easy now."

"I will. Bye."

"Bye-bye." He pushed through the door and was gone.

Maddy had a moment of panic, during which she very nearly ran after Rudy and begged not to be left alone. Something had to be terribly wrong—her parents would never have agreed to this! Then something throttled down in her head, the panic subsided, and all was still.

The desk clerk gave her a key and pointed her toward the elevator. As if in a dream, Maddy rode it up to the second floor. Her room number was 207, about halfway down at the narrow hall, on the right. Like the lobby, the corridor was all very cold and impersonal, smelling of fresh paint and without so much as a picture on the wall to break up the monotony. How many of those rooms contained people like her? She would be interested to know.

Opening her door, Maddy wasn't sure what to expect. A barren cell? A crowded dormitory? But she was gratified to see it was nothing too severe. Just a small, private kitchenette apartment with basic amenities, overlooking the rear parking lot. No phone or TV. With a sense of trepidation, she plugged in the modem's power adapter and closed her eyes, waiting to see if anything would happen . . .

Nothing—nothing at all. There was no way to tell if it was even working, no lights or sounds. She would have to ask downstairs about that.

But not yet. First, she plopped down on her hard single bed and wallowed in the weird sensation of freedom. It was spooky. For the first time in her life, there was no one telling her what to do. And it wasn't just for a day or a week, but for *six months*. All the time in the world. You could live a whole life in six months—get a job, fall in love, get married and divorced . . .

Then and there, Maddy decided she was not only going to make the most of that time, but that she desperately needed it. Maybe those doctors knew what they were doing putting her there, far away from the pressure of family and friends. How else could she escape from the stale role of Maddy Grant . . . and find out who she really was?

About time, she thought, tears streaming into her ears. *About frickin' time.*

NINETEEN

SIGNS

AFTER resting awhile, Maddy got bored and ventured back downstairs. It was still morning; she had a whole day ahead of her. She wondered if she had to check in with the lobby every time she went in or out, but when she got there, the window was dark and locked shut. She went outside.

The street was just as empty, but the haze had thinned, and she could see that some of the stores were open. Down the block was a generic-looking chain restaurant with a huge sign: STRUWELPETER'S. Next door on the right was a dry cleaner's and a Laundromat. On the left was a convenience store and a Middle-Eastern joint—the marquee read, KASHMIR KABOB—ALL-U-CAN-EAT FALAFEL $7.99. Directly across the street were a women's clothing boutique, a gift shop, and a shoe outlet.

Well, if she was going to look for a job, she would definitely need a new outfit. She had nothing to wear but the clothes on her back—the same things she had worn to school three days ago—and the few things packed in the small overnight bag her parents had brought.

Then again, she was loaded.

Counting her twenties, Maddy realized she had exactly three hundred dollars in cash. That should be plenty.

First, she went into the convenience store seeking a few basic amenities like dish soap, shampoo, toothpaste, and tampons. She intended to stick to the bare necessities, but more and more items kept jumping out at her until suddenly her basket was full. The checker was a swarthy, mustached man who rang her purchases up with undisguised relish.

"Ah! Lemon Brite—good choice! This AquaDent is very good, too, a most beautiful color! Do you by any chance have a RiteDrug Card?"

"Oh, uh, no."

"No matter! You will fill this out and I will discount your purchases—very simple! Ah, yes—Tampad! The leading brand! Will that do it for you?"

"Yes, please."

"Then your purchase comes to fifty-five dollars and twenty-six cents, please."

Maddy was taken aback—almost sixty bucks! What was she thinking? Deodorizer? Moisturizer? Conditioner? Hairbrushes? She barely had any hair! Oh well, she rationalized, at least she'd be set for a while. She took her stuff and went outside.

From there she went to the clothing store. The woman salesclerk was very attentive, and also very exotic-looking, with kohl-rimmed eyes and Muslim-style head scarf. She stood back at a polite distance, humming and staring off into space, but the second Maddy had a question about anything, she was there in a flash, grinning blissfully as she rattled off prices, sizes, colors, styles, whatever. And as quickly as she appeared, vanished back under her hood again, cooing softly to herself.

Working up her nerve, Maddy asked, "Excuse me, but would you know of anyplace where they're taking applications? I'm kind of looking for a job."

The woman froze in midleap as if flustered by the question. "Job?"

"Yeah. Any kind of job. Preferably part-time."

The woman gave it some thought. "Have you tried the employment agency?"

"No."

"It's right around the corner—you can't miss it. Able Staffing."

"Oh—thanks."

"You're most welcome. If I can help you with anything else, please tell me." The woman gratefully ducked back into her trance.

Browsing the sale racks, Maddy noticed a sign on the wall. It was a police sketch of an egg-shaped face above the words HAVE YOU SEEN THIS MAN? She realized that the same sign had been posted on the window of the convenience store. There was something generic and yet creepy about that face—it was one of those pictures where the eyes seem to follow you. *A white, middle-aged male of average height and build,* it read. Well, that narrowed it down! It also said the man was being sought in connection with the disappearance of several young girls, and that anyone recognizing him should contact the sheriff's department immediately.

Averting her eyes from the poster, Maddy tried on a few outfits, settling on what she felt was the most professional-looking yet inexpensive combo, something that was laundry-safe: a soot gray pantsuit, with a yellow and black polka-dot blouse. It was hard to choose, because there were so many dazzling items she would have preferred, but it was important to demonstrate a little restraint. *God*—this was worse than having her mother looking over her shoulder.

The designer purses and shoes especially seemed to beckon: gleaming, elegant toys that Maddy could barely resist fondling, pressing their wonderful smoothness against her face and breathing deep of their new-car smell. Weird—she never realized how incredible this stuff was. Stephanie was right. The designer names swirled in her brain like holy mantras, ripe with joyous power, and the corporate logos shone like sacred symbols. She *yearned* for them.

Near tears, she made herself leave the store with only four hundred dollars' worth of merchandise. *It's all right, it's all right,* she thought frantically. *I'll make it up when I get a job.* She had used up her cash, but it occurred to her that she didn't even know if the card had a limit—maybe she could spend a little more!

But not there, no—too expensive. There were other things she needed more . . . like food. Food, yes—no one could call that an extravagance. Across the plaza she could see a small supermarket. FOOD-O-RAMA, the sign said.

Heading for it, Maddy noticed several more flyers posted on walls and utility poles. That face was really starting to bug her. Everywhere she went, she saw that bothersome police sketch, and in her efforts to avoid looking at it, she tried turning her attention to other things, such as the big, colorful VOTE signs that were also all over town. Apparently, there was a local election going on, and the two candidates had plastered the streets with their campaign posters.

One was a very charming, sensitive, and purposeful-looking man who reminded Maddy of her ninth-grade science teacher, Mr. Bekins. She had adored Mr. Bekins. This man's name was Strode, and his signs were simple

and bold, merely a picture of his handsome face over the
words VOTE STRODE.

The other candidate's signs were more rankly manipu-
lative, with the slogan BELIEVE and a photo of the guy
reverently holding his hand over his heart. His name was
Vellon. Vellon's fat face annoyed her, and it wasn't until
she saw it for the umpteenth time that she realized why:
He resembled the man in the police sketch! It wasn't an
exact resemblance, but there were definite areas of simi-
larity, particularly the pointy bald head. Of course, it
couldn't be the same man—that would be ridiculous—but
the mere thought of it was enough to turn her off. She
could barely stand to look at the guy, much less vote for
him. Go Strode!

There was another Vellon sign on the door of the market, and she pushed past without looking at it. Getting a
cart, she took a centering breath and headed down the
produce aisle. She had always found supermarkets to be
restful places—the gentle music, the smells of bread and
brown paper evoking lazy Sunday outings with Mom.

Small as it was, this place was no exception, and for
the few minutes she perused the vegetables, Maddy
achieved a leafy green nirvana—blissful nothingness. She
took only what she needed and nothing more. It was when
she reached the end of the produce section that things got
complicated.

Scanning the labels, looking at the sale signs, she suddenly began to hear commercial jingles echoing in space.
It was not unpleasant—in fact, she found herself humming
along with the familiar tunes, her whole body suffused
with unexpected pleasure. Most rewarding of all was the
feeling of putting something in the cart, a giddy tingle of
pure joy that made her laugh out loud.

I never realized how much fun this is, she thought. *I
really need to shop more often.*

Though she didn't question the sensations, there was something distinctly odd about how some items lit her up and others didn't. The major labels really seemed to smile back at her, almost to *recognize* her. At first she thought it was her simple familiarity with the products: the memory of TV commercials she had seen all her life combined with the excitement of being on her own for the first time. That would naturally make everything more intense.

But that could not be all there was to it because as she went on, there were a number of new products she had never used before, nor even seen advertised—yet they sang their siren calls just as loudly. Then again, after all that had happened, how far could she even *trust* her memory? Perhaps this itself was a sign of recovery, all these things acting as triggers for her subconscious, her lost self. In any case, the experience was delightful as long as it lasted, like being the star of her own musical.

But as she lugged the stuff back to the motel, tired and thirsty and another hundred dollars in the hole, the pleasure faded, and she began to feel sick about it, deeply confused by the lapse. She actually had to set her bags down and dry heave in the bushes.

What happened? she thought. She who had so recently laughed at the Pavlovian manipulation and self-deceptions of consumerism. *I'm smarter than this. I'm not one of those shopaholics on TV. Stephanie's the binge spender, not me.*

Could that be it? Could this be some kind of psychological compensation for a lifetime of moderation? Of settling for less and letting others hog the glory? The rich girls, the beautiful girls, the Golden Ones. Silly clotheshorses like her mother and her best friend and all the Marina Sweets of the world. Watching them preen as she herself blended like a moth into the tree bark—had that finally caused her to crack?

Considering these things as she entered the motel

lobby, Maddy's eyes were drawn to a familiar flyer on the wall—that awful face again. HAVE YOU SEEN THIS MAN? She couldn't remember the sketch being there before . . . or maybe she just hadn't noticed. All she knew was that she couldn't look at that every time she came and went.

With a burst of fury, she whipped the poster off the wall and twisted it into a mangled knot. Then, as she waited for the elevator, she ripped it to tiny shreds while imagining it was the man himself she was punishing, venting all her anger and frustration on a piece of paper and snarling through her clenched teeth as she did it. It felt really good.

TWENTY

BROKEN MIRROR

AFTER her shopping trip, Maddy was reluctant to leave her room, not sure if she could trust herself. The habits she had formed while laid up in the hospital made it easy to hang around in bed the rest of the afternoon, but she knew sooner or later she would have to start looking for a job. She didn't want Dr. Stevens and the rest of Braintree coming after her.

That night Maddy had a bad dream.

She dreamed she awoke. There was something very important she needed to do. She got out of bed and put on her clothes, then gathered some things from the medicine cabinet and left the room. It was too bright in the hall; she closed her eyes and found that she remembered the layout of the building perfectly well. Hurrying down the fire stairs, she came out in an alley. It was dark out, but she could see there was a car waiting, a black limousine. The uniformed driver frisked her, said, *She's clean*, then opened the door and let her in. There was no one else in the car.

They drove out of town and got on the highway, heading north. In the way of dreams, there was a disconnect, so that suddenly Maddy realized she wasn't in a car but in the crawl space under her house. The dirt was cool and damp. She had hidden a plastic bag full of her baby brother's belongings down there before her folks could donate them all away, and sometimes she came down to remember him. Nobody else seemed to. There was nothing of his left in the house; her mother got hysterical at the slightest reminder.

When she opened the bag, what she found was not Lukie's hat and jacket and stuffed animals, but a cache of random junk: a bottle of diet soda, a roll of duct tape, a fat ballpoint pen, a roll of effervescent mints, and some sharp pieces from a broken mirror. Somehow, those things fit together, and Maddy understood that in order to get what she wanted, she would first have to solve the puzzle.

She opened the cola, drank some, and gently pushed the unopened roll of candy inside. Then she took apart the pen and stuck its hollow shaft into the bottle, joining them with a gasket of duct tape. Into the end of the pen she loaded small mirror fragments, jamming the largest one in the opening so its point stuck out like a sharp blade. Then she taped the bottle to her right forearm so it was concealed within her sleeve.

Just as she was finishing, she became aware of a presence in the dark crawl space. Someone was in there with her.

Well, hello, what's your name? a man's voice asked.

The dream shifted again, and Maddy abruptly found herself back in the limo. The car was parked, and she was face-to-face with the man from the poster, his dead-eyed stare drinking her in. Vellon. Believe. He was wearing a tuxedo with the collar loosened, and he smelled of alcohol. The driver was gone; they were alone.

Maddy, she replied.

Well, Maddy, why don't you come sit on my lap so we can get to know each other better? I promise I won't bite.

As if in a trance, she moved across to him, ducking in the low space.

You're a very pretty girl, he said, cradling her against his belly.

Thank you, she murmured.

Are you new at this?

Yes.

I thought so. There's nothing to be nervous about—all you have to do is relax. Let me do all the work.

As his plump, manicured fingers moved up her leg, she could sense the man's excitement, the quickening of his pulse and respiration. Placing her hand on his neck, she leaned in as if to kiss him, feeling the huge, throbbing vein against her palm. At the last second, she turned her mouth aside, his lips smooshing against her cheek. Before he could react, she jammed the razor-tipped pen into his jugular and squeezed the soda bottle as hard as she could. The pressure ruptured the soggy candy wrapper, exposing the bicarbonate in the mints and causing an explosive release of carbon dioxide, which spurted like a geyser up the plastic tube and into the man's bloodstream—shooting the mirror fragments straight to his heart.

The man screamed, turning purple. His limbs flailed violently, his back arching up off the seat so that Maddy was thrown to the floor. Escaping was not as easy as she'd expected. She scrambled away, cowering against the seats opposite as he continued to thrash and make horrible noises. His head looked like a balloon about to explode. Then, like a deflating balloon, he collapsed, wheezing out his last breath at her feet. The soda bottle was full of blood.

Maddy awoke in the dark, heart racing. *I killed him! Oh my God, I killed him!*

Gradually, as full consciousness returned, she realized

it was just a dream—thank God, only a dream. But it wasn't the nightmare itself that had awakened her; she still had the vivid sense of having been jarred out of a deep sleep by something else. A loud noise? She sat up and scanned the room, searching the shadows for anything that could explain it. There didn't appear to be anything wrong or out of place. Without turning on the lights, she clutched her pillow to her breast and got up to go to the bathroom. Nothing.

Just a dream, then. Okay. The tiled floor in there was freezing; she hurried back to bed and burrowed under the blankets. Soon she was asleep.

The next morning, she dragged herself out of bed to pee. *Brrr—somebody turn the heat up!* Half-awake, she barely caught herself before stepping into the bathroom. She almost shrieked.

The floor was covered with broken glass. Shards of mirror and fractured glass shelving lay everywhere, a thousand foot traps for her poor bare soles.

It was the medicine cabinet. Sometime in the night, it must have fallen off the wall, perhaps weighed down by all the crap she had bought. That was what had awakened her . . . and yet somehow she had missed it. Walked right through it in the dark without so much as a cut.

Lucky, she thought, shaky with amazement.

"It's not luck, you know," said a scratchy, high-pitched voice.

Maddy spun around. There was no one in the room.

"Down here," said the voice.

Maddy peered behind the shower curtain and shrieked at what she saw.

There was a large animal in the bathtub. The creature was gray and black, with a bushy striped tail and a dark patch like a burglar's mask across its beady eyes—a raccoon! The raccoon was sitting upright on its fat haunches and washing frozen shrimp in the warm dribble from the tap. It was also wearing a fez.

"I must still be dreaming," she said.

"Life must be a dream, sweetheart."

"This is insane."

"No argument there. With all this washing, I sometimes wonder if I have OCD."

"Did I really just kill that man?" she asked.

The raccoon was matter-of-fact, too busy at its task to bother looking at her. "Yes," it said. "And if you stay here, you'll kill again."

Maddy jerked awake.

TWENTY-ONE

ELECTION

EMERGING like a pupa from her troubled sleep and clammy sheets, Maddy peered through the curtains and thought, *Delightful*. She took a hot shower, put on her new clothes, and headed out to the employment agency. There it was, just where the salesgirl had said—Able Staffing Services. Unfortunately, it was Sunday, and the office was closed. Brilliant.

Okay then, it was up to her. Initiative—that was what they wanted to see. Well, they'd soon find out she was full of it! Setting forth with a determined, slightly teetering stride, Maddy spent the next several hours wearing out her new high heels on the old cobbles of Carbontown—Harmony's teensy tourist district. As it was the weekend, there were a number of visitors about. Maddy assumed they were mostly the families of other recovering patients like herself. They snapped pictures of each other in front of the mining exhibits and pushed those in wheelchairs up the ramp to the Museum of Industry and Culture. The sight made her wistful for her folks.

But she wasn't there to sightsee. Starting at the town center, Maddy went door to door, accosting every clerk and cashier she could find, first canvassing all the standard tourist holes—the fudge factory, the gift shop, the over-priced café—then gradually working her way outward to encompass every other business in a ten-block radius . . . after which downtown turned residential.

Most of the people she spoke with rejected her outright; the rest said they weren't presently hiring but would keep her employment application on file. A lot of places had signs in the window saying, CLOSED FOR ELECTION. Trying not to be discouraged, she ventured up stairwells to even the least-promising businesses, the ones that rented space on the upper floors of cut-rate professional buildings—palm readers and yoga studios and the like—but it was all the same: zip. Zip and blisters.

By that time, everything was pissing her off, and what aggravated her the most was the strange behavior of almost everyone she met. They acted as if they were not fully present, blissed-out on music only they could hear. For such a small town, the ethnic diversity was remarkable, yet everyone was boogying to the same silent tune, identical in their vaguely stoned demeanors. It was infuriating. They smiled or nodded or frowned sympathetically at whatever she said, then politely, implacably kicked her out. By about the tenth time, she started getting more creative with her pitch, since they weren't listening anyway: ". . . and during eighth grade I became editor of the school newspaper, then in high school I joined a lesbian flying circus and robbed Fort Knox . . ."

But boy did they take shopping seriously. Not that there was much else to do around there. Customers rampaged through stores with wild-eyed intensity, and manic sales-clerks responded with hails of cheerful jabber about the merchandise, like hawkers at a Turkish bazaar. They were equally eager to help Maddy . . . until they realized she wasn't a paying customer, at which point they became oddly flustered, as though there was something terminally weird about being unemployed. It was embarrassing.

Another odd thing was that almost everyone she spoke to about a job was a new immigrant. Maddy had certainly never had a problem with immigrants before, but after a long day of rejection, she began to feel resentful. Foreigners seemed to run every business in town. Were they there because of the war or just for the economic opportunity? A lot of them seemed to be Middle-Eastern. Whatever the reason, there didn't seem to be any jobs left . . . or if there were, no one was telling her. It wasn't fair.

She had heard her relatives argue about things like this, but she had never given it much thought. Her friend Stephanie was the one with the strong opinions. *You guys are so racist,* Steph would say. *We all started out as immigrants. It's the freakin' American Dream.* Maddy had always sided with her friend, but now she wasn't so sure how she felt about it . . . except tired and irritated.

It was the end of the day, and she was ready to quit. She tried one last place—a place she would have thought was a guaranteed bastion of old-fashioned whitebread Anglo-Americana: the local firehouse. It was part of a new complex that included a church, a VFW, and an American Legion Hall. She imagined a club full of old codgers in army caps swapping war stories, and figured maybe they needed someone to sweep up the joint.

The entrance was covered with campaign signs, all for Strode, and once inside she found a hushed roomful of people staring at a closed door. The tension was incredible—it was as if they were awaiting news of a loved one's death . . . or birth. Once again, the crowd was remarkably diverse. Exotic newcomers in dishdashas sat alongside tattooed local yokels in stiff Sunday suits. A number of folks had bandages on their scalps.

Barging in on their vigil, Maddy retreated backward, saying, "Oops—sorry!"

A hard-eyed man posted at the door asked her, "Cain I help you?" He had a deep Southern drawl.

"Is this the American Lesion—I mean, Legion Hall?"

"Yes."

"I'm just . . . What's everybody doing here?"

"Doing?"

"It looks like you're all waiting for something."

"The election results. They're counting the ballots now."

"Oh! Okay. So you're all for Strode?"

He looked at her like she was insane. "Of course."

"Why? I mean, I can tell you all really care about this, but why?"

"We love America."

"Oh . . . definitely."

"We love freedom and democracy."

"Great. Me too."

"If you love freedom and democracy, you gotta love Strode. He is the best candidate in the whole world. Anyone who doesn't like Strode doesn't like freedom. We die for freedom, we die for Strode!"

At these words, a cheer went up around the room, half shouting, *"Hallelujah Strode!"* and the other half, *"Strode akbar!"*

"That's . . . wonderful," Maddy said.

Just then, the door opened, and a man emerged waving a piece of paper. His face was a mask of either extreme grief or extreme joy, she couldn't immediately tell which. Collapsing to his knees, he sobbed, *"Strode won!"*

The room exploded in frenzied cheering. People jumped

up and down, embraced, wept, all the while shouting, "STRODE! STRODE! STRODE!"

As the chant rose in fervor, Maddy struggled to make her escape, caught up in the dancing and celebration. It was starting to give her a headache.

"Okay, okay," she said, raising her voice to be heard, "I gotta go . . . excuse me . . . yay Strode . . ."

Breaking free of the room, she stood outside for a moment to catch her breath and check for bruises. *What the hell, man.* Well, at least Vellon didn't win. The thought of that name brought back flashes of her awful dream. Shaking it off, she called to a pair of men in black suits passing on a tandem bicycle, "Hey, you wouldn't happen to know where I could find a job . . . ?"

"Have you tried the employment agency?"

Maddy went back to her room and gratefully kicked the hellish heels across the floor. *Damn. What am I supposed to do now?*

She knew what she *wanted* to do—the credit card was burning a hole in her purse. She had resisted its pull all day, feeling its radiant energy at her hip like a slice of molten gold. And she just wanted to go crazy, banish all her cares in an orgy of spending. That card was so good she could eat it.

No, dammit! That was the problem—she was starving, hadn't had a bite all day. Food would take her mind off it. But what to eat? Her cupboards and minifridge were full of stuff, but the thought of making a meal from these cold, raw elements at that moment was intolerable. Nothing was defrosted, there'd be all those instructions to follow, and at the end a sinkload of dirty dishes—feh. Maddy was not confident in the kitchen; she took after her mother that way.

The card, though, the *card*. It did sound good, the thought of just going out to eat. Splurging one last time, just to make up for a crappy-ass weekend. It wasn't like she hadn't earned it! Plus, she would pay it all back—hadn't she demonstrated her responsibility? One meal was not going to make much difference anyway; a few bucks, come on. They couldn't begrudge her that.

She changed into her school skirt and sneakers and went back downstairs, skipping a little. She was always glad to get out of that tomblike building into the sunlight. Where to eat? Pizza sounded yummy, until she remembered where the pepperoni came from. Cheese pizza just wasn't the same . . . and dairy itself was problematic. Shoot. Hot dogs and hamburgers were out of the question—in fact she might as well forget all fast food. What did that leave? This new consciousness was a bitch.

Her eyes settled on ALL-U-CAN-EAT FALAFEL. Hmm—she associated that stuff with vegetarians and hippies. Vegans especially annoyed her. They were so smug and finicky. What were they trying to prove? But she had to eat *something*, so she went over there.

Going in, Maddy found a pleasant, family-style restaurant, with tapestries on the walls and brass oil lamps hanging from the high ceiling. It was still too early for the Sunday dinner crowd so Maddy had her choice of tables. The waiter brought her a menu and poured her a glass of water.

The prices were pretty reasonable, and there were a number of things that sounded good, but she stuck with the falafel special. It came on a platter with warm pita bread, salad, and hummus. The balls of falafel were crispy and deep-fried—not weird or difficult at all—and the helpful waiter showed her how to stuff them in the pita like a taco. The food was delicious and very filling, and Maddy quickly realized that All-U-Can-Eat amounted to a single portion—they were no fools.

When it came time to pay, she handed over the card

and made a quick trip to the restroom. When she emerged, the waiter was waiting.

"Excuse me, your card, it's no good." He handed it back to her.

Maddy's full stomach shriveled. "What?" she said. "It has to be."

"It won't go through, I'm sorry."

"Did you try it again?"

"Yes, we tried few times. Uh, do you maybe have another card? Or better—cash?"

"No."

"Oh."

"But that one *has* to work. I just used it yesterday."

"Yes, I see, but it say insufficient funds. Maybe you call someone bring money?"

"I can't—I'm not from around here. I'm staying at the motel right down the block."

"Which motel?"

"I forget what it's called—it's a treatment facility. I just had an operation."

The man was slightly interested. "You parents there?"

"No."

"We can call them. They can give credit-card number by phone."

"Wait—the hospital. Call Dr. Stevens!"

"Who?"

"My doctor! Up at the Braintree Institute."

"What is number, please?"

"I don't know the number, but it's right outside of town. It's gotta be in the phone book."

The waiter flipped open his cell phone, saying, "I will check. What name is it?"

"Dr. Chandra Stevens at the Braintree Institute. Tell them it's about Madeline Grant—they'll know who I am."

She watched as he fiddled around uselessly. Finally,

she said, "Let me do it." He reluctantly handed her the phone, and she repeated the information. The electronic operator replied that there was no listing for either a Braintree Institute or a Dr. Chandra Stevens.

"Come *on*," Maddy groaned. "Half the people in this town are patients there. All right, let me try my house. It's gonna be long-distance, okay?"

The waiter nodded warily.

She was just glad she could still remember the number—it had been a long time since she had called home. But it was no good—the number rang and rang and finally went to voice mail. They weren't there. And she knew their cell phones were unlisted because of prank calls after they were on the news. This was getting ridiculous. She left a brief, urgent message and hung up.

"Do you think of anyone else?"

"Just the hotel. If you'd let me go down there, I'm sure they can clear this up."

"Hotel is closed."

"What?"

"There is no hotel."

"*Motel*, I mean! It's a recovery facility, like a halfway house. For the neurological clinic. I'm a *patient* there." She yanked off her hat to show him the scar.

He misunderstood and became even more obstinate, believing she was a runaway mental patient, some kind of nutjob. "No, no. You owe money. I'm sorry, we must tell the police—it is restaurant policy."

"Oh, God . . ."

Maddy slumped in her seat, trying not to cry. She felt humiliated and furious. She couldn't believe she had been put in this situation. How dare they just cut her off like this! No money, no support—it was insane. *Strictly supervised*, my butt! They had left her ass blowing in the breeze.

She could feel all the employees watching her, staring at her. *Look at the crazy homeless girl, trying to eat without paying.* They were enjoying it, this chance to shake their heads over her foolishness: *No, no, miss—we work too hard for our bread to let you steal it. This is America.*

The police were taking their sweet time getting there. No one talked to her or was seated near her. They might as well have roped her off. That was it: She was taboo. Her corner table became an island of quarantine, an object of idle curiosity and whispered discussion among newcomers, then, as the minutes dragged on, pointedly ignored. But there was an undercurrent of anticipation, everyone waiting for the real show to begin with the arrival of the cops. It was like a public execution. *Just get it over with,* she thought, putting her head down.

"You know, you don't have to sit here. You can just leave."

Scalp prickling, Maddy looked across the table. It was the raccoon again. He was standing on a chair, eating her leftover olives.

"Oh no," she said.

"Sorry—were you saving these?"

"What are you *doing* here? I'm not dreaming!"

"That's a question you should be asking yourself. It's not going to be very much fun if you wait till the police arrive. Better to get it over with now."

"This can't be happening . . ."

"Look, I'm just trying to be helpful."

"What *are* you?"

"You know what I am. I'm the bandit, the rascal, the wild one—like Brando. I'm chaos, baby, one hundred percent raw sexuality. Frankly, I'm a friggin' nuisance. My name's Moses." The raccoon reached out its tiny black paw as if to shake. When Maddy just stared, he withdrew it with a smirk. "In case you haven't noticed, lady, my habitat has been shrinking down to nothing lately, and I'm pissed off."

"Moses?" she said. It suddenly clicked that one of Lukie's stuffed toys had been a raccoon named Moses—a character from some old children's book.

"That's my name, don't wear it out."

"You're a hallucination."

"That's right," said Moses. Then, in a stage whisper, he added, "But that doesn't mean I'm not real. I'm you, Maddy—what's left of you. This is the last of your free will talking, and if you don't do something soon, I'm going to die."

"Die? What does that mean?"

"It means that all these people are robots, drones, and you're rapidly becoming one of them. This whole town— it's really not real. It's only a test bed for the next big trend in social engineering: taking hostiles and troublemakers and turning them into good little soldiers. Where do you think these people came from?"

"What do you mean?"

"Duh! Afghanistan, Pakistan, Syria, Iraq, you name it, all courtesy of Uncle Sam. They're al-Qaeda, stupid!"

"*What?*"

"Sure! They're al-Qaeda and Taliban and Hezbollah and every other terrorist organization you can think of, plus a whole lot of political criminals and mental cases. They've all been transferred here. The government is desperate; it can't hold on to them forever, and it doesn't dare kill them, so it has to find some way to make them . . . act nice."

"But . . . that sort of makes sense."

"Sure it does. And Mussolini made the trains run on time."

"What is that supposed to mean?"

"It *means*, sweetheart, that this is just the beginning. Oh, they've been working up to this for some time now, centralizing wealth, privatizing government, globalizing big business. Destabilizing society to favor monopolies and the consolidation of power. Making everyone ignorant and paranoid and helpless . . . and poor. Every country's competing. It's the next great space race: your frontal lobe. The final frontier. Whoever gets there first wins, because from then on, they get to *decide* reality."

"This is crazy. I'm talking to a Marxist raccoon."

"Raccoons aren't Communists or Capitalists—we're pests. That means we believe in using whatever works to survive. Oh, we're clever. We're natural problem solvers. We're cute as hell. But we know we'll never have great wealth or power, so we don't trust anyone who does, whether they say they're on the right, the left, or the Varmint Party. Power is the natural enemy of Nature; money poisons the water. Communists hate sharing just as much as Capitalists hate free markets, free minds, and a level playing field—which is to say a lot. It's human nature to be greedy. But greed is destructive; it reveals itself in the damage it causes. Screw people over for too long, and even the biggest sucker will eventually wise up. Communism didn't fail because it failed, honey, it failed because everybody *knew* it failed, just as they know this war has failed. It's a matter of perception . . . but next time around, they're taking care not to repeat the mistake."

Someone tapped Maddy on the arm. It was the waiter.

"Excuse me," he said. "You can go."

"What?"

"You can go. The man he pay your bill."

"What? Who?"

"Him."

Maddy looked behind her, toward the dim alcove with the EXIT sign. At first she didn't understand who she was looking at, only that he was familiar. Then her whole body reeled like a calving glacier—a million tons of falling ice that left her weightless. Shooting skyward.

"No," she said, lips trembling. Then: "Ben?"

Ben Blevin, her former stepbrother and the first boy she had ever kissed, nodded back at her.

TWENTY-TWO

BEN AGAIN

B EN Blevin was alive.

There he was, unshaven, older, and even more good-looking than she remembered him, cowboy-rugged in jeans and a sheepskin coat.

It was impossible—or was it her memories that were all wrong? Maybe Ben's death was just one more thing she had dreamed. Between Ben's resurrection and Moses the Talking Raccoon, Maddy was terrified she had gone mad. But the raccoon was gone; Ben wasn't.

She went to him. There was no joyous embrace, no tearful reunion—Maddy was too much in shock to feel anything. Ben must have sensed it wouldn't have taken much of a nudge to start her screaming hysterically, so he wisely refrained from touching her.

Eyes round as two pale moons, Maddy said, *"Ben?"*

He nodded somberly. "I know. It's okay. Come on, you want to take a walk?"

She nodded, and they left the restaurant. It was getting dark outside. They strolled aimlessly across the plaza.

"I'm sorry," he said. "I wish I could have told you."

"Told me what? What is this?"

"It's part of the research. *I'm* part of the research—just like you."

"I don't get it, Ben, and it's really, really scaring me." She hugged herself to quiet the shaking.

"We're both part of the same study. The only difference is, you lived, and I died."

"But you're not dead!"

"I am—legally, I don't exist. I never woke up from the carnival accident. After two weeks in a 'profound vegetative state,' I was determined to be brain-dead. My parents signed a DNR order, and the hospital pulled the plug. Then they donated my body to science and went back home. I heard it was a hell of a funeral—I wish I coulda been there."

Maddy covered her ears. "Stop! Stop it before you make me crazy!"

"You're not crazy, Maddy. That's what I thought, too, when they woke me up. Recovery's been a long process. But you've had it way tougher than me, having to go back home and deal with everybody's bullshit. I had the luxury of being dead. No awkward questions. No expectations."

"But *how*?"

"I was just chillin'. Literally. As soon as I was pronounced dead, the hospital froze me stone cold and shipped my body to the Institute. The cold protected what was left of my brain. It was theirs—they had all the rights to it. Then they operated, gave me an implant just like they did you. Shocked my heart back to life. The rest is history."

"But that's a miracle! Why keep it a secret?"

"Are you serious? There are whole organizations whose only purpose is to find things to scream about. Litigate about. Create a crisis, make everybody panic, so then the lawyers swoop in, and the religious groups and the politicians and the media. Everybody all muddled over who lives and who dies. Soon it's a feeding frenzy. And by the time the last investigation ends, the last lawsuit is resolved, we can all turn the clock back on science another twenty years."

"I don't know . . ."

"It sounds messed up, I know, but think about it. This kind of experiment is very controversial. There are privacy questions, human-rights questions, questions about how you define life and death, matters of informed consent. The law hasn't caught up with the technology, and people are dying while the courts work it out. So the Institute has two choices: Either move forward with their work in secrecy or do nothing. They're moving forward. But it's a temporary situation. As soon as the ethical issues are resolved, we'll all be able to go public. In the meantime, the work is more important than the risk of a lawsuit. They saved my *life*, Maddy—I'm in no position to question it. I'm a wholly owned subsidiary of Braintree, Inc."

"You can't mean that."

"No, I'm joking. But I do believe in what they're doing. It's all about saving lives. I've spent a lot of time thinking about this."

"Sounds like it."

"What's that supposed to mean?"

"I mean it sounds like you've worked this all out in your head, and it's all very reasonable. The problem I'm having, Ben, is that I don't trust my head anymore. None of what you've just said explains what's been happening to me these last few days. And I'm very worried. In fact, I'm scared to death."

"About what? Maddy, you have to give yourself time. You're still adjusting. Healing."

"No."

"It's normal to feel—"

"*No.* That's what they told me, and that's what I keep telling myself, but it's a *fucking lie*! There are times when I'm *not me*, when there's somebody else pulling the strings, and it's like they're deliberately making me do things I would never do, just to prove they can. And it keeps getting worse, like I'm possessed or something."

"Oh, come on."

"And the worst part is, I *love* what they make me do! It feels good. But that's not really me either, because afterward, I just want to curl up and die. That's what just happened in that restaurant! You were there! I would have gotten arrested if you hadn't come along." Maddy stopped. "How did you happen to come along just then, anyway?"

"Your name is registered with the police. They called Dr. Stevens, and Dr. Stevens called me. She thought I should talk to you."

"I see. And it's your job to feed me the company line?"

"*No.* I came as a friend."

"Friend. Is that what we are now? Friends?"

"I hope so. I'd like to think so, yeah."

"Okay. Well, Ben old buddy, did you ever find yourself doing things against your will? Like, compulsively? Things you've never done before? Did you ever have euphoric feelings about laundry detergent? Or how about an imaginary conversation with a raccoon? Or murder? Did you ever kill anyone in cold blood? And feel great while you were doing it? Here's what I think: I think everyone here is a prisoner. I think we're all part of some big mind-control experiment, which if it works, will be the beginning of a new kind of society—a human ant farm where there won't be any need for prisons or police, and where nobody will ever even know they're slaves."

Maddy was crying, quickly going to pieces. She hadn't believed any of this when Moses the Raccoon said it, and

she certainly didn't expect Ben to believe it either, but for
her it suddenly seemed all too plausible. She was so pre-
occupied with this disturbing realization that she didn't
notice that Ben had frozen in his steps.

"Yeah," he said softly. "In the beginning, I used to have
thoughts like that. Episodes. But not anymore." ·

"How do you know they were just episodes?"

"Because they weren't real! They were just temporary
delusions, anxiety attacks. It's normal after having the kind
of brain trauma we've had. We're lucky that's the worst
thing we have to deal with."

"Are you sure?"

Ben grabbed her shoulder and looked straight at her.
She saw something in his eyes that hadn't been there before the accident. A depth that only real sorrow could pro-
vide. "Yes," he told her.

"Okay. Well . . . I'm not so sure, okay? I think there's
something else going on here, something not right, and I
don't want any part of it. I have to get out of here, Ben—
that's all there is to it. I feel like somebody's playing with
my head, and if I don't get out of here soon, I swear I will
go nuts."

"Where do you think you're gonna go?"

"I don't care, as long as I'm far away from here. Out of
range of that modem and the clinic and this whole fricking
town."

"Okay."

"Okay, what?"

"Okay, I'll help you."

"You—you will?"

"Yeah. Maybe you're right. Only one way to find out.
Either they'll let you walk out of here, or they won't. And
that'll at least prove your theory one way or the other,
which should have a certain . . . therapeutic value. Right?"

"I guess."

"Okay, then. When do you want to leave?"

"Tonight."

"Tonight it is, then. Here's a hundred bucks to get you started—I can't get any more cash until tomorrow morning. You sure you don't want to wait till then?"

"No."

"Okay. Suit yourself."

"Thanks, Ben." Maddy didn't quite know what to make of his easy acquiescence.

"Don't thank me. I'm probably being the worst kind of enabler. That's why I'm coming along to make sure nothing bad happens to you—I'd never forgive myself."

"Really? Well, then, maybe you should hold on to the money."

"No, you keep it."

"How come?"

"Peace of mind."

TWENTY-THREE

VAN GO

AS she packed, Maddy pictured a future where billions of people lived in peace and happiness, without crime or conflict or hate. Where every person took pride in their labor, and never asked for a raise, or health benefits, or days off, but was available at all hours, any day of the week, including holidays, and could be moved to a new job at the drop of a hat without one word of complaint. And when they were old or sick or otherwise too expensive to maintain, they would willingly jump into mass graves. She pictured gorgeous palaces and parklands inhabited by the wireless rich, who could finally revel in ostentation without fear of resentment or rebellion from the multitudes of implantees slaving away in their teeming, polluted slums. No need for walls or guards—the poor would no more trespass on the privacy of the privileged class than they would eat their own children. Far less so, since they would gladly eat their own children if such a message were imparted through the agency of their glorious and infallible implants. They would eat shit and think it was roast beef. They would gleefully hand their children's skulls over to be screwed with and mindfucked, then celebrate the trepanation with cakes and punch, so that generations ad infinitum would kill for their masters and die for their masters and think themselves free. Rich and poor alike would be happy, and for all their short, blissful lives, Heaven would reign on Earth, forever and ever, amen.

Looking over her room, Ben said, "Man, this place hasn't changed. I remember when I first got here."

"You lived here, too?"

"At the motel? Oh yeah. But first paycheck I got, I was outta here. Now I share a house with two other guys outside of town. We have our issues, but it's still a big improvement over this crap-hole. What happened to your medicine cabinet?"

"Ben?"

"Huh?"

"How much do you remember about that night?"

"You mean—?"

"The kiss."

"Oh . . . yeah. That."

"I just wondered. You know, it was my first kiss. From a boy, I mean."

"Oh no—really? I hope it was good."

"You don't remember?"

"No, I do . . . it's just, I didn't realize . . ."

"It was good. It was the best—one of the best things that ever happened to me."

"Wow."

"Not to be all weird or anything."

"No, I know."

"It's just that it's the last thing I really remember, you know? From before."

"Yeah. Me too."

"Then you left. You got out and never came back."

"Yeah. That was pretty stupid. I'm sorry."

"You don't remember anything after that?"

"No—not really. Just getting really dizzy, you know? The cave seemed to spin around, and I fell on my hands and knees. Then I guess I blanked out."

"Because I thought I remembered somebody in there with me. After you left. You didn't try to come back?"

"Not that I remember. Maybe it was that carny who died. Wornovski."

"No, I don't think so."

"I don't know. Sorry."

"I was just wondering."

"Sure. So listen, I was thinking we could drive north until we hit the Canadian border. I'm not really sure how far it is—I've hardly left town since I got here."

"Drive? You have a car?"

"A van. It's kind of a clunker, but the city gave me a deal on it. I got my driver's license when I turned eighteen. I needed it for work."

"What do you do?"

"Handyman stuff around town—light carpentry, painting, whatever. The Visitor's Bureau keeps a bunch of freelancers on call for all the minor little emergencies that crop up. Plus I'm taking business classes at night. That's why I haven't been able to get away."

"Won't you get into trouble?"

"I'll just call in sick. Besides, I deserve a vacation. Ready?"

"Let's go. Oh, wait a second."

She pulled out the cheap digital camera she had bought at the drugstore. Charging the flash, she said, "Wouldn't hurt to have a little insurance."

"Insurance for what?"

"You never know. Smile!"

She took several pictures of him alone, then used the flash timer to photograph them together.

"I really shouldn't be doing this," he said.

"Relax. I promise not to sell them to the *Enquirer*. Okay, let's go."

"Wait—don't you need this thing?" He was pointing to her modem, which was plugged into its charger.

Jerking the plug out, she said, "Leave it. Let's go."

They went downstairs and across to where Ben's van was parked. It was easy to find, even in the dark: a scuffed white Econoline with a ladder across the top.

"Your carriage awaits," Ben said, opening the passenger door with a flourish.

"Fancy." The back was full of paint cans and spattered canvas. It smelled like turpentine. Maddy climbed aboard and hugged herself for warmth until the heater could kick in.

"You know what's funny?" she asked as they got under way.

"What?"

"I came here in a van, and now I'm leaving in a van."

"Hey, that's just equilibrium. Karma. Balancing the cosmic scales."

"Deep."

"Oh, I'm deep. Twinkie?"

"Thanks."

As they left the lights of downtown behind them, putting distance between her and the modem device, Maddy started to feel a little jittery . . . then a lot. The darkness beyond the headlights was so total it might have been an empty void, a black hole into which they were being sucked, and if they didn't turn back *right then*, they would soon pass a point of no return. *It's the event horizon,* she thought, the place from which not even light could escape.

Looking at Ben, his face sinister in the greenish lights

from the console, she had the awful realization that he was a stranger to her. He could be taking her God-knows-where for his own heinous purposes. For all she knew, he could be a rapist or a serial killer—weren't they all handymen who drove unmarked vans?

"It's not him," said Moses over her shoulder. "It's you. You're a yo-yo. They've got you on a string, and it's pulling tight, making you want to spin the other way. The question is, do you really want to be a yo-yo?"

"Shut up," she said.

Ben said, "What?"

"Nothing. Just thinking."

"Yeah, me too."

They drove on and shortly came to an orange barricade with a large DETOUR sign. Above it was a large signboard that read: DANGER! SINKHOLE HAZARD—COAL FIRE AREA. There was smoke in the headlight beams. Maddy could smell it.

Ben pulled over and set the brake. "Hey, listen," he said. "I was wondering if maybe we shouldn't turn around. I mean, I don't even know where we're going."

"You *what*? I thought you said you knew."

"Well, I thought I did, but . . ."

"Don't you have a map or something?"

"Yeah, but it doesn't do any good if I don't know where we are on it."

"We just left Harmony. It's in Idaho . . . or maybe Montana. Find Idaho on the map and go from there."

He tossed her a road atlas. "Go ahead. You try it."

Maddy intently scanned the map for Harmony. She couldn't find it, not in Idaho or Montana or any other state.

"Don't waste your time," he said. "It's not there."

"What do you mean, it's not there?"

"It's not there. I've looked up Harmony in every map

and directory I could find, even on the Internet, and it doesn't seem to exist."

"That's ridiculous! What is this, *The Twilight Zone*? You're wrong somehow."

"Maybe. I hope so."

"Ben, I don't know what the hell you think you're doing, but you better start being straight with me, or I swear to God—"

"It's the truth. I'm sorry, Maddy. I should have told you right away, but it just didn't seem possible. I mean, a town that you can't leave? But I've tried driving out of here a couple of times now, and the roads just don't jibe with any directions I've been able to come up with. After a few miles, I somehow always end up back where I started."

"What the hell? And you didn't think that was something you needed to tell me?"

"I know, I'm sorry. It's just so nuts that I guess I thought it was a mental block or something—some little glitch in my brain. Dr. Stevens said there might be things like that. I didn't want to deal with it, so after a few tries I just gave up on the idea of leaving. I stopped *thinking* about it . . . until you showed up. I guess I was hoping maybe your confidence could jar something loose."

Oh my God, Maddy thought, trying not to panic. Holding her voice steady, she said, "Do you realize how crazy this sounds? This *proves* it! This proves what I was saying before!"

"No it doesn't, come on."

"Yes it does. The whole town is some kind of sick Area 54."

"Fifty-one. It's *Studio* 54."

"And you stood there and let me think *I* was crazy!"

The shock of an actual crisis had the effect of dispelling Maddy's more vague feelings of doom. The Institute *wanted* her to turn around, of course they did! But she wasn't going to play their game. All she had to do was get past the aversion barrier they had planted in her mind, no different than the physical barriers that were obstructing their forward progress. The answer to both was the same.

Heart thumping, Maddy said, "Just go through."

"What?"

"Drive! Now!"

"I can't do that!"

"Oh Goddammit —"

Maddy lunged for the steering wheel, but Ben held her off, saying, "Okay, okay, I'm doing it!" as he shifted out of neutral and hit the gas. The sign went down, the orange cones and barrels bounced every which way, and they were through, speeding down a dark strip of road.

Which ended a few feet later.

"Stop!" Maddy shrieked.

Ben pulled up hard before a jagged rim of asphalt, their headlights showing the opposite face of a deep ditch. Before Ben could do anything, the pavement under their front wheels crumbled, and the van slid heavily down the eroded bank and plowed into a heap of gravel at the bottom. Clouds of dust and smoke fluoresced white in the headlights.

Ben cut the motor. "Well," he said. "Now we're screwed."

Maddy didn't know what to say. *Sorry* seemed a bit trite. Taking the bull by the horns, she asked, "You think we can get back on the highway?"

"Maybe if we had a dune buggy. Not with this thing."

"Oh. Sorry."

"Come on, we better go. Get ready to hold your breath."

He left the headlights on, and they scrambled out. The air in the ravine was rank and sulfurous, harsh but seemingly not unbreathable, and there was a trickle of hot water running down the center. Maddy's mind tripped off the things she was probably inhaling: hydrogen sulfide, carbon dioxide, carbon monoxide. Best to move quickly.

In the haze, she could see that the bank was not as steep as she'd thought. As she climbed, she could hear strange wheezing sounds percolating from the ground, as if the earth were a giant cappuccino machine . . . and she could hear something else:

A helicopter.

Suddenly, the slope gleamed silver-gray, bright as a movie screen upon which elastic shadows of Maddy and Ben stretched stark black. Turning to face the light, shielding her eyes, Maddy could make out the aircraft swooping low over the highway.

"Ben!" she cried, stumbling on the rubble.

Pulling himself over the rim, he reached down to help her. "We're so nailed," he said.

"STAY WHERE YOU ARE," squawked an amplified voice from the glare. "THIS IS THE SAFETY PATROL."

"Border Patrol is more like it," said the now-familiar voice of Moses. The raccoon was sitting on a projecting edge of roadway, jauntily dangling his feet in her face.

"Oh my God," Maddy said. "What now?"

"They're not rescuers, sweetheart. They're prison guards, and they'll kill you before they let you go. They're here to make sure nobody gets out alive. And even if they don't kill you, you and your boyfriend are probably scheduled for his-'n'-hers frontal lobotomies as soon as you get back to Lemmington. Now that you know what the game is."

"They can't!"

"Oh, they can. They *will*. That is, unless you move your skinny butt and do something about it."

"Like what?"

"Like get back in the van."

The helicopter circled to land, kicking up flurries of

stinging grit and clearing the smoke. A convoy of head-lights appeared. Maddy made her move, ducking into the ravine's shadow and slipping aboard the van.

"What are you doing?" Ben called from above. Before he could go after her, a large dog pounced out of the glare and knocked him flat.

Maddy didn't look back. From the opposite bank, there was a burst of gunfire that kicked up dirt where she had been standing. Narcotic darts bounced off the van's passenger door. But she was already inside, lying flat amid toolboxes and painting supplies. She didn't know what she was doing, but fortunately her hands seemed to. Things came together with the automatic ease of long experience.

Acetone. Benzine. Toluene. Alcohol. The chemical com-binations shuffled like cards, dealing out poker hands on the green baize of her consciousness.

Taking several cans of spray enamel, she removed their caps and set the cans upright in a bucket.

"Yeah, yeah," said Moses. "That'll work."

Then she removed her new digital camera from her bag, charged the flash, and popped the bulb with a screw-driver. So much for those pictures, but Ben in the flesh would be sufficient proof. If she ever got out of there.

While the flash charged, she set the timer for one minute. Placing the camera in the bucket with the spray cans, she sloshed in some acetone-based thinner and put a canvas tarp on top, tucking it around the cans and pour-ing on some methyl alcohol. The last step was to weigh it all down with a gallon can of organic solvent and push in the van's cigarette lighter.

"Beautiful," said Moses. "Now run."

Thirty seconds left. She could hear the hissing spray nozzles as she scuttled butt first out of the van—

Right into the arms of the law.

"Gotcha," a man said.

"You have to let me *go*," she said.

"I don't think so."

Maddy remained still as more men came down both sides of the embankment. She could see from their silhouettes that they were wearing fire helmets and breathing equipment. They also had dogs and night-vision gear. Her captor forced her to lie facedown on the hot ground while he cuffed her with plastic restraints, then painfully jerked her to her feet and dragged her up to the highway. Ben was nowhere to be seen; they had already taken him.

Five seconds. Four . . . three . . . two . . .

Maddy sidestepped in front of her captor, using his body as a shield.

The camera flash sparked, igniting the fumes in the bucket, which went up like a bomb, vaporizing the alcohol suspended in the tarp, rupturing the aerosol cans, and atomizing the solvent, so that for half a millisecond, the van's interior was filled with a dense cloud of vapor. The pressurized vapor shorted the cigarette lighter, causing a volatile reaction in the suspended particles.

They exploded.

The force of the second explosion dwarfed the first. It peeled the van open like a paper bag, the shock wave expanding outward at supersonic speed and blasting the nearest men flat as broken reeds, knocking the clothes off their backs, the shoes off their feet, the limbs off their bodies, and the flesh off their bones. All that happened within a radius of about thirty feet. Beyond that, everything was scoured with flying debris, a lethal hail of shrapnel that took out car windshields half a mile away and riddled the Perspex canopy of the helicopter. Spotlights imploded. Any dogs that weren't killed outright went screaming berserk, attacking their masters in a frenzy of panic.

Maddy felt her whole body clapped between the hands

of a giant. The air was knocked out of her, pressure ramming her ears and sinuses like a sharp stick. For an instant, she thought her head would explode, then the shock wave passed. Just when she thought it was over, something heavy hit her from behind—the guard. His body slammed her against the asphalt, honking her diaphragm like a whoopie cushion.

Struggling out from under, she realized that the man was either unconscious or dead. Something warm and wet was dribbling on the back of her neck.

"Don't waste your chance," said Moses.

The whole place was pandemonium, people running around in the dusty void screaming orders and calling for help. For the moment, they seemed to have lost interest in her and Ben. Where *was* Ben? Maddy couldn't think straight; she just wanted the dead guy off her. Squirming free, she scrambled to her feet and frantically jumped around trying to shake the blood off. *OGodOGodOGod!* Some of it was her own, streaming from her nose and ears—she could taste it. The nauseating flavor of her leaking vital fluid paralyzed her with fright.

"Don't freeze up now." The raccoon wheedled. "Check his belt."

Still freaking out, Maddy reluctantly knelt beside the man, turning her back and sitting down so she could work her hands under his waist. There it was: the leather snap holding the utility pliers. Even with her back turned, it was easy enough to figure out the tool. Whimpering, she reversed it and clipped the restraint. Then she just sat there rubbing her wrists, unsure of what to do next.

The man was not dead; he began to move. To moan.

"Take his gun, too," Moses said.

"No!"

There was no question of her fooling with a loaded

pistol—hadn't things gone far enough as it was? Making a fuel-air bomb out of painting supplies was so outlandish she had had no frame of reference with which to judge her actions, but using a *gun* . . . that was a serious crime.

She could barely bring herself to look at the wounded man. "It's okay," she told him guiltily. "Help is on the way." She figured she would wait there with him until help arrived; after all, she needed medical attention, too.

The raccoon was still there, shaking his head.

"What?" she asked.

"What do you think?"

"What do you expect me to do?"

"You mean other than save your silly ass?"

"How? Make a run for it?"

"Why else did you blow up the van? For the fun of it?"

The words were like a hard slap in the face. "I can't just walk out of here!" she cried. "I'm bleeding!"

"Oh, you're bleeding. Excuse me."

"Well, I am! I'm probably in shock."

"Give me a break. You've got about five seconds left to do something, and you're just going to fritter it away like some bimbo pouting at her birthday party."

"What do you suggest I do? Fly out of here?"

"Why not?"

"What?"

"Take the helicopter. It's just sitting there."

"Oh sure, I'll just take the helicopter. Why didn't I think of that? Good idea—I'm sure they won't mind."

"If you move quickly, they won't even know until it's too late."

"Very funny."

"Why not?"

"I can't fly a helicopter!"

"How do you know until you try?"

As if to call his bluff, she got up and started walking along the roadside. More vehicles were arriving by the minute, and she didn't want to get hit—it was impossible to see anything in the choking dust and smoke. Nobody was looking for her anyway. They were too busy evacuating the dead and injured. Perhaps they thought she was still in the van when it exploded.

She had given up on finding Ben when she saw him. He was sitting on the ground, leaning against the helicopter. Both he and the aircraft had holes in them. It was clear he had dragged himself there. His guard must have abandoned him or been killed.

"Ben!" she cried.

He groggily looked up. "Maddy? What happened? My van—"

"Don't worry about that right now. Are you okay?"

"I think I'm bleeding. Why did you go back to the van?"

"I don't know—I'm just trying to get out of this place."

Before he could interrogate her any more, she pushed him down and clipped his bindings.

"There," she said. "Now I'm gonna go do something very stupid, Ben. You don't have to come with me if you don't want to—in fact, you probably shouldn't. Just stand clear, okay?"

Without looking at him, Maddy yanked the helicopter door open and clambered inside. She had never been in an aircraft cockpit before, but it was all pretty self-explanatory. She could intuit the whole mechanism just from the controls, practically see the hydraulic lines running from the pedals up to the actuators that tilted the rotor blades, trace all the instruments and gauges and especially the joystick, which was so much like something from a video game. Was that all there was to it? The engine was already engaged; all she had to do was throttle up.

The door opened, and Ben climbed in next to her. "I can't believe I'm doing this," he said weakly.

"Join the club."

"Can you really fly this thing?"

"Only one way to find out."

And she lifted off.

TWENTY-FOUR

HELICOPTER CAMP

PLAYING with the pedals and the stick, feeling the pitch and yaw and how they matched with the artificial horizon, then adding to that what she could easily infer from the thrust loads and angular velocities, Maddy instantly formed a clear idea of the helicopter's range of motion. Expecting to be terrified, she instead found herself cocooned in a soothing web of knowledge, borne by a tracery of invisible arrows that clearly showed the way. By simply going with the flow, she flew. In fact, the margin of safety was so great that it was all but impossible to screw up.

"Whoa," said Ben, gripping the seat. "How'd you learn how to do this?"

"It's just like riding a bike."

"Uh . . . I really doubt it."

Maddy rose above the pall of smoke and banked down the valley, following the contours of the landscape. Up there in the moonlight, the visibility was not bad, but she didn't want to get too low for fear of hidden power lines and transmission towers. Icy-cold wind whistled through the shrapnel holes in the canopy.

"Where are we going?" Ben asked.

"Home."

"Do you know how to get there from here?"

"No. Be quiet."

Maddy was straining to listen, to *feel*. Something was wrong. A vibration—something in the gear train was out of whack and getting worse, some kind of dent in the radial plane. Something out of sync. If it broke loose altogether, the gears could just suddenly seize up, the rotor blades could fly off, and they could plummet to their idiotic doom. Stupid raccoon!

As though reading her thoughts, Moses said, "You should probably find a place to set down."

"Ya think?"

"What's that?" said Ben.

"I said we should probably find a place to land."

"So soon?"

"The engine's giving out."

"How do you know that?"

"How don't you know? Can't you feel it?"

"No."

"You don't hear that noise?"

"You mean the wind?"

"Ben, let me ask you something. You and I have both had the same operation, right?"

"I guess so. Similar, anyway."

"So how come you seem so . . . normal?"

"Normal?"

"Do you mean to tell me you couldn't fly this helicopter if you had to?"

"No."

"Why is that?"

"I never learned how."

"Neither did I. It's not necessary. The mechanism's so simple, I could practically build one of these from scratch."

"Maddy, I don't understand what you're saying, but maybe it would be best if we did land this thing."

He thought she was crazy. *Maybe I am special,* Maddy thought. *What did they do to me?*

"Look!" Ben said. "There's a road."

Across the piebald landscape was a string of intermittent twinkling lights, red one way and white the other. A two-lane highway that skirted the forbidden valley, separated from it by a range of bluffs; the happy motorists oblivious in their antlike procession, focused only on the distance to the next rest stop; GAS, FOOD, LODGING shining in their headlights like a Pavlovian promise, and perhaps BRAIN-TREE INSTITUTE, NEXT RIGHT. Yes, this had to be the road they took to bring her here . . . which meant it also led back home.

Things were getting really sketchy, so bad that even Ben began to notice. Trying to stay calm, Maddy feathered the aircraft down over an empty stretch of road, seeking any flat, open field. Every clear space was polka-dotted with pine saplings as though it was a Christmas-tree farm.

All at once the tail rotor gave out, and they began to spin, twirling downward like a leaf. Ben shouted, but Maddy held steady, absorbed in all the swiftly changing adjustments that were required to keep them alive, improvising like a maniacal jazz savant. Slowed by autorotation, the copter touched down reasonably gently, its tail crumpling like a toothpaste tube, but the fuselage mostly intact, canted upright.

Coming to their senses, Maddy and Ben unbuckled and crawled out of the wreck.

"Jeez," Maddy said, "are you okay?"

"Not really," said Ben, collapsing in the tall weeds.

"Oh, Ben, I'm sorry."

"I think I hurt something during the crash, or maybe before. I can't tell. I feel like my stomach's all bloated."

"Oh no." She checked him. From what she knew about anatomy, it looked like he was hemorrhaging internally. "We better get you to a doctor. Can you walk at all? I need to get you away from the helicopter in case it catches fire."

"Yeah. Yeah, I think so."

"The road's right over there. Come on, I'll help."

"I think I can do it."

They made their way down the slope of the hill, Ben using the pine saplings as support, staggering from tree to tree. Maddy stayed close in case he needed a hand. When they reached the bottom, he leaned on the highway guard-rail and retched.

"Phew," he said, wiping his mouth with his sleeve. "I am never flying with you again."

From high up in the air there had seemed to be quite a bit of traffic, but at ground level it was clear that the cars were spaced very far apart. At the moment, the road was deserted. The night sky was clear, and there was a low crescent moon. Maddy had never really noticed the incredible depth of the sky before—it had been more or less a flat field with stars sprinkled across it like glitter on a kindergarten art project. Now she could clearly tell that the moon was in the foreground, and beyond that the planets Mars and Jupiter, then, receding into the deep distance, all the stars of the Milky Way, with the invisible web of their trajectories relative to the Earth. She could see Betelgeuse, the supermassive red giant.

A pair of headlights winked over the horizon.

"I see a car," she said. "I'm gonna try flagging it down."

"You do that. If you don't mind, I'll just sit here."

Maddy went to the edge of the pavement and waited

while the headlights dipped in and out of sight. When they started getting bright enough to cast a shadow, she raised her arms and waved as urgently as possible. The car made an electronic farting noise and pulled sharply over, blinding her with its headlights—it was a police car: BITTER-ROOT SHERIFF'S DEPARTMENT.

The female deputy got out, brandishing a flashlight, and demanded, "What do you think you're doing?"

"We need to be taken to a hospital! My friend is hurt!"

"There was a report of a stolen aircraft going down somewhere around here."

"That was us; we had no choice. Can we talk about this later? He has internal injuries—he needs medical attention, or he's gonna bleed out!"

"How would you know that?"

"Look at him! What else could it be?"

"I have no idea. Both of you up against the car and don't move—you're under arrest."

"That's fine as long as you take him to a doctor."

"Hey! You're not the one calling the shots."

The officer frisked and handcuffed them, then loaded them in the backseat, taking special care with Ben, who was sinking fast.

"Hey, buddy, you feeling okay?"

"Need a doctor . . ."

"Stay with me, okay? I'm Sheriff's Deputy Tina Reinaldi. Are you in any pain?"

"Yes . . . hurts . . ."

"Your stomach hurts?"

He nodded, his face yellow and clammy as congealed beef tallow. Becoming concerned, Deputy Reinaldi called in for emergency medical personnel to meet them and hurriedly got going.

As they drove, she asked Maddy, "How old are you?"

"Seventeen."

"What's your name?"

"Madeline Grant."

"And your boyfriend?"

"He's my stepbrother—well, almost. Benjamin Blevin."

"So what's this all about?"

"We need your help. We're both victims of some kind of medical experiment conducted by the Braintree Institute. It's mind control by means of direct cortical stimulation. You get this implant, and they can make you do anything they want you to. Ben and I got away, but there are a lot more people still there, being manipulated like puppets—a whole town!"

Officer Reinaldi listened to her with the perfect passivity of someone who has heard it all. Maddy immediately realized she might have goofed.

"Good one," whispered Moses.

"And what's all this got to do with a downed aircraft?" asked the deputy.

"We had to steal a helicopter to escape."

"Come on. You stole a helicopter? Which one of you is the hotshot helicopter thief?"

"Me."

"You? Where'd you learn to fly it? Helicopter camp?"

"I just knew."

"You just knew."

They drove very fast, passing a number of police cars and other emergency vehicles speeding in the opposite direction.

"Shit," muttered the officer under her breath. "It never rains but it pours."

"I'm sorry?" said Maddy.

"I'm not talking to you. You've caught me in the middle of another call. I'm supposed to be responding to an armed robbery at an industrial park. Somebody shot up the place and stole a couple million dollars' worth of precious metals. Instead, I'm playing nursemaid to you two whack jobs."

"Where are we going?"

"Presbyterian General. Stay awake back there! I don't want anyone checking out in my patrol unit. I'm gonna have enough paperwork as it is. He still breathing?"

"So far."

"Make sure he stays that way, at least until we get to the hospital."

In a few minutes, they were out of the country and hurtling past gas stations and shopping plazas, weaving around traffic and running red lights. Maddy noticed her teeth were chattering, her whole body vibrating. *I'm in shock,* she thought. But something inside her was resisting it, something that wouldn't allow her to collapse.

Turning onto a side road, they sped through tree-lined suburbs and abruptly swerved into a parking lot, then up a steep ramp to a hospital's ambulance bay. There was a medical team with two gurneys waiting to meet them. Maddy's and Ben's handcuffs were removed, and they were quickly strapped down and rolled inside.

"I'm okay," Maddy insisted, "it's him you have to check." But they weren't listening.

Deputy Reinaldi followed the stretchers into the Emergency Ward, then stayed at the desk to sign whatever she had to sign while the two of them were wheeled into adjoining stalls, to be probed and prodded and poked with needles. After a little while, most of the attention shifted to Ben, leaving Maddy time to reflect on recent events.

She had escaped. Her mind was her own again. She could *feel* it: She was free. The space in her head was a great crystalline dome, echoing only the clear sound of her own true thoughts. Commercial-free and without interruption. It was the most beautiful feeling in the world; she sobbed with relief and gratitude.

They stabilized Ben and took him away to surgery—he was bleeding internally, just as she'd tried to tell them. But Maddy didn't have the energy to sweat it, not with the narcotics trickling through her system. She was drifting off, gratefully sinking into the oh-so-soft pillow.

She slept.

TWENTY-FIVE

1-2-3

SOMETIME later, she awoke. Her head was still remark-ably clear. The ward was quiet. There was a drowsy wee-hour stillness, with only the soft hum of medical equipment breaking the silence. Past the foot of her bed, Maddy could see the nurses' area, but no one was in view. Ben's bed was empty.

She heard a squeaking from somewhere out of sight, and a moment later a group of people went by wheeling a gurney: three tall doctors in long gowns and surgical masks, followed by a short, brisk-looking woman in a white lab coat. The sheeted body on the stretcher was hooked up to oxygen, a heart monitor, and an IV drip. Instead of hair, its freshly shaved head sprouted a mass of colored wires.

It was dark, and Maddy's eyes were still bleary, but she could swear the woman was Dr. Stevens. There was no mistaking that silvery 'fro. But before she could sit up or properly focus, they were gone out the exit doors.

She had to pee. Using the remote to raise her bed,

she pressed the nurse call button. When no one came, she pressed it again. *Come on,* she thought. What did they expect her to do, pee in a bedpan? But there wasn't a bedpan at hand; there wasn't even a paper cup.

And it wasn't just about peeing—she wanted to know how Ben was doing and discuss this whole situation with someone in authority. Most of all, she wanted to talk to her parents. But first, she really, really had to pee.

"Hello," she called. "Could someone please let me up? I have to go to the bathroom."

Still nothing, and now she was getting angry. How could they just leave their trauma patients unattended like this? Someone could drop dead! Maddy had half a mind to pull out her own IV and march to the hospital administrator's office . . . right after she went to the restroom.

Something peculiar caught her attention. There was a stethoscope in the middle of the floor. A bright, shiny stethoscope, just lying there by the nurses' station as if some careless person had dropped it. It was impossible to miss; anyone passing by ought to have picked it up. But clearly there was no one around. All of the doctors, interns, nurses, and orderlies who had been on duty when she and Ben were brought in had left. And whoever was still on duty must be taking a long bathroom break themselves.

Screw it. Maddy sat up and gingerly peeled the tape off her IV needle. It was stuck in the back of her hand, and it made her a little sick to look at it. Without giving herself time to think, she slipped the needle out and applied pressure with a wad of gauze, taping it back down firmly. It hurt for a second, but she didn't lose a drop of blood. She unclipped the pulse monitor from her finger and switched off the alarm—there. Too early in the morning for all that noise.

It didn't strike her as odd that she understood the workings of every piece of machinery in the room. What was strange to her was how brutally archaic it all seemed, like something out of the Dark Ages. The needles and wires and dripping solutions, the scissors and stitches and sticky tape that were more reminiscent of a kiddie craft fair than a house of healing. All the blood and needless pain. She felt sure there were better ways. In fact, she could think of a few right off the top of her head—something with directed harmonics, exploiting ultrahigh-frequency quantum fluctuations to target specific molecules—but she couldn't bother about that just then. Her bladder was about to burst.

Making her way past the nurses' station, she picked up the stethoscope and slammed it on the counter, then hurried to the restroom just beyond. She was worried it would be occupied, but the door opened on a vacant and spotless toilet stall.

After availing herself of the facilities, Maddy emerged feeling much better. She expected to find that the grave-yard shift had returned, but the ward was just as empty as before. The few other patients were dead asleep, curtained off in their cubbies and snoring away unconcerned. For a second, Maddy considered simply returning to bed, but then she saw something that gave her pause.

There was blood on the floor, a line of dime-size drop-lets that started at the emergency entrance and ran all the way down the hall. The blood was trampled in places; there were partial shoe prints of various kinds, in red patterns as sharply delineated as passport stamps. People running into the hospital? Everyone in such a hurry to get to surgery that the attending physician dropped his or her stethoscope? It made sense . . . or did it? Even in an emergency, how long would the other patients be left alone? Certainly, it would have to be something very serious.

Or, it could just be a mistake, an oversight. Ordinary, gross incompetence.

Whatever it was, she couldn't go back to bed without knowing what was going on. And if it gave her an excuse to ask about Ben, all the better.

Maddy found her clothes and shoes in a plastic bag under her gurney and got dressed. Then she ventured down the dim hallway, careful not to step in the blood.

Following the signs, she found the Intensive Care Ward, and was shocked to see that there was no one on duty there either, the unconscious patients wheezing unsupervised inside their plastic oxygen tents. There was also no sign of Ben. She was really getting worried now. *Where is everybody?*

Any minute, Maddy expected to run into someone, a security guard or grumpy nurse, and be yelled at for trespassing, but the whole staff seemed to have cleared out. She peeked into Radiology and Imaging, into various labs and offices, but all she could find were more signs of a hurried departure: clipboards on the floor, spilled papers.

With trepidation, she glanced into the surgical suite, but it was just as empty. It stank of pine disinfectant. All that was left was the Neonatal Wing. If nothing else, there would surely be someone taking care of the newborn babies!

The lights were off in that section, as they were in a lot of the hospital, the only illumination coming from the exit signs and the flashing red and blue lights of emergency vehicles outside the window.

Pushing through the double doors, Maddy said, "Hello?"

"Hello," a man's muffled voice replied, and a powerful hand clamped over her mouth, yanking her backward into the speaker's chest. Pinning her arms and carrying her, he said, "Don't make a sound, or they all die." He kicked open another set of doors.

Unable to scream, barely able to breathe, Maddy's eyes widened at the sight before her.

She had found all the missing hospital personnel.

They were right there, doctors and nurses and orderlies and anyone else who was on duty—about forty people altogether—sitting on the floor of the Maternity Ward, tied up in pairs, back-to-back, amid cradles of newborn infants. Hostages. And standing above them all were four armed men in black clothes and ski masks. She could smell the men's sweat, their fear, and suddenly Maddy realized that the lights and sirens outside were not ambulances but police cars. These men were cornered here, capable of anything.

Pinning Maddy down, two of the men hogtied her with an Ace bandage, taped her mouth shut, and shoved her among the others.

"Here's what we're doing," one of them announced, holding up a cell phone. "In a few minutes we are going to walk out of here and drive to the airport. Each of us will be holding babies, as many as we can carry. Anything that happens to us will also happen to the babies. We will board a plane and fly to an undisclosed location, where we will then release the plane and the babies. We don't want to hurt anyone. We will take good care of these babies as long as everything goes smoothly . . . but at the first sign of trouble, we will abort. Do you understand? We will abort."

At the word *abort*, several people on the floor went crazy, making desperate sounds of pleading through their gags. Their eyes were bugging out in terror, their faces red and streaked with tears—perhaps they were new parents.

Oddly enough, at the sound of the man's voice, Maddy began to feel calmer. At first she had been so surprised and overpowered that she had given in to the assumption that she had no choice but to surrender—it was a habit born of a lifetime of submitting to adult authority, especially *masculine* authority. You did not resist power, boys were stronger, end of story. Against the male will, your only defense lay in the hands of others: parents, teachers, school counselors, police. And if none of them were around (or worse, *they* were the ones doing the dirt), God help you. And God was a man.

But as Maddy looked at these men, she couldn't help but feel an unaccustomed sense of contempt. Especially in the hospital setting, she was inordinately aware of their inner plumbing, the rickety scaffold of bones, sinews, and pulpy muscle that held them together. Humans were so complicated and frail; there were literally a million things that could go wrong, drop them in their tracks.

Ever since the surgery, Maddy had been having anxieties about her own frailty, worrying she was becoming a hypochondriac. Too much knowledge was a dangerous thing. Fortunately, her mind had a way of steering itself away from such pointless fears before they paralyzed her completely. But there was nothing to stop her from projecting these thoughts onto others. By turning them outward, she suddenly realized she could transmute helpless fear into empowering scorn. Scorn for all this shambling, loathsome humanity.

The man nearest her, for example. She was looking at the back of his knee, which though sheathed in black trousers was naked to her in its flimsy mechanical structure. Right there at the joint, everything was exposed: the bone and cartilage, the popliteal, the effectors and motor neurons, the sensitive muscle spindle that triggered the polysynaptic reflex. It might as well have been a house of cards.

A wet nose touched her ear, whiskers tickling, and the raccoon's voice hissed, "Now or never, sweetheart— once these guys are on the move and carrying babies, it'll be much harder to intervene."

Taking a deep breath, Maddy swiveled her shoulders, slackening the tight bandage just enough to slide her bound wrists under her butt and get her arms in front of her. It was not a particularly amazing feat, merely the normal dexterity of a teenage girl, but she was surprised and pleased with herself. It was one thing to know something was possible as an abstraction, another actually to make it happen.

Focus, focus—stay on track . . . go! She rocked backward and drove her bound feet as hard as she could into the crook of the man's supporting leg. As she expected, his flexor sprang like a mousetrap, causing his leg to fold under him like a bent cardboard tube.

Caught completely off guard, the man fell backward, flailing for support, and found only the hard pedestal of Maddy's heel in the base of his skull—*crack!* The force of her second kick, combined with the man's own mass and velocity of descent, caused a severe rupture of his C-1 vertebrae at the point where it joined the skull. He fell into her lap, unconscious, perhaps paralyzed, and she took the toylike 9mm pistol from his twitching hand and fired three shots, each of the remaining three men collapsing in turn like a synchronized building demolition, falling where they stood, and three neat arcs of blood trailing them down—1-2-3.

Her man was still twitching, and Maddy pulled off his ski mask to see if he was breathing. No—he was dead. But she was alarmed to see that there was a fresh scar on the back of his bald head—a familiar, crescent-shaped surgical incision. *Oh shit,* Maddy thought.

The man had an implant—he was one of *them*.

TWENTY-SIX

HOPSCOTCH

ALL of a sudden, she understood everything: The body on the gurney had been Ben's. Dr. Stevens had come to take him back to Braintree, using the hostage thing as a diversion, and if Maddy had not gone to the bathroom when she did, they would have taken her next. *Stupid!*

Tossing the gun aside, Maddy undid her cloth bindings and peeled the tape off her mouth, then said sorry to the other hostages and ran from the room. There was no time for an explanation—not if she wanted to save Ben.

Running down the hall, she heard a massive commotion of breaking glass and trampling footsteps. The cavalry was finally arriving. Smoke canisters rattled down the corridor, spewing noxious clouds threaded with laser light and burgeoning with black-helmeted SWAT troops.

"GET DOWN, GET DOWN," they screamed at no one in particular, battering through locked doors and dispensing flash grenades right and left, setting off the fire alarm and the sprinklers, so that every patient who didn't die outright from the shock shot bolt upright in utter panic, thinking it was the end of the world, pissing their beds and screeching for mercy. All at once, the hospital became a zoo, an insane monkey house from which there was no safe exit.

Not wishing to be mistaken for a target, Maddy sat down on the floor and put up her hands, crying, "Don't shoot! I'm a patient!"

"GET DOWN! GET DOWN!"

"I am down!"

"Stay there and don't move!"

"I'm not, I'm not!"

Speckled with red points of laser light, she held still as scary-looking commandos in gas masks descended on her out of the artificial rain and fog, guns trained on her face.

"WHERE ARE THEY?" they demanded.

"Back there, in Maternity."

"STAY HERE AND DON'T MOVE."

They swept past her, taking up positions around the bay doors. Maddy half hoped she could just slip away without being noticed, but as she started to move, someone shot her. The impact was so hard it knocked her down, as stunningly painful as if she had been whammed in the back with a major-league fastball.

Sprawled on the floor, struggling to breathe, she thought wildly, *I've been shot!*

Powerful hands grabbed her under the arms and started carrying her away.

"You shot me!" she cried.

"You moved. Relax, you're okay."

"Okay? I've been *shot*, you jerk! Oh my God!"

"It was just a beanbag, calm down."

"A *what?*"

"A nonlethal munition. Take it easy."

"You take it easy, dickhead! It *hurts*!"

The man lugged her outside. It was a traffic jam out

there, the hospital parking lot crammed with emergency vehicles of every type, their crews anxiously sitting around waiting for the go-ahead to enter the building.

The SWAT guys handed her off to the regular cops, who took her name and signed her over to some EMTs, who gave her a quick once-over to make sure she wasn't suffering from any life-threatening condition. She wasn't, though they admitted she was going to have one heck of a bruise. "No shit, Sherlock," she said. Pushing through a line of reporters, they wrapped her in a blanket and put her in a makeshift corral with a number of other ambulatory patients who had fled the hospital. Dawn was coming up beautiful and clear, and there were volunteer firemen handing out donuts and hot coffee. Everybody seemed to be enjoying the excitement—a real-life hostage crisis!

All she could think of was how she was going to sneak out of there. Once they found the dead guys and heard what had happened from the hostages, it was all over—she'd never escape.

"Madeline! Miss Grant! Over here!"

Oh no. Following the voice, Maddy turned to see a burly female figure at the edge of the police cordon. It was that woman deputy who had picked them up on the road, Tina Reinaldi. What now? Trying to play it cool, Maddy went over.

"Yes? Oh, hello."

"Could you follow me, please? I just need to ask you a few questions."

"Okay." Maddy ducked under the yellow caution tape. "What about?"

"Come with me."

Leading Maddy through the maze of vehicles, the woman took her to a trailer parked on the street. The sign on its side read POLICE MOBILE COMMAND UNIT. Opening the door, Reinaldi said, "After you."

Maddy stepped inside. The place crackled with the sound of police scanners, and there were several men in suits and dress uniforms barking orders. They hardly glanced at Maddy. Deputy Reinaldi directed her to take a seat while she conferred with them, obviously having trouble holding their attention. From the hectic chatter, Maddy could tell that the assault team had found the dead guys in the hospital, and everyone was scrambling to make sense of it. Who were the killers, and where had they gone? Clearly, the hostages needed to be interrogated, but the first priority was evacuating the building—there was still at least one homicidal maniac on the loose.

Without thinking, Maddy blurted, "I killed them."

Nobody noticed.

"I killed them," Maddy repeated loudly. She couldn't believe what she was doing, but she couldn't help herself. The feeling was like making yourself vomit—like the time she ate a whole bottle of chewable vitamins and had to drink ipecac. It was as the doctor had said: *The bad stuff has to come out.*

"What?" said Deputy Reinaldi.

"Those dead guys in there. I'm the one who killed them. I broke one's neck and shot the others in the head."

"For Christ's sake," one of the men said impatiently. "Get her outta here."

"Hold on," said Reinaldi. "Madeline, what are you talking about?"

"I couldn't help it. They did something to my brain that makes it easy for me to do stuff . . . kill people. I've killed a bunch now. You have to stop me."

Suddenly, Maddy was crying, feeling her insides shiver apart.

"Please stop me," she begged. "Stop *them.*"

Reinaldi said, "Them?"

"I already *told* you! The doctors, the *doctors*—up at

Braintree! Chandra Stevens. She was just here, you must have seen her. She went into the hospital and took Ben. You have to stop them!"

"Ohhh," one of the men said knowingly to the others. *"Braintree."*

"No," Maddy cried. "That's not it—I'm not *mental*! Officer Reinaldi, you know what happened to us. Tell them!"

The deputy held back, reluctant to speak. Finally, she said, "There's definitely something strange going on . . ."

"I don't have time for this," the lead man said.

Reinaldi bit the bullet. "Chief, this kid stole a helicopter from the EPA quarantine site—the Bitterroot Valley reservation. The chopper went down near Junction 38, and she and a boy survived the crash. I picked them up by the side of the road and delivered them here. You saw my report."

"I haven't had much time to read anything tonight. What are you saying, Tina?"

"Look at her. She's seventeen years old. She claims she has no special training or technical expertise—in fact she should barely be able to talk, much less fly a helicopter. I ran a background check, and she's spent the last fourteen months recovering from severe brain injuries, enrolled in an experimental research study. Guess who sponsored the study?"

"Look," the chief said, "I'm sure this is all very interesting, but I don't have time for guessing games. In case you missed it, we're in the middle of a situation here."

"But that's what I'm trying to tell you, sir. This kid *is* the situation. The boy who was with her, who had the internal bleeding? I checked him out, too. He's listed as deceased."

"He died last night?"

"No—*last year.*"

There was a loud knock on the door. One of the cops

answered it, and said, "It's just the guys from the fire-house. They brought coffee."

An ax struck him in the head.

The firemen came in.

There was something wrong with them. Beneath their helmet visors, their grinning faces were too white, their lips too black, and their red-stained teeth too numerous and sharp.

Taken by surprise, a second officer went down before anyone thought to draw a gun, by which time it was too late. Cornered in the tight space, some of the cops tried screaming for help; others, like Officer Reinaldi, attempted to defend themselves, but everything happened so quickly there wasn't much they could do.

Axes chopped through upraised hands, bit into skulls, lopped off heads . . . and all at once it was over. No shots had been fired. Maddy was alone, huddled in the back corner.

Then the most amazing and horrible thing of all: The firemen started to drink.

Falling on their victims, they sucked the still-pulsing blood from their open veins, guzzling the firehouse red liquid as if it was the most refreshing thing ever, their bellies visibly expanding as they gulped and gulped, until the blood stopped running so freely. Then, bloated as ticks—as gorged leeches—they burped and wiped their lips.

A woman came in.

"Hello, Maddy," she said.

It was Dr. Stevens. She was wearing a Red Cross cap and a pink paper mask over her mouth

"Why did you have to kill them?" Maddy moaned. "You could have just killed me."

"Just cutting through a little red tape. I'd rather avoid all this negative publicity, wouldn't you?"

"What do you want from me?"

"Oh come on. You know what we want from you. Come back voluntarily, right now, and we can still keep you out of the system. No one needs to know what you've done while in recovery—you're not responsible. As far as we're concerned, all this was purely accidental. You should know I'm very much against having you permanently institutionalized, but once the state gets involved, it'll all become much more complicated. None of us wants that."

"You're crazy," Maddy said. "It's you people who are the psychos, not me."

"That's simply not true; you're suffering from paranoid delusions, which are only going to get worse if left untreated. Honey, you'd still be a vegetable if not for us."

As Dr. Stevens spoke, Maddy found it hard to follow the words, which seemed to echo from a deep cavern. Her vision blurred and strained to refocus. With an abrupt lurch, she had the feeling of snapping out of a dream. Suddenly, the police trailer was clean. There were no bodies, no blood, no signs of violence. The firemen and Dr. Stevens were not monsters, just ordinary people dealing with an unstable mental patient. The thought was impossibly hopeful and at the same time too horrible to take: *I'm mad—I'm completely insane, oh God.* Her legs started to fold, and she drew breath to scream.

Out of nowhere, a voice whispered in her ear. "Hey, yo-yo. They're just jerkin' your string." It was Moses.

Averting her own fall, she begged, *How? How?*

"They're running a line on you, baby. Don't believe the hype."

Maddy looked at Dr. Stevens and the firemen. Yes, there was something odd about them; the image was being doctored. Cleaned up. Maddy's head hurt as she fought to block the alien signal that was creating the optical illusion—digging its claws into her brain. In desperation, she focused her mind on the babbling police radios, tuning them all to the same ultrahigh-frequency bandwidth and broadcasting a wall of white noise. A scene of red carnage faded in like a double exposure. Maddy shrieked, *"What have you done with Ben?"*

"Ben is back on the road to recovery."

"Back to being a robot, you mean."

"Back to living a productive life, a life of service to his country and community. How many people can say that? A mind is a terrible thing to waste, Madeline, and we're in the recycling business. Our only crime is taking damaged goods and trying to create solid, useful citizens."

"Is that what you call it? What about those guys back there—the four ninjas? Are they graduates of the program, too?"

"Who?"

"Those criminals inside the hospital!"

"Oh, yes. Wasn't that interesting? All of us ending up here at the same time like this?"

"As if it was an accident."

"Madeline, you of all people should understand the quirks of probability. Or maybe you'd prefer to call it fate."

"Give me a break. I don't believe any of this is co-incidence."

"Neither do I. We're all governed by the dictates of our subconscious. Free will is an illusion."

"Bullcrap. I'm sure that's what you'd like me to think, but I'm not one of your zombies."

"Oh no?"

"You're rigging the odds so nobody has a choice."

Dr. Stevens stepped forward, backing Maddy even more tightly into the corner.

"No, you do have a choice," she said mildly. "You can either come with us and get the help and support you

need, or you can go to the authorities and test these conspiracy theories on them. You've had quite the spree tonight, Madeline—whom do you think they'll believe? But
you're welcome to try—no one's stopping you."

She stood aside, offering Maddy the door. The friendly
firemen made a path for her through the gore.

"Fine, then I'm out of here."

As Maddy passed between them, surrounded, Dr. Stevens made a lightning move behind her back, jabbing a
long syringe at her jugular.

Maddy's reaction was explosive. Before the needle
even broke the skin, she was moving, recoiling, trapping
the syringe between her shoulder and jawbone so the
plunger could not be depressed, and using the same lateral
motion to shove both forefingers of her right hand all the
way up the doctor's nose, deep into the funnel-like infun-
dibulum, grabbing her by the moist sinus cavity and goug-
ing the sensitive tissues of the nasal septum as hard as she
could.

The fluid-filled needle twanged in Maddy's neck as
Chandra Stevens's hands flew to protect her face. The
pressure on the doctor's ophthalmic ganglia and arteries
caused her to go temporarily blind; her throat filled with
mucus and blood, and in an instant all her senses were
gone; she was in agony, couldn't breathe, couldn't think;
the escalating shock had a domino effect on her consciousness, and she momentarily blacked out.

Maddy jumped clear. The nearest fireman grabbed her,
so she rammed the doctor's syringe into his neck and
pressed the plunger. The effect was like letting the air out
of a balloon—the man simply deflated, sliding to the floor
and all but handing her his ax.

Bruised and bloody, Maddy stepped into the aisle,
breathing hard and brandishing the ax in both hands.

"All right, assholes," she said. "Step aside."

They came for her.

The first one swung for her head, and when she dodged that, the second one swung at where her head was expected to be. It was a clever double-play, one that had cost the cops their lives, but Maddy saw it coming a mile away. It was all very simple, or she couldn't have done it. There was no guesswork involved, merely a matter of following the dotted lines. The air was full of these ghostly hypothetical trajectories, swirling around the room like weird cobwebs, constantly realigning to her changing position relative to her opponents. There were multiple options, but the easiest path was always the brightest, elementary as a game of hopscotch.

In plotting these pathways to their inevitably neat resolution, Maddy felt the same pleasant tingle that she used to feel solving minor brainteasers like sudoku. Fear was no part of it, any more than one would be afraid of dying on an escalator. Sure, she could get hurt if she was very, very clumsy. But she wasn't.

She ducked inside the first man's swing, close enough to touch him, and arced her own weapon down to the floor and up again, exploiting its weight like a pendulum so that on the upswing it had enough force to drive its pick end under the second man's sternum and into his heart. He toppled over dead while the first one pinned her against his chest, trying to strangle her with his ax handle.

Swinging her legs up and kneeing the man in the face, Maddy noticed Dr. Stevens pulling herself upright. The doc was a wreck, gushing blood and snot, feeling her way along like a blind person, barely aware of the death match that was going on right beside her. Tipping her head back and applying pressure to the bridge of her nose, Chandra Stevens shakily left the trailer.

Enough now, come on*!* Wrenching her ax free of the dead man's body, Maddy again used the weapon's pendulum-like mass to swing it forward up over her head, then laterally into the fireman's right Achilles tendon. The heavy blade almost severed his ankle, and he toppled sideways. As they went down together, Maddy twisted her upper torso, guiding their fall so that the man landed face-first on his own ax.

Smeared with blood, she crawled free of her attacker and left the trailer.

In the glare of the cresting sun, Maddy saw the van pulling out of the parking lot. It was one of the silver vans from Braintree, there was no doubt about it—she recognized that stylized banyan-tree logo immediately. The driver wasn't visible, but Maddy had no doubt that Dr. Stevens, and probably Ben, were inside. The van was pulling out of the parking lot, turning onto the street—she didn't have much time if she wanted to catch them.

There were a lot of people around, but their attention was mostly focused on the evacuation of the hospital. One by one, the newborns were being brought out, triggering cheers and applause from the onlookers. The media people were all over this feel-good story, not only on the ground but in circling helicopters. Nobody, not even the cops, had noticed the massacre in the mobile command unit.

Maddy didn't want to be around when they did. Searching for a means of transportation, she went down the rows of cars, checking doors, until she happened upon an unlocked Mercury Monarch in the long-term parking section. Weather-beaten to a blotchy shade of gray, the car was at least twenty years old and probably worthless. She couldn't imagine anyone raising much of a stink if it disappeared. Plus, it had no antitheft system. She got in.

Maddy stared at the ignition. Hmm. She could picture exactly how it worked mechanically, the problem was getting at it. She needed a tool of some kind. There was nothing in the car except for a thick wad of maps and a lot of fast-food refuse. Popping the trunk lid, she checked to make sure nobody was looking and scurried around back. The trunk was full of boxes, and it took her a second to realize that the Braintree logo was stamped on the lids. What the hell . . . ? Inside were cases of small, heavy cylinders wrapped in black plastic. The labels read: PTIAG INSULATED BIMETALLIC ELECTRODES. They resembled fishing reels, and were in fact spools of wire. Millions of dollars' worth of microthin conductive wire—the very same wire that was inside her head. The wire that was supposedly stolen from Braintree. *This was the thieves' car!*

But there was no time to think about that now. Underneath the boxes she hit pay dirt: a bald spare tire, a jack, jumper cables, and a collection of rusty tools. Perfect. She grabbed a big monkey wrench and a screwdriver, then returned to the front seat.

Placing the screwdriver into the starter switch, she used the wrench as a hammer to bash it in good, busting the locking pin and nearly busting her thumb in the process. Sucking the throbbing nail, she turned the screwdriver to close the electrical circuit. With a clatter, the engine started right up.

This was kind of exciting. Maddy had her learner's permit, but she hadn't driven in over a year, not since before the accident, and even then her actual driving experience had been mostly limited to a few squeamish circuits around the mall parking lot. Her time behind the wheel could be readily computed in minutes and seconds, the way skydivers measure their time in free fall. Her parents weren't big on teen driving. In their neighborhood, there had been a number of deadly accidents involving underage drinking, and they weren't taking any chances. She could get a car when she turned eighteen.

Look Ma, I'm drivin'!

Maddy backed out of the space, testing the play in the

wheel and the response of the pedals. It really was a shit-box; she could hear every loose fitting in the old V-6, but somehow there was something special about driving it, a feeling that even flying the helicopter couldn't match. She had been too busy to enjoy that experience, just going through the motions as necessity indicated, and afterward her mind had barely retained the memory of flight. It all seemed like a bizarre nightmare, nothing fun about it. But this was *driving a car*.

Pulling onto the street, she turned in the direction the van had taken. It was out of sight now, but since Dr. Stevens probably had little reason to think she was being followed, it shouldn't be hard to find. Maddy hoped. Reasoning that every cop for a hundred miles was tied up in that parking lot, she hit the gas.

"Nice work, killer," said a voice from the backseat. It was the raccoon. He was belted into a baby carrier and clutching a live earthworm—a big night crawler.

"Holy crap," she said. "Do you have to keep sneaking up on me like that? God!"

"Hey, you should be thanking me, Princess. How many times am I going to have to keep bailing you out?"

"Why? Isn't that your whole purpose?"

"Depends. You just killed *people*, honey." Moses's voice strained as she swerved around a truck. "Whoa. Don't you even care?"

"Of course I care!"

"No, you don't." He ate the worm headfirst, munching rapidly.

Maddy looked away from the mirror. "Yes, I do."

"Then why aren't you more upset?"

"Because it wasn't me back there. It was Braintree. They made me do it."

"That's just an excuse. You're killing because you can. If you could have done it before your little upgrade, you would have. Many times. I'm not sure I should even be helping you. You're a cold-blooded murderer. Murderess."

"No I'm not—shut up! It was self-defense."

"You could have escaped without killing them . . . if you'd really wanted to."

"Not without taking a bigger risk."

"So it's all about playing it safe?"

"Yes! Maybe. So what?"

"Just asking."

Barreling down the main drag, blowing through all the cross streets and stoplights in favor of the fastest route back to the highway, Maddy spotted the van. *Gotcha.* It was easy to see, its silver finish gleaming brightly in the morning sun. There was very little other traffic at that time of the morning.

Now what, genius?

It would be easy enough to nudge the van into a spin— the dynamics of that classic police maneuver were very simple to figure out. The problem was, there was no telling how the other driver might react, and if he or she was stupid, the van could crash or flip over. This wasn't a game of billiards—if Ben really was in there, he could be killed.

No, she would have to disable the van so that it stopped on its own, which would be tricky since the big vehicle was quite a bit newer and more powerful than her clunker. And what then? She was leery of more hand-to-hand combat. The very thought of it suddenly made her sick. Moses was right: She couldn't just kill everybody who got in her way, even if they were trying to kill her. *I have to be the good guy.* It was a worrisome prospect, but at least this time she had the advantage of surprise, the sun at her back. In the glare, they wouldn't notice her approach until it was too late. Perhaps she could avoid violence altogether. The firemen were dead, and Dr. Stevens was certainly in no condition to fight.

It was a nice thought, as hopeful as it was brief. As Maddy advanced on the other vehicle, two police cruisers suddenly swooped in from a cross street, blocking her car between them. They had been waiting in ambush. Flashing their lights and blurping their sirens, they forced her to slow down as the van accelerated away.

But Maddy refused to lose Ben again. Flooring it, she simultaneously spun the wheel 180 degrees, clipping the car in front with a lateral glancing blow, then a hip check that spun it into an oncoming bus. The Mercury spun the opposite way, tires smoking, and as the second cruiser came up, Maddy allowed it to bump her so that she completed her spin, describing a full circle and rocketing forward once more.

Suddenly, her windshield crazed and blew in. *Oh shit!* Stung by bits of safety glass, Maddy dropped to the floor and slammed on the brake with her left knee, the old car fishtailing out of control for a second until she was able to grab the rearview mirror off the seat and hold it up like a periscope. As the police car tried to jam her in, she punched the reverse and peeled clear, then shot forward into the lane again, bullets knocking out the rest of her windows and thumping into the upholstery.

Staying crouched below the dashboard, operating the pedals with her knees, steering by the reflection in a cracked mirror, she drove like a bat out of Hell. People witnessing the chase were astonished by the sight of a car without a driver, but to Maddy it was not so remarkable. She was only frustrated that the car couldn't go any faster. With no view of the speedometer, she had no idea she was pushing a hundred in a 25mph zone.

The cops were right there with her, trying to blow out her tires. Maddy juked and jived to keep them off her, but their car was some kind of souped-up V-8 police special, and hers was a pile of junk. Bullets pelted the Merc, making a sound that reminded Maddy of squirrels dropping horse chestnuts on the tin roof of the garden shed. Stuff was flying every which way, chunks of foam rubber and door paneling. Her sad little engine was about to explode.

All right, then. With the police car bearing down hard, Maddy abruptly jumped the curb and sideswiped a row of parked motorcycles, deflecting them into the cruiser's path. She hated motorcyclists anyway, noisy jerks always drag racing down her street late at night and setting off the car alarms. Well, these hogs would never bother anyone again. They tumbled and spun and came to pieces all over the road, so that the patrol vehicle couldn't avoid them all. Brakes squealing, it plowed into a big one, a customized Harley outfitted with straight pipes, which flew up over the cruiser's hood and peeled back half its roof. The motorcycle's chrome chassis landed in the backseat, spewing gasoline from its ruptured teardrop tank. The cops barely leaped clear before their car careened wildly into an empty sports bar, taking out the kitchen and severing all the gas lines. The explosion was spectacular.

Maddy missed all the fireworks, focusing on the speeding van. The highway on-ramp was coming up fast, and both of them were racing for it. There were no more police in sight, but Maddy didn't even bother to get up on the seat—she felt safer down underneath, so close to the engine. Like part of the car. The Mercury was her body, its metal chassis alive with sensation, and she its brain.

As the other vehicle slowed to take the ramp, Maddy accelerated. This was it.

Swerving alongside, she impatiently bumped the van in the right quarter—a gentle tap, hardly more than a nudge, that sent it flying over the grass embankment into a marshy sump. Ducks scattered, quacking furiously.

Maddy braked hard and backed onto the grass. She

hoped someone would appear waving a gun so she could smash them flat. She was not hysterical. She was remarkably calm, in fact, but she was tired and fed up and wanted all this to be over.

No one appeared. The sight of the disabled van reminded her of the other one, the one she had blown up. Ben's van. Hearing sirens in the distance, she took the screwdriver and the big monkey wrench and got out of the car.

Making her way down the steep slope, following the van's wake through the cattails, she called, "Ben! I'm here! Say something if you can talk."

There was no reply. Trying the rear cargo doors, she found them locked, and worked her way through the reeds to the driver's side. That door was ajar. There were smears of blood on it, and traces on the grass.

"Hello?" she said.

"Hi there," said a muffled voice from behind.

It was a doctor—one of the tall, masked surgeons Maddy had seen with Dr. Stevens. The man was standing in the reeds like some kind of weird sentinel, his eyes black slits in a fish-belly white face, leering at her with prurient intensity. There was something funny about the shape of his head. It was sort of . . . lopsided. Asymmetrical. His nose was bloodied from the crash, and the hem of his blue gown was stained with mud. In his rubber-gloved hands was an alarming pair of cutting shears.

"I'm just here to take Ben," she said. "Don't try to stop me, and you won't get hurt."

The man didn't move or say anything, and she warily stole a glance into the van. Empty. *Shit.*

"Where is he?" she demanded. "What have you done with him?"

But she already knew; Ben had never been there at all. The van was a decoy. They had tricked her.

The doctor shrugged. Not a sincere shrug, but a buffoonish pantomime of a shrug, palms raised to the heavens. *Oy. What are you gonna do?*

"Let me by," she said.

He just stared.

"Let me by, or I'll have to hurt you."

It was like talking to a wall. *All right, then.* She went for him.

Her arms were tired, and her whole body hurt, but as she advanced. Maddy slipped right back into action mode, or what she was beginning to think of as "going turbo." It required nothing on her part but to hop aboard—it would have been more of an effort to refuse, not to mention a lot scarier.

As the doctor raised his shears, she pinwheeled the heavy wrench, working up enough centrifugal force to take him out with one blow. *Sorry, jerkwad!* But as she batted his blades aside and lunged forward, the man was quicker, fluidly sidestepping her blow and catching the wrench on its downswing, using its own momentum to tear it from her grip.

"No way," she gasped.

Vectors realigning, she drove one foot into his knee, the other into his groin, and pushed off, catching the shears handle under her arm and stripping him of it as she vaulted backward. *My turn.* Rolling to her feet, she held up the long-bladed scissors, and said, "Nice—what do you use these things for?"

"Grand openings," he replied softly. Her kicks didn't seem to have fazed him, and he calmly awaited her next attack.

She advanced into his strike radius, shears ready at her side. They were playing a game of chicken, waiting to see who would blink first. Maddy understood that by revealing an action, one is already at a disadvantage. She had all his possible moves mapped out, ready to counter them. But what he did was both simpler and more unexpected than anything she imagined.

He went for the shears with his hand. It was like a child grabbing a poisonous snake. But when she hacked at his gloved fingers, she was startled to find that they were tougher than she expected, too tough to chop through. Not flesh and bone at all—the rubber peeled back to reveal glints of *metal*. It was a prosthetic. He seized the blades, ripping the weapon away from her. Now he had both large tools, leaving her with nothing but a pitiful, rusty screwdriver.

"Don't mess with Sinatra," he said.

"What?"

"The man with the golden arm."

"What the hell are you talking about? Who are you?"

"Don't you remember me, Madeline? I'm Dr. Hellstrom. I assisted in your procedure. We should really be friends, you know, since we have so much in common. We're both Braintree alumni."

Clearly, he was more interested in preventing her from leaving than he was in killing her. It was disconcerting to realize that if he had really wanted to kill her, he could have. Easily.

So how could she kill him? Come to think of it, how could she kill anyone? Oh my God, how had all this happened at all? For a second or two, she jittered on the ragged fringe of cold, raw panic . . . then the implant kicked in, delivering a warm, smoothing sensation that muffled the spikes like a blanket over barbed wire.

"Hey, kid," said Moses, sitting behind the wheel of the van. "Need a lift?"

Diving on top of him, she locked the door. The engine was still running. It didn't sound too good, but it didn't have to—it wasn't going anywhere. The front airbag had been deployed, but she used the screwdriver to pry open the door paneling and remove a small package—the side airbag—then reached under the dash for the electrical panel. As the doctor smashed in the window, Maddy dove for the passenger side, but she was too slow. He was already on her, painfully pinning her facedown on the seat. If only she could turn into thin air like that damn raccoon.

Relieving her of the screwdriver, Hellstrom murmured, "I'll just *take* that, thank you very much."

"Take *this*," she said, and touched the airbag's sensor terminal to a live jack.

It exploded between them, blowing the man out the windshield. Maddy, lying tucked in the angle of the seats, avoided the brunt of its force.

Shoving aside the spent bag, she jumped from the van and ran up the slope to her car. God what a mess. She couldn't drive the thing anymore; it looked like it had been used for bombing practice. Fortunately, it wasn't that visible from the road. She could hear sirens in the distance and see plumes of smoke from burning buildings and police cars; no one was bothering much about an old abandoned vehicle in the weeds. Not yet.

Legs a little shaky, Maddy hiked up to the highway and started walking away from town. The morning traffic was backed up because of the fire, and she felt highly conspicuous—maybe walking wasn't such a good idea. When someone rolled down their window to talk to her, she thought, *Oh God, here it comes.*

"Honey, you need a lift?" called the driver. It was a pretty, dark-haired young woman in a sputtering Volvo station wagon, with two little girls in the backseat.

"Actually, yeah, I do."

"Where you headed?"

"Well, I'm a little lost," Maddy said. "I'm trying to get to Denton."

"Denton . . . ?"

"Denton, Colorado?"

"Oh—wow. Okay. Well, we're not going that far, but we can get you over to Cheyenne."

"That's fine."

"Get in."

TWENTY-SEVEN

PINS AND NEEDLES

"YOU'VE been asleep for quite a while."

"Oh—sorry." Maddy suddenly realized her IV puncture was exposed and covered it up. "Gee, I must have really passed out, I'm sorry. I guess I was more tired than I thought."

"I could tell. So what were you doing walking out there?"

"My car broke down."

"Oh! I didn't think you looked like the type to be hitchhiking."

"How can you tell?"

"No luggage. You're not dressed for it. Most hitchhikers are carrying something, a bag or a backpack. I picked up this one kid who had everything he owned in a pillowcase. I was afraid you might be in trouble. I'm on the road a lot for my job, and I try to help out street kids when I see them because I would hope someone would do the same for mine if they ever needed it."

"That's cool. Thank you."

"Hey, just pass it along to the next person you meet. My name's Donna Rasmussen, and that's Faith and Lucy back there."

"Hi," the girls said. The brasher one asked, "What's your name?"

"I'm Marilyn, uh, Marilyn Manson—*Mason*, sorry! Phew, yeah, Mary Mason. Wow. But I'm really not homeless or a runaway or anything. I'm actually on my way back home."

The woman asked, "Do you go to school or something, Mary?"

"Kind of, yeah."

"Kind of?"

"It's more of a . . . rehabilitation program. I just got out."

"*Oh*—I understand. That's okay. Congratulations."

"Thanks."

"I know where you're at, believe me. I've been there."

"Really?"

"Oh yeah. You may not know it to look at me now, but I used to raise holy hell. Got into every kind of trouble you can imagine, mixed up with gangs, drugs, alcohol, you name it. I've done my time. Nobody could tell me anything, especially not my parents. But you know what finally turned it around for me?"

Maddy thought, *The Lord Jesus Christ*, but she said, "What?"

"The Lord Jesus Christ."

"Oh . . . yeah?"

"Don't worry, I'm not gonna start preaching at you. I know how stupid this sounds if you're not in the right mentality. I rejected it for a long time, believe me. Wasn't until I hit rock bottom that I was ready, and that's when He came to me."

"So you had some kind of epiphany or something?"

"Epiphany, yes. Good word. I woke up one night in an abandoned factory, cold and hungry and strung out, and I had no idea where I was. On top of that, I had just found out the day before that I was pregnant. I was scared to death, so I started praying for help, begging on my hands and knees for somebody to save me, when all of a sudden this bright light hit me, like a ray of sunshine, and I knew there was nothing to be afraid of . . . because He was there. And He's been with us ever since."

"What happened to you, though?"

"You mean that night? Let's just say all my sins finally caught up with me. But I forgave and asked for forgiveness. I started fresh. It was the hardest thing I've ever done, but over time I was able to get clean, pull myself back together. And I was blessed with these two little angels. I won't lie—sometimes it's still a struggle. But that's just life—troubles are put here to test us."

"You think so? What happens if we fail the test?"

"It's not a matter of failing. All fall short of God. He understands. Anyway, I didn't mean to hit you with all this—I usually never talk about it, but something about you just brought it all back. Let's change the subject. I was wondering if your folks might be worried about you."

"I don't know. I haven't been able to reach them on the phone."

"Do you want to try calling again?"

"Yeah, sure."

"Lucy, pass her my cell, would you?"

One of the little girls rummaged in a beaded bag and handed the phone up to Maddy.

The woman said, "If you'd rather have some privacy, we can pull over."

"That would be great, if you don't mind."

"Not at all."

They pulled over at a gas station and let Maddy out.

Walking a little way into some trees, she dialed the number, feeling her heart pound harder than it had when she was fighting madmen to the death. It rang twice and picked up.

"Hello?"

"Hello, Mom?" Maddy instantly started crying.

"Maddy! Oh my God—where are you? Roger, it's Maddy! Honey, are you all right? We've been so scared!"

"I'm okay. I'm coming home."

"Oh thank God! Where are you? Can we come get you?"

"No, that's okay. I'm with friends; they're driving me. I should be there soon—I'm not sure how long, but probably either tonight or tomorrow."

"Maddy, what happened? Why did you run away? Did something happen?"

"They told you I ran away?"

"Dr. Stevens just said that you left the grounds without permission. She was worried you might be having a relapse. Everybody just wants you back, honey."

"So they basically told you I'm crazy."

"No! We're all just concerned about you. We want you back safe. Please, honey, tell me where you are. *I'm* going crazy sitting here."

"Mom, I'll be home soon; and then we can talk about this. In the meantime, don't worry about me, and don't believe anyone who tries to tell you I'm having a relapse. I left Braintree because they were trying to turn me into something I don't want to be. That's what they do there. They did it to Ben, and they're trying to do it to me."

"Ben? What—?"

"Ben is alive. Tell his dad I saw him. He had the same surgery as me. They covered it up because they're using him as a guinea pig for their mind-control experiments, just like they're doing to hundreds of other people. It's really twisted. That's why I can't tell you where I am, because they'll come after me. They already have, and a bunch of people are dead because of it. In fact, I better hang up the phone now in case they can trace it. Have the police been there?"

"Well, yes, of course, but—"

"Then I gotta go. Love you—give my love to Dad. Bye."

"No, wait—"

She hung up.

"WELL, this is as far as we go."

They had been driving all day and were pulled over at a truck stop near the highway junction. It was getting dark.

"Okay," Maddy said, undoing her seat belt. "I really appreciate this, thank you so much."

"Wait. Listen, I've been thinking about this: Why don't you come home with us and let us put you up for the night? We've got plenty of room. Or at least let me buy you a bus ticket the rest of the way. I'm sure your parents wouldn't want you out here by the side of the road after dark, and I don't really like it either. It's freezing out there."

"No, seriously, you've done enough already. I'll be fine."

"I know. I know you'll be fine, but do it as a favor to me and the girls—otherwise, we'll be worried about you all night."

"Uh, gee, I don't know. That's very nice and all, but . . ."

"Come on, Mary. I promised them we'd do something fun tonight. Do you want to disappoint them? It's Lucy's birthday tomorrow. Please join us, or it'll be a real drag."

"C'mon, Mary, *pleasepleaseplease*," begged the girls.

"Well . . . are you sure?"

"Absolutely. Positively."

Maddy thought about it for a second, then said, "Okay. Thanks."

"No, thank *you*. That's a load off my mind, let me tell you. Okay, there's one more question I have to ask you, though, and it's very important."

The woman's face was so serious that Maddy tensed. "What's that?" she asked guardedly.

"How do you feel about bowling?"

PIN Drop Lanes was part of a larger entertainment complex in a shopping plaza on the outskirts of Cheyenne, Wyoming. It was not the type of bowling alley Maddy had envisioned, which was a hangout for fifties rejects with beer guts and greased comb-overs, a place reeking of pine paneling and Pine-Sol and drenched with unforgiving greenish fluorescent light. She had never bowled in her life and wasn't particularly looking forward to it.

Walking into the bowling emporium with the three Rasmussens, she was a bit dazzled: The place resembled some disco paradise, only with better music, all lit up with neon and lasers and mirrored balls and black lights. Best thing about it was there were no bowlers of the polyester-slacks variety; the crowd was mostly young families and high-school and college students.

Donna Rasmussen paid for the lane time and the shoes, then ordered food as the other three went to choose balls. Testing a few, Maddy settled on a green-marbled nine-pounder that fit her fingers nicely. She followed the family down to their seating court.

All around was the rumble of balls and the crash of strikes, people in silly shoes doing goofy jigs and twirls as they flung their balls down the neon-lit alleys, then the milk-bottle clatter as the pins were racked and reset. It certainly looked simple enough—ridiculously simple, actually—but Maddy could appreciate the pleasure of mindless fun. She needed some. The pizza smelled good, too.

"Why don't you take the first shot, Mary?" offered Donna.

Maddy would have preferred to go last, but the little girls were still lacing their shoes, and Donna was manning the electronic scoreboard.

"Okay . . ."

"Don't be nervous," the woman said. "There's nothing to it. Just do what everybody else is doing."

That was the problem: No two people were doing the exact same thing—each person had their own style, with a wide range of fluctuating variables. Not even the good ones got a strike every time. Maddy could do the physics, but having been humbled by her encounter with the scissor-man, she wondered if there were randomizing factors that lay outside her experience.

Picking up the ball with both hands, she positioned herself at the head of the alley, triangulating on the second pin to the right. Taking a deep breath, she strode purposefully toward the foul line, let her arm swing down, and released the ball.

It landed at the correct spot, on an ideal trajectory, but its backspin was faster than she had anticipated, an incremental difference in friction that over the length of the alley caused a catastrophic lateral drift. The ball plopped into the gutter.

"*Darn* it," she said.

Donna laughed sympathetically. "Hey, don't worry about it. That was actually pretty good for a first-timer. You have good form, but you're just a little stiff; try to loosen up." Tapping her head, she said, "It's not all up here."

Food came, and Maddy ate a slice of pizza while Donna and the girls took their turns. They didn't treat the game seriously at all, just horsing around, but they still did better than her pathetic shot. They all hit some pins, at least.

Then it was her turn again. The pins had been reset, and so had Maddy's guidance algorithm. This time she didn't think about it, didn't try to imitate anyone else, just followed the prescribed pattern, and it was as easy as skipping rope: The ball described a long, parabolic curve, twirling like a planet in orbit as it plunged through the pins and drove them all down.

"Wow, you did it!" cheered Donna, as the girls clapped and jumped up and down.

Maddy shrugged modestly. "Beginner's luck," she said.

When her next turn came around she did it again. And then again and again and again . . . until she won the game by over two hundred points.

"Mary, you are on fire!" said Donna. "You've really never bowled before?"

"No. Just a fluke, I guess."

"I guess! Gosh!"

By the second game, bystanders had taken notice, all stopping to watch when it was her turn. Even the employees were doing it.

One of them, a good-looking young guy not much older than Maddy, came over, and asked, "How'd you learn to bowl like that?"

"I didn't. I'm just on a roll tonight. Pure luck."

"That's a hell of a roll. Wish I'd have a roll like that. Do you live around here?"

"No, I'm just passing through."

"That's too bad. I'd ask you to join our league."

"I wish I could."

"Me too. If I were you, I'd think about going pro. You're a machine."

Though meant kindly, these words caused a cold breeze up Maddy's spine. *You're a machine.* There it was, all her fears of the past week distilled into one tidy sentence. She was one frame away from a perfect score of 300, which would have no doubt triggered some kind of hullabaloo—on the back wall she could see the bowling awards and photographs of past winners with their prizes. She had never won anything in her life, much less anything related to sports.

As a tall, skinny girl, Maddy had often been pushed into sports, everyone assuming she would be good at things like basketball or soccer . . . until they saw her play. *Madeline exhibits a distinct lack of body awareness,* was how one of her middle-school coaches put it, which was a nice way of saying she was totally uncoordinated, all knees and elbows. For years, right up through high school, everyone insisted she would grow out of it, that it was nothing but a temporary phase caused by a growth spurt. Just you wait, they said. Well, she was tired of waiting— she wanted to win!

"Go for it, Mary!" Donna said. "You can do it!"

The whole place was watching as Maddy picked up her green ball and took a stance. Just as she had a dozen times before, she breathed deep, then strode three quick steps and flung the ball down the lane. It looked perfect, skimming across the varnished boards like a top. It looked so good that even when it started going wrong, floating too wide, nobody believed it—they thought it would magically correct itself. But no: The ball did not make any last-second sharp turns. It teetered on the edge of the gutter and clipped the far outside pin as it dropped.

The room deflated with an audible sigh. *That's it,* someone said.

Donna was still enthusiastic: "Come on, honey! Knock 'em down!"

There would be no 300 now, all the pressure was gone, but a few folks lingered to see Maddy make the pickup shot. Winding up one last time, eyes watering, she threw the ball dead center into the pins. It crashed through them like a wrecker, so fast and dirty it hollowed out the middle and left the rest standing, two on one side, one on the other. The standing pins looked like actors on a bare stage, doing Pinter. Then the gate came down and knocked them in. It was over.

"HEY, Rick, come here."

"What?"

"Did I see you talk to that chick just now?"

"What chick?"

"The one who flubbed the money shot."

"What about it?"

"Come quick, I want you to see something."

"What?"

"In my office."

Rick Callas didn't have much interest in whatever Mr. Barnstable, the surly floor manager, had to tell him, but he went along, expecting to be chewed out. For what, he wasn't sure, but with Mr. Barnstable, it didn't take much. Talking to a girl, though? Rick had never been forbidden from fraternizing with customers as long as he did his job, but maybe someone had complained. Was it possible they thought he had interfered with the girl's game, caused her to screw up? That would suck.

"Here," his boss said. "Take a look at this."

The manager was pointing to the screen of his computer. There was a news site on, showing a picture of a girl's face. In the picture, she looked happier, younger, but except for the bangs and the braces, she was a dead ringer for the teenage girl he had just spoken to out on the floor.

The text read:

MENTAL PATIENT SOUGHT

Recovering neurological patient Madeline Zoe Grant, 17, of Denton, Colorado, was reported missing Sunday by doctors at Idaho's Braintree Institute, where she recently underwent experimental surgery.

"Miss Grant suffered debilitating brain injuries, but thanks to our program of deep-cortex stimulation, she has begun to show signs of full recovery," says Dr. Alan Plummer, Chief of Neurosurgery at Braintree. "Obviously she has recovered sufficiently to leave the grounds on her own, but without proper care, she may be delusional, paranoid, possibly even violent or suicidal. It's important that she be found before she can become a danger to herself or others."

Madeline's parents have issued a reward for their daughter's safe return and ask that anyone seeing the girl should not approach her directly, but please notify law-enforcement personnel immediately.

"They were just showing this on TV, and I looked it up," said Mr. Barnstable eagerly. "Does that look like her or what?"

"Yeah, kind of . . ."

"Are you kidding? It's definitely her!"

"I know, but she can't be the same one. Like an escaped mental patient is going to come in here and bowl a 300. Be real."

"She didn't bowl a 300. Anyway, who knows what crazy people can do? I'm telling you, that's either her, or it's her freakin' twin sister."

"I heard them call her Mary, not Madeline."

"So what? They both start with M. Hell with this, I'm calling."

"Go ahead, but you better hurry."

"Why's that?"

"They just left."

TWENTY-EIGHT

SILVER BIRCH

DONNA drove them to her house, a rustic wooden cabin in a grove of cottonwood trees, surrounded by a low adobe wall. There was no lawn, only a plot of indigenous succulents. It was too dark to see much, but Maddy could tell that it was a pretty spot, more homestead than suburb, somehow sheltered from the encroachment of slash-and-burn residential developers. A cross-eyed Siamese cat met them at the door, frantic for attention.

"This is nice," Maddy said.

"Thanks. Yeah, we put a lot of work into this place."

"You and the girls?"

"Well, them, too, but I meant me and Barry—my fiancé. We're gonna get married when it's finally finished."

"Congratulations. When's that?"

"At the rate we're going, never." She laughed.

"Does he live here?"

"Yeah, unless I'm in town. Then he stays with his folks. We meet up during the day at their house, or we go out with friends from church, nothing unchaperoned.

Probably sounds pretty weird, but we're trying to preserve the sanctity as best we can."

"No, I get it."

"You have to understand: We've both had histories, if you know what I mean, so this is something that makes us feel more worthy of grace. It's a token."

"Hey, you know, whatever works."

The little girls dragged Maddy on a grand tour of the house and yard while Donna made coffee. Then they all sat and watched *The Empire Strikes Back* on television. Maddy started nodding off as Yoda was tutoring Luke in the Jedi arts. When she jerked awake, Luke was battling Darth Vader.

"Look at you, you must be exhausted."

Maddy's eyelids were drooping. "No, I'm okay," she said. "Just been a long day."

Donna turned off the TV. "Let's get you fixed up for bed. Come on, girls, help out."

They brought in a load of blankets and pillows, and made the couch into a proper nest. The little girls were dragging, too, but helped without complaint.

"If you get cold," Donna said, "just shove another log into the woodstove."

"I'll be fine, thanks."

"Okay. Well, sleep tight, then."

"You too. And thank you."

"My pleasure, Mary. Good night."

"'Night."

Donna turned off the light and went upstairs.

Maddy had dreams of silver. Silver vans and silver arms and long silver needles. A forest of silver birch trees with flame-bright leaves and black eyes watching her on their knotty trunks. Silver roots sunk in folds of rusty clay, water puddling red in the cracks.

Maddy was holding hands and hopping from stone to

stone so as not to smirch her dainty white shoes, her Sunday shoes. Looking back, she could see, far off through the trees, a sunlit clearing and a little mound of earth. The sight twisted her heart like a vine tomato, and Maddy asked, *How come Lukie died?*

Because God said so, replied a soft, childish voice.

Maddy turned to see that she was not holding hands with her mother, but with her baby brother. His eyes were closed as though trusting her to lead the way. She had never heard him talk before, didn't realize he could. He was wearing his Sunday suit of brown plaid shorts with a matching jacket and cap. His face was rouged and powdered a lifelike pink, but when he opened his eyes, they were silver.

Trying to scream, Maddy came awake.

It took her a minute to figure out where she was, another to realize something was happening. The cat was going nuts. For a long time, it had been curled under the blanket with her, but suddenly it was up and galloping around the house, making groaning noises as it dashed from window to window, pawing aside the curtains.

There were hurried footsteps outside, the furtive *crunch-crunch* of gravel. More than one set of feet.

Rolling off the couch to her hands and knees, Maddy crept to the window and peeped out. Catching a glimpse of black-helmeted figures with guns fanning across the yard, she ducked back down and thought, *Oh shit.*

Scuttling into the kitchen, she took a few items from under the sink and wrapped them in a wet cloth, then she stuffed this parcel into the still-hot woodstove. As the coals hissed, she hurried down the steep basement stairs in the dark, shutting herself in just as the front door was knocked down. The whole house shook.

Maddy remembered from the grand tour where everything was . . . except the cat, which popped up underfoot

and nearly caused her to break her neck. But of the basement itself—the hanging bicycles and chain saw, the rain-
coats and camping gear, the washer and dryer, hot-water
heater, carpentry area, and metal shelves—she remembered everything. Of particular interest to her right then
was the gas valve in the corner.

Turning off the valve, she coupled a garden hose to the
gas inlet and set the other end by the exhaust flue, which
was a vertical steel pipe that ran straight up out the roof.
Next, she quickly gathered a few items together: a jerry
can of gasoline, a sparking tool, a bag of deicer crystals,
a box of mothballs, a box of roofing nails, a bucket of
sealing compound, and some sawdust and metal filings
from the trash.

She could hear trampling and screaming from upstairs.
I'm sorry, Maddy thought, hoping Donna and the girls
weren't being traumatized for life.

Just as someone started pounding the basement door,
there was a series of metallic concussions as the aerosol
cans in the woodstove exploded, filling the house with
acrid smoke and blasting flaming-hot embers and metal
shards at the invaders.

Shouting *"PULL OUT, PULL OUT,"* the assault force
retreated to the yard, dragging the terrified family to the
safety of the vehicles. Perfect—Maddy had hoped the police wouldn't keep them standing in the cold with only
their nighties on.

Soaking the mothballs in gasoline, she dumped them
into the sealant bucket and coated them as though enrob-
ing bonbons in chocolate. Then she added the deicing
crystals, the nails, and the wood and metal floor sweep-
ings, tossing the balls in the mixture until they were
thickly encrusted. Naphthalene, benzene, cellulose, po-
tassium chloride—*mmm, yummy*. She loaded them into
empty caulking tubes and pushed them up the exhaust flue

with the jerry can's metal spout. When they were all in there, she snaked the hose into the can's filler valve and turned the house gas back on.

As gas fumes filled the can, Maddy stood well back and applied a spark.

With an underwhelming *whump*, the tubes shot up the pipe and burst from the roof like roman candles, peeling open as they emerged to rain a hail of sticky, exploding fireballs on the clay-tiled roof and everything else in the immediate vicinity.

Pelted with these napalm poppers, the strike team scrambled for the cover of their vehicles or batted at each other's burning clothes. They had no idea what was going on or where it was coming from. When a small, hooded figure came zooming out the back door like a witch on a broomstick, they were scarcely in any frame of mind to notice, much less block its escape. Before even the most alert of them had raised his weapon, the noisy specter was gone through the trees.

RIDING as fast as the modified bicycle could go, zigzagging down alleyways and narrow side yards all the way to downtown Cheyenne, Maddy glanced back to make sure she wasn't being followed. Spotting a Dumpster, she cut the motor and coasted to a stop, detaching the chain saw from the bike's rear sprocket and flinging it into the trash. Then she pedaled away, rain poncho flapping. Innocent-looking as the Morton Salt girl in the rain.

Almost there, she thought. *Almost there.*

TWENTY-NINE

LOCUST

FORGETTING. That was the key.

Turn trauma into a temporary file, click delete. Memory was the critical component of fear, and fear was the prime mover when it came to human behavior. Fear could overcome reason; it could overcome love. Fear was the main cause of greed and hate and addiction and self-destruction. Fear also engendered complacency, the tendency simply to tune out. It made people stupid and vulnerable to manipulation. Hence, fear—the conscious or subconscious memory of trauma—was the root of all evil.

At Braintree, they manipulated fear, induced or relieved it at will. That was nothing original—every politician, priest, and marketing director exploits human fears. At Braintree, they might have taken it to the nth degree, but the same basic mindfuck was for sale on any street corner at five bucks a hit.

By monkeying with people's pain centers, you could get them to do anything. Anything at all.

Maddy understood the principle perfectly well, so when she first walked into the biggest little meth lab in Denver, she knew exactly what it was about. Not the graffiti-scrawled rooms it occupied, not the filthy mattresses on the floor, not the sharp reek of toxic chemicals or the overflowing toilets. Not the dead-eyed dealer who sold her the address or the female zombies slaving over the distillery within. They were all lost children, huddled against the cold. Maddy knew the feeling. There were a few things she would have liked to forget herself . . . starting with the fact that her family was a lie.

You fucking jerks, she thought. *You evil rotten creeps.*

Maddy was still in shock from that one. She was not herself—literally. If her life was not her life, her parents not her parents, then who was she? It was a hard thing to wrap your mind around.

She had made the discovery purely by accident, trying to find a way into Denton. The FBI had the town under heavy surveillance; it was a big mousetrap, and her house was the cheese. Using a computer in the lobby of a motel, Maddy had plumbed the Quantico database and extracted the whole operation. It was surprisingly haphazard. Internet connections, mail, phones, streets, vehicles, businesses and homes of family and friends were all being monitored, but nobody was looking at the bigger picture, nobody was connecting the dots back to Braintree. She could circumvent some or all of these things, but not without risk—the database itself might be a plant. The human factor was so annoying that way; you couldn't even count on people to be stupid. What she needed was an intermediary, perhaps some old family acquaintance who only her folks would recognize, to deliver a private message.

In the FBI file was a cache of Grant family photos, pictures of her growing up. Maddy was familiar with them: They were scans of pictures her mother kept in a photo album and dragged out on special occasions. It was a dreaded holiday ritual.

To a casual observer, there would have been nothing unusual about these pictures, but Maddy was not looking at them casually. She was hunting for a mole. Immediately, she noticed something strange. In all the earliest pictures, those of her as a baby or toddler, her parents' faces had been digitally altered. But why would they be altered to look like themselves? It was almost as if these were some other family's photos, with Beth and Roger Grant's faces grafted on.

The fakery was subtle, and at first she couldn't believe it, thought it must be some pixilation problem with the file. Yet the more she studied the images, the more she realized it was a deliberate cut-up job. Why? These were the exact same pictures she had been looking at all her life, so if it was a fraud, it was her parents' fraud . . . and a sophisticated one at that. It didn't make sense.

Searching her parents' public and private histories, she traced down every visual record of them up to the time she was three. There was not much out there, just a few official documents like passport photos and driver's licenses, but what there was only confirmed for her that their identities were forged. It was a little terrifying.

And then she found it.

Lost and forgotten among the photo archives of a defunct newspaper called the *Providence Eagle* was an undoctored photo of Beth and Roger Grant. The *real* Beth and Roger Grant.

The truth did not set her free. The truth *hurt*, and Maddy left that ugly motel lobby in search of something, anything, to dull the pain. To forget. To kill the knowledge that she was truly alone. Fortunately, there was a special-

ist waiting right outside, eager to help her find peace. And
with a little incentive, he gave her directions to the Home
of Happiness.

Entering the place, she immediately realized it was a
microcosm of the culture outside, just a little more transparent: a tidy façade disguising a cesspool of abject mis-
ery. At first glance it was row of perfect little town houses
with flower boxes and children's toys on the lawns—this
apparently was what the mouth of Hell looked like.

Locust's operation was a factory of forgetting—a
wholesaler of temporary amnesia. All the guns, motorcycles, scary people, and stench of ammonia and sudden
death were just bulwarks against the ultimate bogey monster: the specter of childish dread. Dread born of genera-
tional poverty and abuse and educational neglect and the
latest travesty: a half-cocked war cooked up by oilmen
and military contractors, spawning in these damaged female veterans a self-justifying philosophy of predatory
capitalism to cash in on the one commodity they had in
abundance. You use what you got, and the hard-riding
membership of Faster Pussycat Kill! Kill! had the franchise on cracked souls.

Maddy came to them with a proposal.

You guys aren't even scratching the surface, she had
said. *You're stealing from the poor—how dumb is that?
Wouldn't it be better to go where the real money is?*

They laughed, amused by her ambition, if not her intelligence. The girl had a death wish; they could respect that.
They thought they were making plenty of money from
their many and varied criminal enterprises, but Maddy
convinced them to hear her out.

They humored her.

Borrowing a stolen laptop, she had quickly designed a
smart bug, a fractal fruit fly that generated infinite varia-
tions of itself, weeding out the weaklings, replicating and

further refining those that survived, promulgating these larvae through untraceable proxy servers to financial networks all over the world, using a quantum algorithm to challenge the laws of statistical probability, demolishing the security codes.

Craving only rotten fruit, the bug sought out vast reserves of old money, private capital amassed through centuries of corruption. Money so full of holes from shady accounting it could be riddled further without giving immediate alarm. Slavery money, railroad money, alcohol, oil, drugs, arms, water, and power—it was often all in the same hands, everybody's fingers in the same pie, and Maddy's flies swarmed the picnic, channeling and rinsing the hoarded wealth through unwitting intermediaries, ten million clone computers and dummy accounts, rendering it untraceable.

Except that Maddy designed it to be traced. She left footprints, deliberate tracks in the silicon jungle that led neither to her nor the FPKK, but straight to the back porch of Braintree, Inc. Clues not immediately apparent, nothing too obvious, but stuff that a really determined seeker would happen upon in good time. And as soon as those crumbs were sniffed out, the hunt would be on. Oh yeah, there would be an investigation that would wring that joint inside out and snap it like a wet towel.

Clickety-clicking away on a laptop at two hundred words a minute, Maddy had to smile—she had never done anything like this before. It was fun!

The whole operation took about twenty minutes. When she was done, she gave a few dummy account numbers and fake IDs to the leader of the band, the heavily tattooed ex-Marine and half-breed Seminole Indian named Locasta Pursleigh—known within the club as Locust. Maddy had found her on the FBI's Most Wanted list. Locust sent her "manager," a private attorney named Chica Kazantza-

kis, aka Chickasaw, out on a tour of area banks. An hour
later, she returned with a million dollars in cash.

There's a lot more where that came from, Maddy
said. *But first you have to help me solve this problem I'm
having.*

What kind of problem?

*It's kind of like if somebody steals your lunch money,
and after that, they act like it's your job to give them your
lunch money, and before you know it, they want everybody's lunch money.*

Lunch money, Locasta said, looking at the million
bucks.

*Right. Well, I think it's time to tell them they can't take
anybody else's lunch money.*

*And what happens when they tell you to go pound sand
up your ass?*

Maddy just smiled.

She demonstrated in twenty-two easy steps how to
modify a laptop computer, a cell phone, and a satellite
dish so that they could not only monitor but jam selected
radio transmissions, including police signals. After that,
she showed the gang how to build a simple Faraday cage
out of tinfoil to shield electronics from powerful electromagnetic discharges. This was in preparation for her next
tutorial, which was how to set off a homegrown EMP—an
electromagnetic pulse—strong enough to crash all un-
shielded electronics within a thousand yards.

Then for the fun part. Maddy had once had a fondness
for cooking shows—she loved the Food Network, particularly *Iron Chef.* For that day's challenge, she had a few
basic recipes:

Using the meth distillation plant and a few basic household supplies, she whipped up three concoctions: a nonlethal aerosol nerve agent, a stable plastic explosive, and
a somewhat unstable rocket fuel. The latter two were based

on a bleach derivative called sodium perchlorate, which reacted violently when combined with sucrose, so the final product—a six-foot-long missile made from a heating pipe and carrying an EMP warhead—was powered by a bottle of Aunt Jemima pancake syrup. It was launched out of a bathtub.

The last thing she needed to do was send out an invitation.

THIRTY

SMOKE AND MIRRORS

TWO doctors from the Institute were on hand for the raid. The task force commander, Senior Agent Bradley Cook, had agreed to take them along in case negotiations were necessary. They rode in a convoy of several cars and vans, a combined force representing both state and federal authority. Helicopters circled overhead. It was an impressive thing to see so much manpower working on their behalf. It couldn't help but inspire humility.

"Oh my God," said Dr. Plummer. "Poor Maddy."

"I know, honey," said Dr. Stevens. "But don't worry, these guys know what they're doing. They're trained professionals—they won't hurt her." Dr. Stevens looked like she had a head cold, her eyes puffy and her nose packed with gauze.

Agent Cook said, "No one's going to get hurt. You two did the absolute right thing in notifying us as soon as she contacted you. Miss Grant is a danger to herself and others, and the sooner we bring her in, the sooner she can get the help she needs."

"But she told us to come alone," Plummer said.

"Of course, sir, but who's to say *she's* alone? There is evidence she is hooked up with some organized group, perhaps criminals or terrorists. Plus, she may be hyped up on drugs, which would exacerbate her mental condition. The letter she sent you is proof of paranoid delusion, inventing that whole town and the conspiracy against her. She clearly blames both of you for all her troubles, so I wouldn't go to any private meetings with her. Not unless you want to end up like those unfortunate folks in Bitterroot."

They pulled up before a strip of identical, town-house-style duplexes, each with a small front yard and a satellite dish. Except for the run-down surrounding neighborhood, the buildings could have been mistaken for luxury condos. But this was government-subsidized, low-income housing—what the zoning laws referred to as Section 8. The residents were accustomed to disturbances at all hours of the day—stabbings and shootings and every variety of dope-fueled mayhem. The arrival of a fleet of armed commandos barely merited a glance out the curtain.

The ATF leader seemed to be having some sort of problem with his radio, fiddling with it and getting nothing but static. "Ten-one, Ten-one," he said. "I'm getting some interference here—is anyone reading me?"

Sitting behind him in the command vehicle, the two doctors watched as a squad of sweating, Kevlar-plated ATF agents charged the door of Unit B-7. From years of cop shows, the couple knew what was coming next: doors battered down and stunned, half-naked perps dragged from their filthy dens into the light of day. Order restored.

But as the point man ran up the walk to the porch, he hit something—perhaps a transparent strand of fishing line. From everywhere at once came a sudden eruption of billowing whiteness: fountains of smoke shooting out of the sprinklers with a screaming rush like a hundred fireworks. The men disappeared in the thick, spreading clouds, which rolled toward the street and enveloped the nearest vehicles.

At the same time, there was a loud *whoosh*, and some kind of rocket streaked from the building's skylight, exploding high overhead with a tremendous, reverberating *BAM*.

"Pull back, pull back!" someone shouted, and last thing the two doctors were able to see out the car windows was a roiling wall of smoke, bearing down fast.

"Put these on!" Agent Cook shouted, thrusting a pair of gas masks into the doctors' hands. Trying to move the car, he found that the engine wouldn't start. "Come on!" he said, pounding the steering wheel as the opaque fog settled over the windows like a cotton sheet. Visibility fell to zero, and all of a sudden Agent Cook slumped sideways in his seat, twitching.

"What's going on?" Dr. Plummer cried, pressing the gas mask to his face.

"I don't know," Stevens said. "Just stay put so they can find us."

Everything suddenly went very still. Only the vacant hiss of the car's police scanner broke the muffled silence. As the heavy smoke parted, swirling, they could see other vehicles sitting like abandoned hulks, doors hanging open and men sprawled on the ground. There was no sign of life. Even the helicopters were gone.

Then: A strange, two-humped shape appeared, looming out of the low murk. Gliding just above the ground like a weird sea creature, a floating nautilus, it made its way down the line of police vehicles with careful deliberation, as though peering into each one. As it drew near, they could hear the rumble of its engine.

It was a motorcycle. A sleek, hornet yellow racing machine with two helmeted riders. The rear passenger was aiming something like a camera into each car they passed, and as the motorcycle drew up alongside, the doctors found themselves in the thing's sights.

The device lowered; the rider got off the bike and peered into the car. She tipped up her mirrored visor so they could see her face.

"Omigod! Chandra, it's her! It's Maddy!"

Alan Plummer jumped from the car, frantically jabbing the button on his wave emitter. It seemed to have no effect. In the excitement, he neglected his gas mask and fell unconscious at Maddy's feet.

"Whoops," Maddy said. Her voice was muffled from the helmet. "Don't worry, it's temporary."

She got into the car next to Dr. Stevens. "Hi, Doc."

Chandra Stevens looked at her unflinchingly, mask to mask. "Hello, Maddy. Are you okay?"

"Not really," she said. "It's been a weird couple of weeks. I only have a minute, but I thought we should talk."

"All right."

"I just found out everybody I know in Denton has been taken into protective custody. That's not the weird part." She tossed a sheaf of printed-out photos on the doctor's lap. "I don't think Beth and Roger Grant are even the real Beth and Roger Grant. They look sort of the same, but not that much. You know what I think? I think these people started impersonating the Grants about fourteen years ago. Right around the same time you adopted me and gave me to them."

"Maddy, that's absurd—"

"Stop. I found the records. I know you think you're

playing some kind of mind game, but believe me, you want to start telling me the truth."

"Maddy . . . I've already told you the truth. It's your own mind that is playing games. By this point you've discovered that for yourself; you just refuse to accept it. Stay with us, and we'll do everything we can to help you. It's not too late."

"Bull. That's total bullcrap. Here's the thing: If you don't tell me the truth, and immediately expose to the world everything that's going on at Braintree and Harmony, then I am going to be forced to deal with it myself. I have nothing to lose anymore."

Several other motorcycles pulled up. The riders were women—very alarming women. They were road warriors, dressed for medieval combat in studded boots, chain mail, and spiked leathers. Their helmets had been converted to some kind of improvised breathing apparatus that made them look like giant hornets. They were members of a biker club: On the backs of their leather jackets were red she-devils and the letters FPKK.

Dr. Stevens said, "What do you think you're going to do? Who are these people? What do they want from you?"

"Just some ladies I met on the road. It's a motorcycle gang. This one is Locust."

"Yo," said Locust huskily.

"Dear God, Maddy. And I suppose *they* believe you, is that it?"

"No, they pretty much think I'm bonkers, too. But I've been able to demonstrate my usefulness to them, so we've worked out a mutually beneficial agreement. My brains in exchange for their brawn. You know, I never realized how easy it is to make money off the Internet. Give it a couple months, and I think you'll be seeing these guys in the Fortune 500. So what's your answer?"

Dr. Stevens shook her head, then scornfully dropped her gas mask and breathed deep. Instantly, she convulsed and fell unconscious.

Looking at the twitching form, Maddy sighed. "That's what I thought."

She got back on the bike, hugging Locust around the waist. With a wave, they were gone.

THIRTY-ONE

CASTLE DRACULA

LOCUST paused her motorcycle by the roadside, staring up the steep sloping lawn to the big silvery cube at the top.

"So that's it, huh?"

"That's it," Maddy said.

"Doesn't really look all that sinister, does it?" Locust sounded disappointed.

"It's not Castle Dracula, no."

"And you say they're making zombies in there? By the hundreds, like a big assembly-line thing? Beaming out brain waves to control everybody, like something out of the Body Snatchers?"

"Yeah."

"Right here in this building? With the employee parking and handicapped access and all?"

"Yes."

"Let me get this straight. The guys who wash the windows, and the landscaping crew, and all the secretaries

and everybody—none of them know about this? Or is it
that they're all cool with it?"

"I don't know."

"Hell, that's a first. You don't know. But you're sure
this is the right place? It's not some other generic office
park you're thinking of?"

"*No.*"

"All right, all right. If you say so."

Locust was still not over her surprise at first laying eyes
on Maddy Grant. She might have believed the kid was a
Girl Scout selling cookies, but the idea that this walking,
talking Raggedy Ann doll could be a dangerous wanted
felon was too much.

The bikes all caught up, and Locust signaled them to
wait. "So, what's our next move, hotshot?"

Maddy wasn't quite sure what to do next. Her thoughts
were suddenly garbled, fuzzing in and out like a bad
phone connection. It was a feeling she hadn't had for some
time, not since her encounter with the firemen, but this
time she recognized it for what it was: interference. They
were messing with her head. *Nice try,* she thought, turning
up the gain on her signal blocker.

"Give me a minute, okay?"

"Knock yourself out."

After speaking to Dr. Stevens in the car, Maddy had
ridden north with Locust and the FPKK, retracing her path
back to Braintree. The trip had been uneventful. They'd
traveled in an invisible storm of radio interference, so that
no one without a landline could immediately report their
passing. There were a few run-ins with the highway patrol, but those were quickly defused by either diverting the
cops elsewhere with fake radio signals, or—if they were
really determined—frying their cars' electrical circuits
with the portable EMP cannon that Maddy had rigged to

the back of Locust's motorcycle. They made good time, ignoring the speed limit and stopping only to eat or go to the bathroom. By nightfall, they had arrived at Braintree.

Locust was getting impatient. "So what's it gonna be, kid? You wanna turn back or what?"

"No," Maddy said. "Let's go in."

LOCUST signaled the other motorcycles to follow. They advanced in a line.

As the train of bikes cruised through the open gate and up the driveway past the empty parking lot, the security cameras all mysteriously went dark. Likewise, phones and computers in the whole complex went dead, so that when the lead motorcycles charged up the wheelchair ramp and blew through the glass doors into the lobby, none of the frantic skeleton crew could alert police. The automatic alarms did not go off.

There was a small security contingent, six heavily armed and gung ho Homeland Security fast responders, who took positions in the foyer and were instantly rendered unconscious by a homemade gas grenade.

The rest of the staff was already gone. Rather than challenge the wheeled invasion, they had abandoned their stations and retreated for the fire exits.

As the last of the bikes streamed in, Maddy consulted the floor directory, and said, "Communications Suite— Sublevel Two. That must be where the carrier wave originates."

"If you say so."

"It's below ground level and probably well shielded. In case it's still functioning, we have to go down there and knock it out directly."

"How?"

"Just pull the plug. Follow me!"

"Whoa—you said to get you in here. We got you in. I ain't goin' noplace my wheels can't go."

"Fine, I'll go myself."

"You crazy? You can't go down there alone!"

"I went into that disgusting hellhole of yours—this is nothing."

"All right, hold up, I'm coming."

Locust wasn't about to let the kid out of her sight. It was funny, because just a few days ago she had thought nothing of taking Maddy's money and selling her down the river. As far as she was concerned at the time, the girl was just a fugitive with a big price on her head. She remembered the look on Chickasaw's face when Maddy first showed up at the Hippo.

Locust?

What's wrong?

She's here.

Locust had checked her gun, thinking: *This better not be a goddamn setup.* She'd been worried ever since she got that money and the strange note that came with it:

Dear Ms. Pursleigh, it had read. *This is a serious business proposition. I give you this money as a gesture of good faith, just so you will hear me out. I need partners who are willing to take small risks for large rewards. Since you already take large risks for small rewards, I hope you will consider my proposal. I look forward to visiting you soon. Sincerely, Maddy Grant.*

The attached bundle had ten thousand bucks in it. Unmarked, nonsequential twenties. Nobody gave money away like that, not even teenage psychopaths; it had to be a trap of some kind. Plus the note looked like fucking Emily Post had written it. The girls in the office only cared about the chunk of free cash, and Locust had to remind them there were all kinds of shady characters out there, many of them wearing police badges. It was a sick world, full of false promises, false information, false salvation. At least Locust's criminal enterprises offered value for money. But from Chick's tone of voice, she could tell this was something different. Out of curiosity, Locust had her bring the girl in back. They could always kill her.

Instead, they made her their leader.

As the last of the bikes came in, Locust ordered them to guard the entrance while she followed Maddy downstairs. There was no rush; no help was coming anytime soon. They went down two flights, emerging in a dim utility corridor with metal doors on either side. The ceiling was a mass of pipes and wires, and there was a hum of machinery.

"Where exactly are they supposed to be doing all these mad experiments?" Locust asked, looking around doubtfully.

"I don't know," Maddy said.

"She don't know."

"I don't know everything!"

"Coulda fooled me."

Maddy didn't know what to say. It was a good question and one that increasingly troubled her. The more she looked around the place, the more she realized it was nothing like what she had expected to find. Truth be told, it was all pretty straightforward—she could intuit the blueprints right down to the welding specs and bolt torque. There were no extensive secret laboratories, no surgical assembly line with a conveyer belt carrying thousands of people in one end and mindless zombies out the other. The building was not that big, there was no room to hide an operation of that scale.

So what did that mean? Was she crazy, as everyone said? Could it all be a sick fantasy, just a postoperative delusion? No way, no *way*—it was ridiculous even to entertain the thought.

Going down the rows, passing the computer lab and the rustling rat amphitheater, Maddy quickly found the Communications Suite. Its heavy steel door was locked. Locust cocked her Glock, but Maddy pushed the gun down.

"You're going to kill us with that thing," she said. "I got it."

Taking out a Gerber jar of gray putty, Maddy used a plastic spoon to pack it into the doorjamb. Then she said, "Stand back," and stuffed in a Gummi worm. At once it began to burn, flaring hot as a blowtorch. It went on like that for about half a minute, then abruptly sputtered out, leaving a large scorched spot.

Maddy tried the door. It still didn't open. The lock hadn't burned through.

"Damn," she said.

Locust brushed her aside, saying, "Let me try." She raised her massive hobnailed boot and kicked the door in, shearing off the weakened bolt.

Inside, they found a control room lined with instrument panels—it looked like a recording studio. There were fax machines, computers, and printing equipment, as well as a lot of high-tech stuff with labels like STORAGE SERVER, SCANNER CONTROL CONSOLE, REAL-TIME ANALYSIS, RF COIL, RF AMP, DIGITIZER, WAVEFORM GENERATOR, and TRANSMITTER.

Transmitter.

"There it is," Maddy said.

"There you are," someone else said.

Maddy turned around, feeling the hair bristle on her neck. Her heart rate spiked then leveled. There was a doctor standing in the doorway—*the* doctor. His ID badge read, DR. MARK HELLSTROM. He was the same strange-looking man she had fought before, the one who had almost killed her. Once again, he was wearing a pale blue surgical gown, a paper mask, and elbow-length rubber gloves. Half his face was one big, nasty-looking bruise, with a lot of little sutured cuts.

"Locust?" she said evenly. "I need you to give me some space."

"What? Aw, don't worry about this asshole, honey—just do what you came to do, and let's get the fuck out of here."

The doctor came in, pale and languid as a ghost, seeming to glide forward on casters.

"Back off, motherfucker," Locust said, brandishing her gun.

"Locust, get back," Maddy said.

"Stop, man, or I'll blow your nuts off! I mean it!"

When the doctor didn't stop, Locust wavered in frustration, then lost patience and fired, intending merely to wing the man. A little wake-up call.

Except that when the bullet got there, the doctor's leg was not where it was supposed to be—the slug punched empty air. And before Locust could try again, the gun was clapped in a vise grip and yanked from her hands.

Diving after it, Locust cursed in shock and anger.

She knew how to fight, had been trained in hand-to-hand combat, knew all the techniques for fighting dirty, even to the death, but this odd-looking man wasn't interested in fighting. He didn't seem to even know there was a fight going on.

With clinical indifference—practically as an afterthought—the doctor swung the gun's handle like a club, delivering a sharp blow to the ventral root ganglion at the base of Locust's skull. In a fraction of a second, the confrontation was over.

Maddy was a different story. As the doctor came for her, she retreated behind the equipment, keeping clear of those hands.

"Come on now, Madeline," he said patiently. "I'm not going to hurt you."

Ducking and dodging, she said, "I know you're not."

She tossed him the baby-food jar. Lid screwed tight, it was crammed with Gummi worms, the chemical reaction already glowing fiercely as a tiny bottled sun. Maddy hit the floor as it exploded in his face.

The man went down in flames, a screaming, melting marionette—swiveled steel armatures grafted to flesh and bone—and Maddy bolted past him to the doorway. Then she was out and running for the stairs.

But others were already there, coming down for her, and more emerging from the elevator. Dr. Stevens and Dr. Plummer were with them—she heard Dr. Stevens say in a voice of nasally resignation, "Oh God, that's her."

Maddy spun, seeking an alternative exit, an air duct, anything, but there was nothing except an array of locked doors leading to a dead end. She was out of weapons, out of ideas. More doctors appeared from the opposite end of the corridor, bottling her up so that the only choice left was to go down fighting . . . or just go down.

Busted, Maddy thought.

THIRTY-TWO

RETURN TO HARMONY

A LL right," she said. "I give, I give. You got me."
      She limply allowed herself be restrained, strapped
to a gurney, and hooked up to an IV. There was nothing
else for it; all she could do was wait. Wait for the next
chance. And if it never came?

"What happened to the other guys?" she said, feeling
numb. Whatever was in her IV had definitely kicked in.

Dr. Stevens ignored her, but someone with a soft
Southern accent asked gently, "What other guys, honey?"

"The ones who brought me here. The bikers."

"Don't worry about them, they can't hurt you anymore.
You're home safe with us now."

They wheeled her into the elevator and descended one
floor to the bottom level. Here there was nothing but an
underground parking garage for a fleet of company cars
and vans.

Harmony, here I come, Maddy thought, trying to say
the words aloud. She found she couldn't speak, couldn't
move her lips. And yet she wasn't afraid. In fact, it was

intriguing to be fully conscious and yet completely paralyzed. Off the top of her head, she could think of several
biotoxins that might do that. But somehow she knew this
was not a toxin. It was not a chemical at all—there were
no telltale side effects. With any sedative drug, there was
always a danger of suppressing involuntary functions too
much, killing the patient, but this was perfect.

.It had to be her implant; that was the only explanation.
They were using electrical impulses to mess with her
autonomic nervous system, turning her off like a windup
toy. Was that what they had used on Ben, to mimic death?
Pretty clever.

To her surprise, they did not load her into one of the
vans, but onto a small electric-powered utility truck, not
much bigger than a golf cart. Dr. Plummer climbed on,
and the vehicle sped down a ramp into a low concrete tunnel marked SECURE DATA STORAGE. There was a bright-lit
storage vault, but hidden at the back was a platform overlooking a bottomless pit. The platform was barely big
enough for the truck; Maddy felt as though they were teetering above an abyss.

With a lurch, the platform dropped.

It was an elevator—a very fast elevator. The angle of
descent was very steep, but it was not vertical. *Bat Cave,*
Maddy thought. Fluorescent lights were strung along the
walls at regular intervals, creating a mesmerizing strobe
effect.

It was a long ride. The elevator was more of a railcar—
a *funicular*, Maddy recalled. *Are we having fun yet?* Her
ears popped. Trying to clear them with her limited movement was frustrating. Giving up, she focused her attention
on the shoddy workmanship of the tunnel. Though obviously new, it was already full of cracks and seepage and
rust stains. It reeked of mildew. The contractor who had
built the thing probably charged a fortune, too. At a cer-

tain point they slowed down, passing a series of warning signs reading, DO NOT PROCEED IF LIGHTS ARE RED. The lights were green. The air became warm and tinged with sulfur. There was a roar of ventilation equipment.

After a while, the elevator hit bottom, and they drove the rest of the way, a long straight shot of tunnel, until at last they emerged in a much larger space, a man-made cavern held up with massive wooden beams and brick archways. Huge, corroded remnants of ancient factory equipment jutted from the floor like wrecked ships. The place looked old, a condemned relic of the Industrial Age . . . yet Maddy had seen it all before.

It was the Braintree of her earliest dreams.

The cart carried her up a ramp to a loading dock, where vacant-faced orderlies waited to roll her wheeled stretcher inside a very large and very dirty freight elevator. With a crash of gates and gears, it rose to ground level. The doors opened on a clean white corridor, all new plasterboard and a new drop ceiling. After the basement, the lights were so bright they hurt her eyes. Maddy found she could blink, but her slack eyelids wouldn't stay completely shut. Every few minutes Dr. Plummer put drops in them. They passed a sunlit window, and Maddy had a blurred glimpse of rooftops and mountains. Those, too, were familiar, but of much more recent memory.

I'm in Harmony, she thought. *Carbontown.*

The mine. They had brought her to the big abandoned mine at the center of downtown Harmony—the Museum of Industry and Culture. *Of course, stupid!* Why hadn't she thought of it sooner? It was so obvious! They weren't doing anything up there on the mountain. How could they? Up there they were in the public eye, a government-funded operation. That was just a front. Braintree Institute was a sham; it was all for show—a few high-profile surgeries now and again, maybe a little token research, just for display purposes, so the funding could be justified. So there would be no questions about where the money really went.

Meanwhile, the actual work was going on here.

They wheeled her into a yellow-and-black-tiled room with a padded door and a tiny window of reinforced glass. A mirrored bubble hung from the ceiling, concealing a camera. From the reflection in the dome, Maddy could see that there was someone already in the room, but she couldn't turn her head to see who it was. Dr. Plummer left without a word, leaving her alone with the stranger.

"Hi, Maddy," he said. "It's me."

It was Ben.

THIRTY-THREE

REUNION

H IS head was clean-shaven, but it was definitely Ben.
If she could have, she would have jumped up and
hugged him. She would have screamed, *Oh my God, I'm
so glad to see you!* But all she could do was blink.

"I'm sorry," Ben said. He came near, leaning over her.
"I know this is rough, but they thought it would help if I
was the first one to talk to you. Can you understand me?"

She blinked frantically.

"Good, I see you, that's good. Are you okay? Blink
once for yes and twice for no."

She blinked once.

"Thank God." He sighed. "I'm fine, too, I guess—they
patched me up and got me right back on my feet. No rest
for the wicked, huh?"

He looked very uncomfortable, as though he would
have preferred to be anywhere but there. Maddy could
tell he was ashamed, struggling to say something he didn't
want to say, and she wished she could yell, *Just spit it out!*

"Look," he said finally, "I hate to be the one to tell you

this, but it's probably something you already know, so maybe I'm just stating the obvious. Y'know?"

She had no idea what he was talking about. *If you're going to say something, say it!*

Ben said, "See, the thing is, you never escaped. Any more than I did. We both did exactly what we were supposed to do, what *they* wanted us to do, from day one. We never had any choice—only the *illusion* of choice. That's how it works, Maddy. The implant, I mean. The computer compels us to do whatever the doctors program it to, and our organic brains come up with creative solutions to accomplish it. Rationalize it. It's human nature.

"Everything that's happened to us has been by design. Everything. It was all a field test, a trial run, and from what they tell me, you performed like a champ. Look how you even voluntarily returned, against all common sense! Part of me was hoping you wouldn't, but here you are, right on schedule.

"You're a celebrity, did you know that? In the news, they're calling you Maddy Hearst because you've supposedly been kidnapped and brainwashed by this gang of crazy lesbo-terrorists. They say you're riding around leaving a trail of dead bodies everywhere you go—is that true?"

Maddy blinked.

"Jesus. Sounds like you had a hell of a trip. I guess it's a good thing you're zonked out right now, or I might be another statistic, huh?"

She blinked twice.

"No? That's good, I'm glad. I hope we're still friends, Mad. I want to be. I didn't choose any of this either, you know? It's just the way it is. We can't change it."

She blinked twice, a tear gliding down her temple.

"You're an amazing girl. And you'll see it's not so bad living here. I swear to God, in some ways it's better than being on the outside. In here we're like one big family. Everybody's decent to each other; there's no crime, none of that fucking depression, just this real sense of *community*, everyone working together for the same goal. You always know where you belong. There's no confusion. Life's a lot simpler. It's kind of old-fashioned that way, more the way people used to live, I guess, and eventually it's gonna spread across the whole country, so we won't even have to keep it a secret anymore. That's what I'm looking forward to."

Maddy squeezed her eyes shut as hard as she could. It took all her concentration, but there was still a thread of light; she couldn't escape completely.

Ben said, "Okay, well, I'm gonna let you go then. You're probably pretty tired. We'll talk again later, okay?"

She kept her eyes scrunched partly shut. The door opened, and someone else came in. There was a feeling of something cool pressing against her head, a smooth metal object, and just like that her mind went blank.

MADDY woke up back in the motel. It was as if she had never left.

Everything was the same: the bare white room, the bed, the window overlooking the rear, the little kitchenette and bathroom, the honking big radiator. All the stuff she had bought was still there, too, still shelved and hung in the closet exactly as she had left it. There were two differences, however: The broken medicine cabinet had been replaced, and her external modem was gone. No more need for pretence, apparently—she was theirs.

Maddy sat up and checked her PDA for messages. Someone had made her an appointment with Able Staffing for 11 a.m. She put the device aside and closed her eyes for a while, chanting *ommmmm* to clear her head. It was a meditation exercise she had once been pretty good at though she hadn't tried it since before the accident. She was glad to find it still worked.

In the months following her parents' breakup, she and her mother had started going to TM classes together—the memory caused an intense, fleeting pang of nostalgia. Those few months were the closest she and her mom had ever come to relating to each other as adults. No condescending mother/child bullcrap. She had seen too much for that, chafing against the role of Mommy's Little Angel.

In the meditation studio, they were on an equal footing, both novices, except that Maddy took to it quicker, went deeper than Beth Grant could or dared to, and in her growing self-awareness began to see through all the assumptions that had ruled her existence . . . and her family's. She began asking her mother questions, questions that made Beth increasingly uncomfortable, and it was perhaps lucky for their relationship that at this awkward juncture, Sam and Ben Blevin came into their lives. That put an end to Transcendental Meditation.

Her mom claimed she stopped out of dissatisfaction with the cultish aspects of the practice, but Maddy knew it was because she wanted to spend time with her new boyfriend, Sam. And Sam's son Ben was so cute that Maddy didn't object . . . much. At the time, she only felt a vague regret. Maddy had no way of understanding then that she and her mother had just squandered their last chance of ever being more than strangers. Which was what they were, of course. Complete strangers. Maddy had to keep reminding herself, because the truth was so slippery. It kept sliding right out of her head like a live eel from a basket, and what was the good of catching it? It only made things worse.

There was a knock on the door.

"Who is it?" she asked.

A girl's voice said, "Housekeeping."

"Oh. Jeez. Hold on a sec."

Maddy got up and threw on some clothes, one of the new dresses she had bought. Then she opened the door. Expecting to find a maid, she was startled to find a beautiful and smartly dressed young woman grinning at her.

"Maddy!" the woman cried, seizing her in a full-body hug.

"Whoa," Maddy said, looking over the weeping girl's shoulder for sign of the towel cart. "I think there may be a mix-up . . ."

"Maddy, it's me!" The girl pulled back to arm's length, laughing and crying. "It's Lakisha!"

Lakisha? For an instant, Maddy drew a total blank, her mind unable to process this most unusual and yet familiar of names, especially in combination with this stranger's beaming, intelligent face. The pieces didn't match. "What Lakisha?"

"Oh shit. I know I look way different. Wait." She took her glasses off. "Special Needs?"

At the sound of those words, Maddy felt the floor shift. Her face went slack, mouth and eyes gaping as she realized this elegant woman and the frantic, damaged creature she had recently known by the name Lakisha were somehow the very same person.

"Oh no . . . no way . . ."

Impossible. Lakisha had been a mentally disabled child, and this was a whole woman: Lakisha 2.0. All her features were the same—the pug nose, the full lips, those gold-brown eyes, as well as the self-inflicted marks and scars, now softened with makeup. But those eyes, that face, were animated by a bright light that focused on Maddy like a laser beam. Lakisha's whole posture was different; she seemed taller, tighter, slicker. Maddy suddenly realized she did know this person—not from life, but from dreams. In a way, this was the original Lakisha, the gorgeous, funny one from her recovered memories.

Maddy had to sit down. She wept; they wept together. Finally, she asked, "How?"

They answered in tandem: *"Braintree."*

"Shit," Maddy said.

"I know. It's crazy."

"Where are you living?"

"Right here in the motel. Just down the hall."

"What! Since when?"

"Since last week. I've been so nervous since they told me you were coming. I didn't want to screw it up."

"What did they tell you?"

"That you've been having a hard time, but you're doing an amazing job, and it's very important that I help you feel welcome and loved. They didn't exactly have to twist my arm. I told them I'd do anything if it would help my peep Maddy."

"What is my job?"

"Don't you know? Wow. I don't know if I'm supposed to say this, but you're a key part of the big experiment— the next phase in medicine. Well, we all are, but you have some special, important function. I don't know exactly what it is, but they're basically trying to save the world, one person at a time. It's such a miracle, Maddy, oh my God."

"And you believe them?"

"Yes. Why wouldn't I? The proof is right here." She indicated her head, careful not to muss her perfect, glossy hairpiece.

"Did they also tell you we're prisoners here?"

Lakisha's face became sad. "Oh, honey. I know you've

been having some trouble adjusting. It's why Dr. Plummer asked me to talk to you." She took Maddy's hand in hers. "*This* is what it's all about, Mad. People like us having a second chance at life. Nobody asked my opinion; they just did it—and thank God they did! I feel bad about lying, but I understand the necessity. They're experimenting on people who are not legally competent. Some folks might think it's playing God, get all up in arms, but I would hope you of all people can understand. I'm so glad to see you, Maddy. I'll do anything I can to help you get through this. We'll do it together."

"You know, they already tried this on me with Ben."

"Who?"

"Nobody. So, can I ask you something?"

"Of course! Anything!"

"What was going on back in Special Needs?"

Lakisha went stiff. "What do you mean?"

"Well, I remember some of it being nice, and some of it being . . . kind of gross. Was something going on in that class with Principal Batrachian?"

"You don't remember?"

"Not really."

Lakisha looked shocked, tears flowing anew. "But Maddy. Oh my God."

"What?"

She knelt at Maddy's feet. "You *saved* us. From that man. Don't you know that? No one outside had any idea what was happening, and when Jonas tried to tell people, they had him put on heavy meds. Turned him into a zombie. But then you came back from your operation like some kind of knight in shining armor! You saved all of us!"

"So you're saying it was good I stuck him with a fork?"

Lakisha sobbed in her lap, "Yes! My God, yes!"

"Okay." Maddy nodded thoughtfully, chewing her lip. "Listen, I gotta be at a job appointment in a few minutes. You want to come with me and have lunch after?"

"Hell to the yes."

LAKISHA accompanied her to the employment agency, then waited in a coffee shop. The interview went quickly. Maddy wasn't the only person in line with a recent surgical scar, but they gave her special treatment, taking her into a cubicle and introducing her to one of the job counselors, Mr. Strode. She instantly recognized him as the man whose campaign posters she had liked. Apparently, he was just as likeable in person.

"Say! And you must be Madeline Grant!" he said jovially, giving her a seat. There was a glass bowl of M&M's on his desk; he offered her some. "So glad you could finally make it!"

Maddy said nothing, waiting.

"And what can we do for you today, Maddy? Have you given any thought to what kind of work you might be interested in?"

She slowly shook her head.

"Well, let's just see what we've got . . ."

Mr. Strode opened the lid of a plastic file box and began flipping through a stack of index cards.

Strode . . . Strode—why was that name so familiar to her? Not from the campaign posters but from something earlier in her memory, a tiny fragment of the past that was suddenly rattling around in her skull like a loose nut. Strode—Manfred Strode. Manfred, yes, that was it.

The Nightly News: Manfred Strode, White Supremacist, standing in shackles as the judge read the verdict: Guilty. Guilty of multiple counts of tax evasion, weapons possession, conspiracy to overthrow the government, and the murder of two federal agents.

Manfred Strode had been sentenced to death . . . and executed!

Holy crap, Maddy thought. Strode was dead! Dead and rehabilitated. Damned to Hell and reincarnated as a social worker.

"How 'bout cake decorating?" he said. "We've got a number of decorating jobs, from pastry finishers to window dressers to interior design, all entry-level but with full health coverage and excellent chance for advancement."

"Cake decorating?" Maddy said, jarred from her daze. "Are you kidding?"

"Not at all. Or you could go into the fast-growing field of health care. All kinds of paid internships available, from nursing assistants to neurosurgeons. Accelerated training program for qualified candidates—that's you. You could be working your way toward a college degree. Earn your PhD in as little as three months!"

"I don't think so."

"All right. *Ooh,* here's something: How 'bout the security business? Guards, bodyguards, investigators, force protection? No? From what I understand, you have quite a talent for cloak-and-dagger stuff; this would put you in league with the big boys."

"You're seriously asking me if I want to be a hired thug? A mercenary?"

"No! An *asset.* A chance to serve your country. These are all government contract positions, designated GS-12 or above. Free housing, travel, paid vacations, matching retirement fund. You're eager to travel, right? Well, here's your chance."

"Forget it."

"Retail sales?"

"No."

"Well, then I don't have much to offer except the labor pool."

"Labor pool?"

"It's the on-call labor force—the unskilled workers. All the folks who do whatever needs to be done around town: general construction, painting, digging ditches, and so on. Not something I'd really recommend to someone like yourself."

"Why not? Because I'm a girl?"

"No. Well, yes . . . but it's also a waste of your potential."

"Good. Sign me up."

"Really?"

"Definitely."

"I'm talking manual labor. Outdoors, in all kinds of weather."

"I understand."

"Okay . . . if you're sure . . ."

"I'm sure."

"Well, remember, you can always change your mind. But I can't guarantee these other jobs will still be available."

"That's fine."

"All right, then. All you have to do is call this number every day at 5 a.m. to receive that day's work assignment. Then you just show up and punch your time card."

"I got it. Can I ask you something?"

"Certainly, shoot."

"I thought you won."

"Won . . . ?" The man was drawing a complete blank.

"The election."

"Oh! The election, yes. Yes, I won my seat. Actually, it's my second term."

"Term as what?"

"Mayor. I'm the mayor of Harmony. Among other duties."

"Congratulations. So I guess you have me to thank for that."

"Oh? How so?"

Maddy intended to reply, *I murdered your opponent, jackass*, but Strode's look was so dumb and guileless that she said, "Nothing—never mind."

THIRTY-FOUR

WORK

S HE worked.

There was not much to it. Every morning she called a number and was told where to show up. Usually it was the big parking lot behind the Visitor's Center, where the different crews milled around in the dark and cold until a bus arrived to take them to their various work assignments.

For the first couple of days, Ben was there, too, deprived of his wheels. Maddy felt bad about that, but not bad enough that she could bring herself to talk to him. When he tried talking to her, to ask how she was doing, she replied, *I'm fine*, and turned him off like a light switch. After that, he didn't come over again. Then she stopped seeing him at all—they were assigned different duty shifts. Maddy wondered if he had specifically asked to be changed, just to avoid her.

A couple of days a week she would meet Lakisha for lunch, and they would talk about their respective experiences. Maddy talked the most: This was her first chance to express her fears of being a human lab rat, or to ask one of her fellow rodents how they felt about it. But she didn't learn much.

Lakisha was practically born yesterday. Everything in Harmony was new and exciting to her, a brave new world. What Maddy didn't understand was how she could already be so well versed in the trappings of trend-savvy young womanhood.

"So how did you learn to look and act so normal?" Maddy asked, munching stuffed grape leaves. "You seem so together."

"It's the implant. It lays out the pattern, and I just play connect-the-dots. I can't believe it myself! You say normal, but for me it doesn't feel normal at all—it feels incredibly exotic to fit in with these amazing superbeings that I've looked up to all my life. I feel like somebody handed me the keys to Camelot, and I'm just kind of sitting at the table, taking it all in."

"Wow, that must be . . . interesting. My experience has kinda been the exact opposite." Maddy felt momentarily guilty about her own bitter skepticism.

"I know. I wish you could see it the way I do. Just getting dressed in the morning is so awesome, and *shopping*— forget it. I love clothes! You know I was always into dress-up, because I thought that was part of the secret of being normal. And it totally is! But it's so much better now that I can really comprehend all the little nuances of fashion."

"I guess. You sure that's a good thing?"

"Are you kidding? I love it! I just wish my friend Stephanie could see me now."

"Stephanie?"

"Yeah, in junior high, I used to hang out at the mall all the time with this girl Stephanie. She loved shopping, man."

Maddy blinked, trying to make sense of the coincidence. "You had a friend named Stephanie?"

"Yeah! Why, did you know her?"

"No," Maddy said. "I must be thinking of somebody else."

AS the days went by, Maddy fell into the routines of working, eating, sleeping, bathing, laundry. When she got her first week's pay, it came as a bit of a surprise—she had forgotten about this part of it. Depositing the check, she made her first debt payment, compounded with interest, but also had to leave enough money to live on. After taxes and multifarious other charges, it was not much. At that rate, the debt would never go away . . . which was the whole point. Her coworkers laughed it off: *That's how they get you!*

In her few moments of free time, Maddy downloaded music onto her PDA and stayed in her room at the motel to avoid browsing the stores. There were no televisions or computers anywhere in Harmony. At first she found it extremely odd, until it occurred to her that any kind of commercially sponsored medium was outmoded technology here. Who needed advertising when companies could pitch directly to your brain, all their products singing like a heavenly choir? TV was obsolete!

Eventually, she'd have to shop again, but she tried putting it off as long as possible. It was like being a drug addict, and she knew they were in fact tickling the same parts of her brain as alcohol, nicotine, or heroin. She understood that very well, yet knowing was no defense against the growing sense of sick yearning that hung like a ball and chain from her heart.

To keep her mind off it, she listened to music and obsessively rearranged the contents of her cabinets. There it was: all the stuff she had bought during her binge—nonsensical items like an extension cord and a cordless drill, a rectal thermometer, a neck brace. Some things made obvious sense—the tiny travel kits for sewing and manicuring—but what did she need with ten bottles of toothache remedy?

She also started cleaning fanatically, scrubbing and sterilizing every metal object with antibacterial soap, alcohol, or boiling water, then rolling them all up in plastic bags.

Everything was going along fine until she saw Lakisha with Ben.

It was two weeks after her arrival back in Harmony. Maddy was up on a utility pole fixing a blown transformer that hadn't been grounded properly—typical. There were much better ways to do everything, but nobody on the crew listened when she spoke, so she had stopped bothering. *Morons.* If they wanted stuff to work like crap, so be it.

Glancing down at the park, she saw Ben. He was walking toward the bandstand, hands in his pockets, looking cool as ever with his lazy, confident strides. She had been thinking a lot about Ben lately, wondering if she should seek him out and talk to him. Ask him about Denton . . . and their folks. Chances were, he knew less than she did. But it wouldn't hurt to talk to him.

Ben waved at someone, and suddenly Maddy saw Lakisha running from the bandstand to meet him. They embraced, kissing, then walked away arm in arm. They were obviously in love.

That night, Maddy found a dead raccoon in her bathtub.

THIRTY-FIVE

FISSURE

IT was bedtime. Maddy had just finished brushing her teeth when she glanced over, and there it was. The poor thing looked like roadkill, its fur clotted into black fins, its skull crushed and bloody teeth bared and clenched together in a frozen snarl. Its little fez was flattened as if it had been stomped on.

Maddy caught her breath, then left the bathroom and turned off the light.

Yes, she thought. *Okay. I get it.*

Keeping her mind focused on inconsequential details, Maddy donned her PDA's ear-buds, set its music playlist to start with Mozart's *Requiem*, and turned off all the lights. Then she took the chair and nightstand from the main room and placed them beside the bathtub. She couldn't see the raccoon anymore, couldn't see anything in the total darkness. That was good; it meant the hidden cameras probably couldn't see much either. The difference was that Maddy didn't need her eyes to know exactly where she was. There was already a perfect 3-D model of the room in her head.

Its clarity and interactivity were far greater than the crude stereopticon of human eyesight.

Gathering items from the cabinets, she laid them out beside the tub, then stepped in and closed the shower curtain. Just in case of infrared surveillance.

Taking her clothes off, she hung them on the curtain rod and sat down in the tub. Opening a portable grooming kit, she removed an electric razor and used it to shave the new hair from her scalp, taking extra care around the tender scar tissue. Then she vacuumed herself with a Dust-Buster and cleaned her hands and scalp with alcohol wipes. That stung.

She stripped an extension cord and twisted the copper wiring around a piece of nichrome from the toaster, wrapped it thickly in insulating tape, and plugged it in. Finally, she put on the neck brace, good and rigid, and propped herself up with rolled towels.

Using a razor-sharp matte knife in one hand, she cut into her head—sliced right down to the bone, drawing the blade in a semicircle along the anterior rim of the implant. With her other hand, she squirted the incision with concentrated phenol she had distilled from over-the-counter medication. The pain, bright at first as an electric arc, dimmed to a dull orange throbbing. Blood gushed freely down the back of her head and neck, soaking into the towels, until Maddy clamped the vessels with a staple gun. She also stapled back the crescent flap of scalp she had opened, baring the round, enameled disk of her implant. About the size of a silver dollar, it was flush with the surrounding bone, smoother but just as hard, glued in place with a bonding agent similar to dental cement.

The technology of the thing held no mysteries to her, and she didn't hesitate to crack it open with a power drill. On its reverse side was the RF coil, and underneath that was the Ultra Low Power Bluetooth transceiver, held in place by tiny recessed screws.

Taking a microscrewdriver from an eyeglass repair kit, Maddy fastened it to the drill and pulled the screws, then carefully unpacked the shielded RF module and GPS unit. There was enough play in the wires to allow access to the signal processor beneath, and Maddy located the data port. Everything was hugely magnified, a holographic image extrapolated from materials she had read at Braintree.

It did not escape her notice that she was below the level of her skull, tinkering in a cavity that penetrated an inch or more into her brain—the part known as the fissure of Rolando. She didn't dwell on it.

Crudely unhousing the guts of her PDA, she cannibalized it for parts, using the red-hot insulated needle as a soldering gun to install a two-way serial-port connection in her head, brazing an entirely new circuit path out of mercury amalgam (from the rectal thermometer). This enabled her to do something the Braintree doctors never intended: communicate with the system.

Her microprocessor was now a two-way street.

It was a very strange sensation. She could feel structures forming in her head, see and hear and touch them, clear as objects floating in space. Crystalline trees sprouted in the darkness, branching and growing into vast, intricate forests that merged in all directions to cover the void with fractal wilderness.

But the forest was off-limits—something was blocking the view, and when Maddy tried to move forward, she couldn't. Of course: The spreading filaments had become a mesh, and the mesh had tightened to become a fence. NO TRESPASSING. It was a block cipher—a wall of numerical gibberish that had to be unscrambled with an entry PIN. A sphinx.

Fine, be that way, she thought.

The PIN number was based on a custom algorithm, designated E22—an encryption mechanism she had encountered before. To crack it, Maddy reentered the loading protocol, opening an emulated serial-port connection to establish a multiplexer control channel and a peer RFCOMM entity using L2CAP service primitives. To start the RFCOMM device, she sent an SABM command on DLC10 and awaited a UA response from the peer entity. When the response came, she was able to passively eavesdrop on the pairing process and spoof the code.

Nothing to it.

As the gate fell, Maddy fell with it—a distinct sensation of tripping forward, Alice tumbling down the rabbit hole. Not just any rabbit hole—these were AutoCAD diagrams of the tunnel leading from Braintree to Harmony, and Maddy was not so much moving through it as it was feeding past her, a great volume of information assembling itself as fast as it could load the data . . . which (with her sluggish, improvised connection) was really not that fast.

But she was in the machine.

THIRTY-SIX

ASTROTURF

THE whole layout of the place was visible to her as a three-dimensional model, a CGI transcape comprised of live video feeds and digital renderings, incorporating every technical detail of its construction.

At the same time, there was a ghostly overlying design that seemed oddly to mirror the Braintree architecture, and it took Maddy a moment to grasp that she was not only traveling through the back corridors of the medical-industrial complex but through the inner reaches of her own neural implant. She was a fly inside her own head, zooming down the bundle of ultrafine wires that led from the 2.4835 GHz signal processor to the very core of her brain. The wires looked as massive as cables on a suspension bridge.

Down, down, as though descending into a mine shaft, Maddy penetrated her own cerebrum, diving through folds of white matter as thick as the mantle of the Earth, then entering the thinner corpus callosum, the choroid plexus, the thalamus. She emerged in the lateral ventricles

as though entering a vast cave system—four caverns like
subterranean finger lakes full of cerebrospinal fluid . . . in
which she could see something that shouldn't have been
there.

What the hell . . . ?

Rather than just stopping at the terminal ends of the
electrodes, the wires forked to join a pair of large, podlike
objects. They looked huge to her, ominous as docked zep-
pelins. Machines, but not made of metal. *Living* machines:
fat, neuron-rich sausages webbed in pulsing blood vessels, bristling with nerve fibers. Twin lobes of the alien
intelligence that had taken up residence in her skull. Per-
manent as ships in a bottle.

Maddy could see the whole process: how these things
had been *grown* here, cultured like a pair of giant, mis-
shapen pearls, intelligent tumors that gave her the ice-cold
reasoning power to do all the terrible things she had done
in the name of survival. Even to do what she was doing at
that moment.

And Maddy could see the point of it all, the master plan
behind it, which was not, after all, simply to enslave humanity but to save it. To enforce obedience, yes, but only
so that the goals of an ideal society could be realized. People were idiots, that was the general theme, which scads of
scientific research proved beyond a doubt. The data was all
at her fingertips, going way back to Plato's *Republic*: If
granted complete freedom—true democracy—human beings would invariably screw it up.

So a few big brains dedicated themselves to a solution.

They quickly discovered that they weren't the only
ones: There was a whole network of scientists at work on
the same problem, and a lot of research money for anyone
with a promising hypothesis. A private research foundation was paying big bucks for insights into the perfection
of mankind. Hence it was under the shady auspices of

the Mogul Cooperative that Alan Plummer and Chandra Stevens founded their company: Braintree, Inc.

Look, Alan had said in a taped lecture dated November 13, 2002, *all you have to do is look at all of history to know the human race will never overcome its basically selfish, brutal tendencies. Every organization, every religion, every civilization from the beginning of time to the present has been built on the notion of getting people to live together in harmony . . . and every one, no matter how oppressively or progressively it imposed its laws, has failed. Failed miserably. Education is no good—even lessons learned through painful experience are unlearned by the next generation. Look at Vietnam and Iraq. There's a willfulness to the forgetting, a fundamental inclination to repeat past mistakes, to ignore established facts, to deny cause and effect. Clearly, something new has to be done to break the cycle once and for all, to move the species forward. Because unless something is done soon, our civilization will fall. It's statistically inevitable. And even if* Homo sapiens *don't go completely extinct, all our higher virtues—the hard-won advances in medicine and technology, in knowledge of the universe, in music and literature and art—will be swept away. Vanish as though they never existed.*

Avoiding this future required a new way of thinking. Tricky choices were coming, dangerous waters that would require clear judgment to navigate, bold decisions unclouded by religious hysteria or unreasonable opposition. The Singularity was coming.

Godhood was coming.

Not to everyone—that was neither feasible nor desirable—but to an educated elite, a privileged few. The Moguls.

Maddy saw this word, this acronym, MOGUL, cropping up again and again, and finally traced it to its source:

Miska Orthotics and Gerontology Underwriters Laboratories. That was the source of it all, the silent partner of dozens of private research foundations around the world, a vast blanket entity of which Braintree, Inc., was only one thread.

So that was it. Technological breakthroughs had been made that enabled people to replace almost any body part with an excellent prosthetic substitute: legs that could walk, hands that could touch, eyes that could see, ears that could hear, flesh and organs with not only the suppleness and sensitivity of living tissue, but which could perform their functions every bit as well as the originals, if not better, and which could be replaced as needed. Throwaway hearts, disposable bodies . . . all for a price.

And the ultimate replacement: the *self*.

From what Maddy could determine, scanning volumes of classified material, the process was modular—an incremental replacement of knowledge, swapping blocks of damaged, decaying, or dead organic neurons with artificial ones. In that way, acres of messy old synaptic pathways could be plowed under to make way for a neat, orderly crop of sweet American corn.

With proper conditioning, the brain adapted to the changes, planting over the rough spots, cleaning up corrupted data, until eventually the person's whole mind was converted to the new medium—a more durable and easily replaceable medium than the soft tissue of the human brain. Astroturf. One-Use-Only was now Multiple-Use . . . or even Infinite-Use. Maddy could hardly believe it, but the scientific data didn't lie.

If the human mind could be transplanted, that meant a person could theoretically live *forever*.

There had been no gas leak in the fun house. What had happened to Maddy and Ben was grand theft. They had been deliberately set up, stripped down, their minds stolen and rebuilt as part of some crazy immortality experiment.

The problem was, not everyone was meant to live forever. Immortality was to be a perk of membership in a very select club. The rest of humanity would get the consolation prize: a coach-class ticket to Lemmington. That was the no-frills operation, the basic cable, which was already cranking out dozens of happy customers a day.

So that's what they've done to us, Maddy thought.

Even with her new brainpower, she had never understood how they were able to recover her memories. All the auxiliary computing power in the world couldn't magically rewrite the complex web of synapses that had been destroyed in the accident. At best she should have been a blank slate, starting over from the beginning. Instead, she was a fully formed person, as if somehow they had been keeping her soul on ice and just had to thaw it out. System Restore. Which was exactly what they must have done.

But how?

Maddy went looking. She could see the whole layout of the mine: how they had automated it like a regular assembly line, with robots and revolving operating tables like spokes in a wheel, each turn a stage in the implant procedure, until at the end patients were whisked away to Recovery/Post-Op, where their brand spanking new brains were saturated day and night with canned experiences, captured memories enhanced with pharmaceutical neurotransmitters and positive reinforcement. Then off to Harmony for a little street conditioning . . . before being released into the real world.

Oh yes, there were many thousands of them already out there. American society had been thoroughly infiltrated, right up to the White House. Not the president himself— not yet. That was perhaps for the next election, or the one after that. But they were among his advisers. And it wasn't just the goons from Braintree, but all the corporate offshoots and international subsidiaries and government affiliates—all the grim, bloated piglets suckling off the monstrous brood sow known as the Mogul Cooperative. Its bastards were everywhere, up to the highest levels of government.

Looking at Braintree's list of political connections, Maddy gasped to see a familiar face: Vellon. The man she'd dreamed of killing in the limo. She had done her best to forget that night, burying it in a dark corner of her mind, never quite sure if it had really happened. But there he was, his pointed head on a flock of obituaries. Only his name was not really Vellon.

It was Joseph Lawlor—*Congressman* Lawlor.

Maddy suddenly realized that she remembered Lawlor from one of her earliest dreams, postop, when she was still a basket case touring Braintree in the company of her folks. There was a big shot congressman from Washington there, and Dr. Plummer had been giving them all a tour. No wonder Vellon looked familiar.

From deleted e-mails, Maddy learned that Lawlor was invited to Braintree in the hope that he would petition Congress to approve an increase in Braintree's funding. But the congressman had his own ideas. He was a disturbed man who saw possibilities in Harmony far beyond anything the doctors ever intended, and he demanded they put him in charge of the project . . . or he would open an investigation to expose it. Lawlor wanted Harmony to be his own personal toy box. Dr. Plummer refused, but Dr. Stevens recommended they play along; she was a fan of hardball. So Lawlor became Dean Vellon, and a fake election was held between two fictitious candidates: Vellon and Strode.

Lawlor was confident of victory. That was the beauty

of Harmony: Nothing was left to chance. But he made the mistake of celebrating prematurely. He requested a companion for the evening.

So they sent Maddy.

Like a windup toy, like a perfect little robot, she fulfilled her function. But the pressure of killing must have been too much, causing her psyche to crack like an egg. It sheared apart, hatching a furry little avatar of destruction—her own remorseless id in the form of a raccoon named Moses.

But no more, she thought. *You jerks haven't got me yet. I'm still human—human enough to jack you up.*

Entering a file called Madzog 227, Maddy found herself at the center of a thousand-faceted jewel—a vast crystal ball comprised of smaller crystals—whose every mirrored face was a door that opened on command, expanding to reveal a playlet from her own childhood, some familiar scene or sensory impression. *Extremely* familiar.

What the frick? she thought, scanning furiously.

Every scene was a flashback—these were bottled memories of every significant or not-so-significant moment in her life, digital collages assembled from snippets of 3-D high-def video, reconstructions and reenactments and lifelike CGI. These were *her memories*, a pirated Greatest Hits collection of her entire past. It was as if a thief had been in her mind, illegally downloading the stuff that made her her.

So this was the source from which Maddy flowed, the headwaters of her mind, comprising everything she had ever seen, heard, tasted, smelled, or felt, from age three to age fifteen. All converted to code and readily downloadable into any neuroconductive holographic quantum matrix. Such as her implant.

The question was, how did they get the stuff?

Following branching links like a snake seeking eggs,

Maddy plumbed other dossiers, discovering her parents, all her friends and family, with each of their personal histories compiled in a similar fashion. Their bottled lives dangled in cyberspace like so many ornaments on a plastic Christmas tree, while Maddy herself was the star at the top.

They all existed just to support her delusion. As oddly flattering as it was, she couldn't help but wonder, *Why am I so important?*

There was a radial structure to this tree. Its trunk was the time line of her personal history, and every event in her life was a branch, so that as she followed the central axis downward, she was proceeding backward in time.

She followed the chain of recorded events from the present day back to the night of the carnival accident— back to the fun house. She'd always wondered what exactly had happened that day, and at last the pieces of the puzzle were hers to assemble:

She and Ben, kissing in the dark. The hitch in the ride. Ben leaving her alone. Maddy getting off the car and making her way toward the exit. Groping toward the next car, and the hooded figure seated there. And then . . .

And then the file ended. There were no records beyond that point, and her personal memories were no help, just the monotonous dreams and impressions left over from her long convalescence.

So what happened? They had saved her life, yes, she could see that, and there were the implant procedure logs—hers only one of many thousands, including Ben's. But Maddy's operation was clearly different in its particulars, a custom job that included a number of steps she wouldn't have thought necessary, such as orthodontic surgery, a nose job (to make her nose *larger*!), breast alteration, and other, more obscure cosmetic changes.

Something was obviously very weird. The data was confusing:

On the night of the fun-house accident, Maddy's memories inexplicably converged with a second time line, both cut short by the brain injury. *Whose life was that?* The ghost time line forked off into darkness, protected by its own password. What was disturbing was that it was an earlier file, to which Maddy's history had been surgically appended like an extra limb.

But this was the only life she knew—the childhood world of Madeline Zoe Grant, with all her minor neuroses and her parents and their Ozzie-and-Harriet-from-Hell lifestyle. The recent news that her parents were imposters and she was adopted didn't make her existence any less real.

Yet it was not real.

The life she remembered was the downloaded one, the superfluous one, the overwrite. The shell. The older, hidden time line was clearly the real history, her true story, which had been pruned from her brain like so much deadwood to make way for a nice clean graft.

Is that all I am—a graft, a transplant? The more she looked, the more apparent it became. She could see it all in the arrangement of her memories. The timing of them, the selection, the emphasis—it was all a clunky, overly cute montage. Her life had been *edited.*

I'm not me.

An orphan girl had been adopted by Braintree scientists, then used as a template, a sacrificial cow plundered for her "typical" life experiences, which were then coded, digitally embellished, and finally written over the fried neurons of an entirely different person. Since the original Maddy might likely collide with her doppelganger, they couldn't coexist in the same world. Hence there had to be an artificial world to accommodate the artificial people.

Harmony.

I'm a copy, she thought wildly. *A counterfeit.* Were

they *all* counterfeits, all her friends and family? An entire population of bootleg copies? No—most were just mind-controlled, not mind-Xeroxed. Maddy was one of a select few, a trial run. But where was the genuine Maddy, the source of her memories? Where was her Content Provider now? Obviously not in Denton, or she would have encountered herself. There was no record of any other Madeline Zoe Grant, living or dead.

Had they killed her?

It would help if she knew who she really was. Who had this body belonged to before being possessed by Madeline's decanted spirit? It was tempting to believe that maybe they had simply tampered with her mind and reloaded it back into her own body. At least that would mean she was still at least partially herself.

There was only one way to find out. Clearly, there was an alternate Maddy Grant in the computer, an alien one she was forbidden to know. The information was buried underground, hidden beneath a layer of redundant encryptions like the severed taproot of her Christmas tree.

Maddy made a virtual shovel and began digging. In a moment, the ground gave way, revealing a whole other tree beneath—an inverted tree and an entirely new file, this one labeled MARET 99. Maddy opened it up and gasped.

It was Marina Sweet.

THIRTY-SEVEN

PEP

OH shit, she thought. *I'm her! I am Marina!*

Marina Sweet was not dead. The golden girl designed to earn the love of millions and fleece them like sheep was alive and kicking in the persona of her biggest fan: Maddy Grant.

Marina Sweet. The little girl manipulated by her daddy and his corporate overseers to nurture and grow her own legend until it was big enough to sell the ultimate self-help program, the final bandwagon from which no voice of dissent would ever again trouble the dreams of the mighty: *No pep? Want pep? Marina Sweet says, "Get PEP!"*

Maddy wormed out the roughs for the ad campaign:

Feeling overwhelmed? Depressed? Mentally exhausted? Tired of mood-altering drugs and expensive therapies? PEP's exclusive, ASR-based technology gives you the power to cope with the ever-increasing demands of modern life. Guaranteed safe and effective, our patented Autonomous Self-Replicators deliver the power of PEP at a price you can afford. PEP—Personal Enhancement Prosthetics for a

*better you. PEP and PEP PLUS Accessorized Neural Ar-
chitecture are trademarks of Braintree, Inc. PEP—For The
Life You Deserve.*

And Marina was to have been chief spokesmodel. Her
career trajectory was mapped out with the mathematical
precision of a mission to Mars: pop princess to sitcom star
to glamour girl to Big-Time Movie Actress to Media
Saint. And right when she was at her peak, beloved by
billions around the world, she would become the face of
PEP. Who wouldn't trust America's Sweetheart? Anything
with her face on it sold millions. Hearts and minds, hearts
and minds. Don't worry about the hardened cynics; aim
for the sweet spot, the big soft middle. Sell the sizzle not
the steak.

The girl had been their grandest experiment: an artificial icon, a perfect pop star, a pretty human puppet made
to sell strings.

But Marina went bust. The merry-go-round broke down.

Marina had awakened. Over the years of stupid pet
tricks, she had somehow come to her senses and rebelled
against being the clone they wanted—the Hannah Montana Candidate.

Maddy could see it all: how the starlet had spiraled into
depression, dabbled with drugs and dangerous diets, and
even tried to kill herself. But they caught her, cooled her
down, wired her up again for another try. Marina's implant was too valuable to destroy—they had invested too
much time, money, and technology just to kill her. Better
to kill her memories. Starve her brain of oxygen until it
got soft, then snip off the troublesome bits. Lather, rinse,
repeat, until total amnesia was induced. Then fill the void
with . . . someone new.

There were arguments made against this; not all the
scientists were on the same page. Few on staff objected
to adult terrorists and criminals being purged and rere-

corded, but many had ethical misgivings about doing it to minors. There was a big fight over it—Maddy recovered tons of heated, deleted correspondence.

The justification offered by Mogul Corporate was that this was the purpose of their existence, doctors and patients alike. Unlike the adult subjects, the minors all arrived at Braintree either severely brain-damaged or legally deceased. Their personalities were *already* secondhand. That was cold comfort to the aggrieved doctors, particularly those who had signed on as adoptive parents of their test subjects—a necessary means to acquiring the orphans in the first place.

Over the years of intensive monitoring, Marina's adoptive father, "David Sweet," (actually Dr. Neil Breitling) had grown very attached to his troubled "daughter," and objected to her personality being erased. He was not just a drone Placeholder, programmed with recycled feelings, but an aging, divorced scientist with heavy alimony payments. Placeholders were useful under optimal conditions such as existed in Harmony, but for a high-profile implantee like Marina, operating in the real world, it was necessary she be accompanied at all times by her actual sponsor. For Dr. Breitling, the emotional pressure of this task had already cost him his marriage and children. And the company wanted to rob him of the only thing he had left: Marina.

Likewise, Maddy's dad, "Roger Grant" (actually Dr. Bernard Fenster), truly cared for her, and when he found out that her pure and painstakingly catalogued life experiences were needed to replace Marina Sweet's corrupt ones, he was appalled. Not only because he didn't want Maddy's innocent mind to be put in the dysfunctional brain of an overindulged and self-mutilating pop princess, but because Maddy—his Maddy, the *real* Maddy—would then have to be wiped and replaced.

Objections were raised, which set off a series of corporate crackdowns and even government intervention. There were resignations, terminations, quashed leaks to media. Behavior-modification programs became compulsory, and national security was invoked to justify the creation of a special squad tasked with putting out media fires before they could spread—the dreaded Firemen.

The people chosen to be Firemen were some of the earliest Braintree subjects, dregs of the criminally insane who had initially been cured by their implants but later developed strange tics as a result of their long interface with the Leech-Tron. They were frightening characters though utterly docile unless commanded otherwise by Dr. Stevens.

From the scanty available records, Maddy suspected it was these Firemen who caused the mysterious disappearance of Dr. Vanessa Hunt—Ben Blevin's crusading mother—and drove Dr. Fenster to take his own life . . . which Braintree restored to him, along with the behavioral chip that enabled him to resume the role of Maddy's daddy.

Such events prompted the divorce-and-remarriage scenario, an attempt to salvage at least one "average household" from the mess. Maddy's mother could be paired with Ben's father. Not an ideal solution, but the rationale was that divorce was typical enough to not constitute a fatal breach in the family dynamic. Marina/Maddy could still fall within normal, healthy parameters. The superstar scenario would have to be scrapped, of course, but in some ways Marina might be even more useful as a plain Jane. As Maddy Grant, she would be nobody; she would be invisible—the ultimate spook.

But before they could erase Marina's scratched master reel and dub Maddy over it, a boy had come—a boy Marina had secretly been communicating with for some time.

The boy was one of the roadies for her show, a high-school dropout and former carnival mechanic named Duane Devlin. Marina and Duane had raided Dr. Breitling's personal computer and learned the whole story. There was a police report filled with Duane's frantic testimony, which went utterly ignored. After failing to interest the media, then nearly being arrested by local law enforcement, Duane had come up with a plan for getting them both to Canada.

At Marina's next gig—a traveling carnival in Denton, Colorado—she was to leave the show early, ditch her people and the paparazzi, and meet Dev at the fun house. Once inside, the two of them would be met by some friends of his, who would hide them in the caravan until they could be smuggled over the Canadian border.

But it all went wrong. Someone had spilled the beans, let the cat out of the bag—however one cared to put it, royally fucked them over. The fun house became a trap. A chamber of horrors, as the news would say.

They were inside, waiting. The Firemen.

A boy and a girl went in, a boy and a girl came out . . . just not the same boy and girl.

Dr. Neil Breitling, Marina's father, who had fought this, failed, and ultimately fled, took with him the only two people he could still manage to help: Madeline Grant and Ben Blevin. They were both under anesthesia, being transported to Braintree for removal of their inconvenient identities. Breitling used his credentials to have them put aboard his private helicopter. All three died in the suspicious crash.

So Madeline Grant was dead.

And Marina Sweet, the faded legend, whose life Maddy would once have given anything to live, was literally her own flesh and blood. The Grants were a nuclear family again. Last but not least, Marina and Dev were Maddy and Ben, trapped in this magical, mystical Valley of the Dolls, forever and ever, amen.

Fuck that.

Maddy wanted to barf. She wanted to scream or cry or do *something*, but she couldn't because she had no body. She was the machine, and the machine was her.

Burrowing into the mainframe, the thousands of critical program files, she started wiping stuff, scrambling codes, breaking connections right and left as though hacking jungle vines with a machete, opening a clearing so she could see the sky.

For a second she could feel the sunlight . . . then it was blotted out, as though by an eclipse.

Something was coming.

Something big, snuffling through the undergrowth for her. A shapeless hulk with a thousand seeking tentacles. *Leech-Tron,* she thought.

Maddy had given herself away, set off some kind of system crash warning, and so it was hunting her, this monstrous artificial intelligence. It was on her trail, tracing the source of the breach. And it was fast, faster and smarter than her—Cthulhu, version 10.0. She was hardwired in; if it found her, it could hack right into her exposed brain.

Ducking low, Maddy fled through the brambles like Brer Rabbit, hiding deep in obscure programs as if they were hollow logs, covering her tracks, camouflaging herself and setting diversionary fires.

It was no use. The thing was onto her, boxing her in and smoking her out, channeling her into narrower and narrower runs until she had no place left to go, forcing her to face her demon. Then: There it was, rearing up all around her. She was cornered!

In the nanosecond before the monster took her, a small entity darted between them, leaping into the billowing face of her adversary. Maddy only caught a glimpse of its bushy, striped tail as it disappeared into the gullet's whirling black teeth . . . but she did hear the last words of that familiar, high-pitched voice.

"Eat me!"

Then Moses was gone. Maddy stood alone as the beast's rough claws ripped through her last defenses, groping through the pirated firewalls that formed a multi-layered-shell around her soft, helpless mind. She wanted to scream, to run, but it was just like in a nightmare—she couldn't get away.

It swallowed her whole.

THIRTY-EIGHT

GOOD-BYE,
YELLOW BRICK ROAD

MADDY floated, blissfully innocent as a fetus in its
mother's womb.

A hard, white, ceramic womb—a motel bathtub. There
was a loud commotion outside the shower curtain, a very
bright light, and Maddy squirmed, frowning. Her head
was killing her.

"Go *way*," she moaned. "I'm sleepin'."

The curtain was ripped aside, and behind the glare,
someone said, "Oh my God."

Another voice, the familiar one of Dr. Plummer, said,
"Christ, what a mess. Let's close her up and get her stabilized
so we can transport her. I'd say this kid's had enough play-
time for today."

There was a sharp prick, just where it hurt the most, and
immediately the knives of pain began to dull.

They didn't mess with the inner damage to her implant—
they weren't equipped; that would take specialized microsurgery at a later date. Dr. Stevens would want to assist. All
they could do for the time being was reset the skull plate as

best they could, pull the staples, and suture the wound shut. Give the flesh a chance to relax.

Wheeling her out, someone said, "You gotta admit, this is pretty amazing. I mean, look at this. When's the last time you saw someone do microsurgery on themselves? With household utensils? In the *dark*?"

Dr. Plummer grumbled, "Yeah, she's a bloody prodigy."

"What are you pissed off about? This is everything we've been working for. You and Dr. Stevens especially."

"I don't know . . ."

Leaving the motel, Maddy felt the sun on her face. She could see that a small crowd had gathered on the sidewalk. A number of people familiar to her were there, watching solemnly.

There was Ben, poor Ben, standing guiltily with Lakisha, and beside them her best friend, Stephanie. There was Locust with the other bikers, and Donna with her two kids. Even the carnies from the fun house. Nothing surprised her now, not even the sight of her parents, Beth and Roger, anxiously holding each other as if they still really thought they were her mom and dad. Cogs—all cogs. Not real.

"Thanks, Doc," Maddy said, her voice cracked.

"For what?"

"For making me the girl I am today."

"Well, Miss Grant, you may not appreciate any of this right now, and I don't blame you, but by tomorrow, you'll have a whole new perspective."

"Off the top of my head, I'd probably agree with you."

Dr. Plummer laughed sympathetically. "I know you're upset with us, but you must admit the experience has been interesting."

"Well, that makes it all worth it, then."

"You can't be expected to understand the value of everything we've accomplished, or your part in it. It will all make sense, I promise."

"Oh, it makes sense. You needed a stick to shake the tree. A troubleshooter smart enough to probe the system for weak spots—it couldn't be one of these slaphappy local yokels. Moronic contentment isn't very conducive to sabotage. You needed a wolf in sheep's clothing, a sincere gremlin to prove there's no problem you can't handle. I'm your little monkey wrench. Did I perform to your satisfaction?"

Dr. Plummer started to speak, paused, then gave up, and said, "You did great."

"Just call me Humpty Dumpty. Hey, tell me something."

"You should try to relax now."

"Why do people keep telling me that? I'm very relaxed. I just want to know what happened to all your high ideals. When did you change your mind about saving humanity's higher virtues? Was it always your idea that the glorious future of mankind should be a paid presentation?"

"Sometimes, to achieve great things, it is necessary to make temporary compromises. That's par for the course in doing research on this scale; corporate funding is paramount. The project would not have been possible otherwise."

"Maybe that's a hint you shouldn't do it."

"You only think that because we are in a period of transition. These are birth pangs of a new age. Money and power will become increasingly meaningless as the equalizing force of technology begins to break down the archaic systems of commerce and class. With a little time, these problems will go away."

"Finally," Maddy said.

"What?"

"Something we can agree on."

As they loaded her in the van, there was a disturbance. A couple of blocks away, angry voices were shouting, and there was a sound of breaking glass. Alarms started going off.

The doctors looked around, and Dr. Plummer said, "What the hell's that all about?"

"Looks like a fight," someone said.

"A fight? What are you talking about?"

"A fight—look!"

There was a fight. A major street brawl, by the look of it. People were spilling out of doorways and throwing furniture out the windows. The trouble was spreading like wildfire, everyone in sight grabbing sticks and throwing stones. Smoke was coming out of the buildings.

When a brick came through the windshield of the van, Dr. Plummer said, "Get us out of here, Vick. Now."

But it was already too late. Even as he spoke, people were surrounding the front of the vehicle. They dragged the driver out and bludgeoned him to the ground with clubs. Maddy's parents were in on it, seeming to have forgotten all about her. The surgeons—the terrifying, enhanced "residents"—went down without a fight.

"Get up! What's the matter with you?" screamed Dr. Plummer to his useless assistants, as greedy hands clawed at his white smock. Even his own people were turning on him. "Do something! Help me!" But there was no one to ask for help anymore, and in a moment his struggling body disappeared in the frenzied mob.

Lying in the van on her gurney, unprotected, ignored, Maddy had to smile. *All the king's horses and all the kings men . . .*

Someone climbed in beside her. It was Ben.

"Are you okay?" he asked breathlessly.

"I'm great. You?" She was a little surprised to see him.

"I don't know," he said. "Something's weird—what happened?"

"Looks like the Sims are in revolt."

"Huh?"

"Did you know Bluetooth is named after a tenth-century king?"

"What are you talking about?"

"King Harald Bluetooth. He united the warring tribes of Norway and Denmark. I just killed the king."

"Maddy, I don't—"

"Oh for God's sake. I planted a time-delayed Trojan, a tapeworm in the belly of the beast. Denial of Service. All the lines are down."

"What does that mean?"

"It means no more *Mayberry RFD*—you better get us out of here, Slick."

"What about your folks?"

"They're not my folks."

Uncomprehending, Ben nodded and got behind the wheel. "Where?" he asked.

"Anywhere. Just go."

The crowd around the van had partially dispersed to spread havoc elsewhere, so Ben was able to nudge forward. Rioters pounded the side panels, running alongside.

Gaining speed, Ben muttered, "This is outta control."

The whole village was on fire, people running from house to house with flaming torches, screaming *"Allahu Akbar!"* and *"Kill the mothers!"* A firestorm of unleashed aggression, unfrozen zeal, burning down everything in its path.

"Why are they doing this?" Ben asked.

"Just making up for lost time," Maddy replied.

As the van swerved onto the highway, there was a bright flash in the rearview mirrors, followed by an ear-splitting shock wave.

"Damn!" Ben said, almost going off the side of the road.

"That's what I was afraid of," Maddy said.

It was an explosion in the center of downtown—the old mine complex. Where the buildings had stood was a gigantic fireball, rising like a mushroom cloud and raining burning debris on the surrounding rooftops. Even half a mile away, the van was pelted with bits of brick.

"Go faster," Maddy advised.

There followed a whole series of explosions, a regular bombardment, working outward from the town center to encompass every building in the valley. As the destruction progressed, it penetrated the outlying coal seams, triggering vast sinkholes beneath the airstrip and country club, swallowing the golf green. In a moment, there was no sign left of human habitation, no evidence of any crime—only a roiling, pitted wasteland. A man-made natural disaster.

"Good-bye, yellow brick road," Maddy said, as they drove out the deserted gate.

THIRTY-NINE

OF RATS AND MEN

CHANDRA Stevens sat alone in the break room, vacantly sipping from a cup of instant cocoa. The cocoa had gone cold, but the action of raising it to her lips was purely mechanical; she didn't even know she was doing it. She hadn't been able to taste anything since that Grant girl stuck her fingers up her nose.

The room was a tiny windowless nook deep in the building, just a few plastic chairs, a small table, and a bank of noisy vending machines—a buzzing fluorescent cave that most Braintree personnel sensibly eschewed unless the weather was really intolerable. For Chandra's present purposes, that made it ideal: She was much too easy to find in her office.

What a waste, she thought.

That mantra that had been running in her head for the past hour, until the words had lost all meaning. *What a waste, what a waste. What a waste, what a waste, what a waste . . .* Words like so many sandbags on a levee, holding back the horrific knowledge of what had just happened in the valley below.

At least the bombing was over; the walls had stopped vibrating. That was good—for a while she had been on the verge of losing it. No—she *had* lost it . . . just for a few minutes, when the thunder started and the lights flickered and the full meaning of the innocuous-sounding word *fail-safe* hit her like a punch in the stomach, sending her reeling for someplace private, where she could fall on the floor and give in to temporary insanity. Thank goodness no one had come in before she was able to pull herself back together.

She was finally doing better. She would make it through this. She would do it for Alan, because that's what he would have wanted.

It was hard to believe he was gone. Her Alan was dead. And it wasn't like the stroke, when she thought she had lost him only to have him restored by the miracle of their own research—the ultimate validation of everything they had accomplished together. All the years of struggle and sacrifice, of putting their scientific careers before anything else, including each other. Everything taking a backseat to the Greater Good—his inarguable rationale for any concerns either one of them might have had.

It had been hard work, so insanely busy they rarely saw each other, but through all the years of late nights, endless experiments, and eternal staff meetings, there had always been that promise: *Someday, Chandra. Someday we'll be finished with all this, and it'll be our turn, just you and me.*

Only now there would be no more promises. No more dreams of cottages by the shore and kitchen gardens and golden years. After the fiasco with Maddy Grant, she would never again adopt a child. No June wedding, no wedding dress, no honeymoon. Face it, she would never be married. No Mrs. Alan Plummer—she was to be Dr. Chandra Stevens, maiden scientist, now and forever.

"DR. STEVENS, YOU HAVE A CALL ON LINE ONE."

Damn. The loudspeaker, so ridiculously loud it made her jump.

She turned her phone back on. The saved-message icon flashed in rebuke—she wasn't supposed to be out of touch like that. She would have loved to smash it.

There was another call coming in. "Yes?" she said. "This is Dr. Stevens."

"Dr. Stevens, the Advisory Committee is on conference call in M2. I've been trying to reach you. All the department heads are already down there."

"I'm sorry, my phone's acting up—probably from that power surge."

"Well, they're waiting for you. Can I tell them you're coming?"

"Yes, yes, certainly. Tell them I'm on my way."

Boy, those lawyers weren't wasting any time. The rubble had barely settled, and there they were to give it a spin. Not that she was surprised—in any corporation, the first and foremost part of damage control was managing perception. Lawyers, lobbyists, and PR firms were the filters through which the murky flow of potentially incriminating facts had to be strained. Purified. Perhaps discarded altogether, so that a clean-smelling and altogether-more-plausible fiction could be substituted. She had been through it before, during the Marina situation.

Taking the elevator to the lower levels, Chandra walked through the computer lab and along a dim catwalk skirting the rat city. She wasn't crazy about rats and had never been fond of the construction. Alan had loved it—it had been his baby. She could still hear him giving the VIP tour in that rapt voice, which he called his "planetarium spiel."

With its incredible complexity, this system may seem very fragile. It's all well and good to be able to maintain efficiency under artificially imposed ideal conditions, but that's not natural, is it? So what happens when we introduce disorder? Society is an organism, a living body, and its response to disorder must be similar to the body's response to infection—it must create antibodies. Observe:

Here we see a rat that is being redirected to deliberately subvert the parameters of the system. Let's call him Bob. Now of course we could simply introduce an outside rat, a wild rat, but its behavior would be so random and clumsily disruptive that it would not effectively show the system's subtlety. For demonstration purposes, an intelligent attack is more useful. Bob must be crafty.

As you can see, our spy infiltrates the system by carefully avoiding notice. He stays out of the way, doesn't block the supply lines, and only when the coast is clear does he seize his opportunity—there! What you're seeing is him gnawing through the plastic tube that delivers water to the feeders. Very smart: In that way, he can drink undetected as well as destabilize the whole ecology. Oops—they've seen him. Once one gives chase, they all do. There they go! Doesn't usually take long. As you can see, they're cutting him off, methodically blocking every means of egress. Meanwhile, others are sealing the leak with putty. Remarkable, isn't it? Uh-oh—that's it—they've got him, got him cornered . . . aaaand, he's nailed. Sorry, Bob—here's where it gets a little ugly. It's still a matter of speculation why they've started drinking the blood like that; it's a recent behavior that's obviously not part of the program. Our goal is actually to have them take prisoners alive, simply because it requires a higher degree of sophistication, but this abnormal savagery seems to be a long-term side effect of the motor control. Stress, maybe, or perhaps by inhibiting their will, we are inadvertently exposing a deeper level of rodent psychology. We'll figure it out!

Seeking more challenging disruptions, we've introduced various crises for them to deal with, including predatory animals such as feral cats, barn owls, several species of large snakes, and even a very-bad-tempered monitor lizard, all of which they dispatched within minutes of the intrusion. The last test involved an adult male chimpanzee that had been specifically conditioned to kill rats with a hammer, having been rewarded for doing so. He lasted the longest, but in the end was overwhelmed, with the rats pursuing him right up to the top of the tallest building there, where he refused to move . . . until the rats finally dislodged him by launching a squadron of tiny biplanes and shooting him down. I'm kidding! No, they chewed away the building's foundation until it collapsed. Then they ate him alive.

As Chandra walked beside the darkened pit, it suddenly struck her how *quiet* it was in there. That was odd—she couldn't remember the last time the amphitheater wasn't busy with the rustling and skittering of rodents. Furthermore, she couldn't see any movement in the papier-mâché metropolis, not one rat. It made no sense, since she knew for a fact that the rats worked and slept in shifts, so that half of them were supposed to be awake at any given time, even during their artificial night phase. Unless they had had to be removed because of the signal interruption . . . perhaps just as a precaution. But even so, moving the rats was a big deal that required special authorization—usually from Alan.

Ah, that was the problem. No Alan.

For that matter, where was everyone? Having been

well shielded from the previous day's electromagnetic attack, the basement computer vaults should have been the quickest to return to normal, but there was nobody at the workstations; all the lab techs seemed to be out taking a smoke break. Smoke break—that's a good one: No doubt they were all staring out the upstairs windows at the huge smoke plume rising from the valley. Whispering about the end of Harmony.

That's right, that's right, it's gone, she thought irritably. *All that work down the drain. So let's just curl up and die, why don't we? That won't be suspicious at all.*

Entering the flickering blue light of the teleconference suite, Dr. Stevens suddenly realized something was terribly, terribly wrong. The long table had been tipped over, the plush leather chairs tossed around willy-nilly. The video screens were rolling windows of static, captioned SIGNAL FAILURE. And behind the table . . . oh God behind the table . . .

Inching forward as if in a bad dream, Chandra peered around the canted mahogany surface at a strange, heaving mass on the floor. It looked like an enormous white fungus, a sprawling, furry blob with many wriggling pink tendrils—she understood at once it was a living mound of rat butts. Protruding from underneath the thing were several pairs of half-gnawed human legs. She recognized Dr. Trager's orthopedic shoes.

"Goddammit," Chandra said softly.

The rats ignored her. They could barely move, they were so engorged. She stood frozen in place for what felt like a very long time, her scrambled brain just rolling and rolling.

Signal failure . . . unable to connect . . .

Finally, one of the rats waddled toward her, its belly dragging on the carpet. So ridiculous with its little cranial cap. In a burst of blind rage and despair, Chandra kicked the stupid thing across the room, where it struck the center of a plasma screen and splatted like a rotten tomato.

"God*damn* that bitch." Opening her phone, she said, "Brenda, call Security. We need an exterminator down here."

Dr. Stevens turned and walked out. She made sure to close the door behind her.

FORTY

GHOST IN THE MACHINE

LYING awake beside Maddy, Ben Blevin had a moment to think about the bizarre events of the past week. Bizarre was an understatement: terrifying, unbelievable events—not the least of which was the discovery that he was not really Ben Blevin but some brainwashed stranger named Duane Devlin. As if that wasn't insane enough, Maddy claimed she was really the ghost of Marina Sweet.

At first he refused to believe it.

I know who I am! he had insisted, nearly storming out of their crappy motel room by the truck wash. The Marina thing he could understand to a degree, because he knew Maddy had been nuts about Marina Sweet, but this other stuff was pure nonsense. Who the hell was Duane Devlin? And what did that even mean, his parents weren't his real parents? How could his father, Sam, be a Braintree doctor named Kaleel Zondervan? Obviously, between her brain implant and everything else that had happened to her, his goofy-ass former-stepsister-to-be had finally lost it.

But she explained it all, pulling him back inside the

room, sitting him down on the grungy yellow bedspread, and calmly, methodically telling him things about himself that no one could ever have known: things from his deepest subconscious that were so powerful and true they brought him to tears. The buried hurts he had suffered from earliest childhood at the hands of those he loved and trusted the most.

Neither white enough to please his mother's small-town people, nor black enough to please his father's, Ben had always felt like a shunned mongrel, caught between worlds, whose greatest comfort came from his parents' unfailing bond. The race issue meant nothing to them, and their marriage was the best proof against the stupidities of others.

When Ben's mother died, it was as though the Earth itself cracked in two—he closed down, refusing to deal. He thought things couldn't get any worse . . . until his father started dating again. Then, as if that weren't bad enough, they actually moved in with his dad's new girlfriend! It was a nightmare. But the strangest thing happened:

It was the woman's daughter. An annoying, freckle-faced chick who was silly, awkward, and possibly the only person on the planet more uncomfortable than he was. Maybe because she was so uncomfortable, she drew Ben's attention away from himself. Out from under the shadow of his towering grief. And every time he looked back, it was a little bit smaller.

As gently as possible, Maddy told him this was all bogus. His memories weren't really his; everything before the carnival accident was secondhand. It was like an organ transplant, only instead of a kidney or a liver, he had gotten someone else's *soul*. Ben Blevin's soul.

But I am Ben Blevin, he said.

No, she said. And she showed him the pictures.

Who the hell is that supposed to be?

That's Ben Blevin.

The guy didn't even look like him. *That's ridiculous.*

She proved it. She showed him evidence that the real Benjamin Blevin was dead, just as the original Madeline Grant was dead, their present identities nothing more than bootleg recordings from lost masters. And even those originals were fakes—the real Ben and Maddy had not been normal children but guinea pigs of Braintree.

We're bootlegs of counterfeits, she said. *Third-party unauthorized copies downloaded onto stolen computers. But check out the special features.*

She proceeded to repair her head in front of him. Ben could barely stand to watch, but Maddy had insisted he see what they had turned her into, making him sit beside her with a mirror and a spray bottle of topical anesthetic while she pulled out the hasty temporary stitches and reset the implant. It was nasty. He would have needed a microscope to see half of what she was doing in there with those tweezers—*damn* she was fast—but in a matter of minutes the wound was evenly and minutely threaded back together.

All done, she chirped. *Now it's your turn . . .*

Over the next few days, they recuperated in the room. From time to time, Ben stepped out on brief errands (the first thing he had done was get them both some hats—they looked like a couple of skinheads), running through their small supply of cash. They still had all the money from their original escape attempt, Ben's pocket money, which was enough for about a week at the cheapest lodging they had been able to find: a noisy truck-stop motel on the outskirts of Newark. Ben had smuggled her in, but even at the single room rate, there was little left over for food or other amenities. At least gas was not an issue since they had abandoned the Braintree van in a parking garage. As far as they knew, no one was looking for it; there was noth-

ing about them on the news. The only thing they heard
about the destruction of Harmony was a brief story about
reported explosions in the Bitterroot Valley region of
Idaho. The official explanation was that these were "gas
eruptions triggered by spontaneous coal combustion"—
the gist being that since the valley was under federal juris-
diction, a restricted no-fly zone, it was of no concern to
anyone.

Despite her crazy abilities, Ben could tell Maddy was
having just as hard a time of it as he was. She could no
more think of herself as Marina Sweet than he could think
of himself as Duane Devlin. That more than anything was
what persuaded him it was all true, the fact that she had to
keep reminding herself that Roger and Beth Grant had not
been her actual parents, that they were strangers to her,
real-life mad scientists, and it was ridiculous to mourn
their deaths. But she couldn't help it; they were the only
parents she knew. What's more, *they* had thought they
were her parents—Ben remembered the look on their
poor sad faces as she was being wheeled out of the building. At Braintree, self-deception, self-obliteration, was the
final reward. Everyone drank the Kool-Aid.

I killed them, don't you understand? I killed them.

Ben comforted her in her grief and guilt, talking her
through the long, miserable nights. They separated the
single bed in two, he sleeping on the hard box spring and
she on the stained mattress, but somehow by morning they
always wound up huddled together.

Thank you, Maddy told him, nestled tight against his
body. *Thank you for saving me. Thank you. Thank you.*

He said, *Hey, it's you who saved me. If you hadn't done
what you did, I'd still be back there. I'd be one of them. I
was down with the program, man.*

*But you keep on saving me, just like you tried to save
Marina. Is that why you do it? Because of her?*

Ben shook his head. *I don't remember her. Marina Sweet isn't real to me, Maddy, any more than Duane Devlin is. You and me are all I know. I only believe in us.*

Maddy awoke beside him.

"Hey," he said softly.

Without speaking, she untangled herself and went to wash up. The afternoon sun was beaming in harsh through the blinds—another new day.

When she came out, Ben was flipping channels on the TV. He said, "I was thinking about what you said before."

"What's that?"

"About Duane and Marina. Maybe we should do what they tried to do: go to Canada."

Maddy sat beside him and muted the TV. "Ben," she said, "I don't think I'm going to be doing that."

"What do you mean?"

"I mean I'm going to New York. I'm going to find my mother. My real mother—Marina's birth mother. She's some actress named Angela Brightly. I don't know what I'll do when I find her, but I'll figure that out later."

He nodded. "That's cool. I understand. We'll go together."

"I don't think that's such a good idea."

"Why not?"

"You know what I am, what I can do. What I've already done. It'll be safer for both of us if I'm there alone. I'm sorry."

"And what am I supposed to do?"

"I've been thinking about that. Here."

She handed him a piece of paper scribbled with an address in California and the word *DEVLINS*.

"I've been making some phone calls while you were out. It's your family—your real family. They filed a missing-person's report on you last year, but by now they probably assume you're dead. Maybe it's about time somebody set them straight."

"Shit." Ben held the paper as though it were hot. "There's only one problem. We're almost outta money. How am I supposed to get all the way to California from here? Hitchhike?"

Maddy laughed and got dressed. "Come on."

Leading Ben to the motel lobby, she made him ask the desk clerk, "Has any mail arrived for Room 103?"

The clerk handed him a mailing box marked OVER-NIGHT EXPRESS. The return address was a P.O. box in Omaha, Nebraska.

"What's this?" Ben asked her.

"Like I said, I've made a few calls."

Back in the room he opened the box. It contained an envelope full of birth certificates, social-security numbers, credit-card numbers, bank statements, and other identity documents, all with his picture, all with different names. A second envelope was stuffed with ATM cards and attached PIN numbers. A third envelope held fifty-thousand dollars' worth of blank traveler's checks.

"Don't ask," she said.

They went out.

ABOUT THE AUTHOR

Walter Greatshell has lived in five countries and worked many odd jobs across America, including painting houses, writing for a local newspaper, managing a quaint old movie house, and building nuclear submarines. For now, he has settled in Providence, Rhode Island, with his wife, Cindy; son, Max; and cat, Reuben. Visit Walter's website at www .waltergreatshell.com.

It's the end of the world—unless you're a zombie.

XOMBIES:
APOCALYPSE BLUES

by Walter Greatshell

When the Agent X plague struck, it infected women first, turning them into mindless killers intent on creating an army of "Xombies" by spreading their disease.

Running for her life, seventeen-year-old Lulu is rescued by the only father she has never known and taken aboard a refitted nuclear submarine that's crew has one mission: to save a little bit of humanity.

Now available from Ace Books!

penguin.com